LEFT AT THE MANGO TREE

A Novel

STEPHANIE SICIARZ

PINK MOON PRESS
Left at the Mango Tree
Stephanie Siciarz

Cover Art: Patti Schermerhorn
Cover Design: Andrew Bly

Published in the United States by Pink Moon Press
ISBN: 0989686302
ISBN-13: 9780989686303
Library of Congress Control Number: 2013912672

For Barry

WANTED: information concerning circumstances surrounding recent pregnancy of Edda Orlean. If you were party to/witness to/privy to details/events/evidence explaining origin of daughter of Edda Orlean, you are urged come forward. Call evenings 45468.

My name is Almondine and I grew up in black and white. I didn't *live* in black and white or *see* in black and white—no home was more colorful than mine—but somehow it always seemed to boil down to that. At first, my lack of color was only whispered about, but as I grew and everyone got used to me, it came to be discussed as plainly as two neighbors might talk of their chickens or the summer rains: Where did she come from? What brand of magic is this?

My face was the problem. It was as white as the moon's, and where I come from, the moon makes us all a bit nervous—and the faces all tend to be black. My mother's is, and my father's, and my grandfather Raoul's. Everyone I've ever known on the island of Oh is black, except for me.

You see now why the islanders should wish to debate my very existence. I puzzled over it myself for a long time, struggled with my impossible reflection in the mirror, and finally determined that the flesh of an almond could no more camouflage itself against the dark shell of the nutmeg than could the sun's orb against a nighttime sky. When I was old enough, I left. Trouble is, you can't know where you're meant to be going, if you don't first make out where you've been, and my unfinished tale was loath to let me get away so easily. Soon enough it came knocking—quite literally—and looked me in the face.

I gave it hot chocolate and listened to what it had to say, every word a tile in a quickly-forming mosaic that was me. But still there were holes that wanted filling in, and the tiles missing could only be got back home: in the island sand, in old pockets and bureau drawers, in intimations blown about by tattletale winds. I collected them all. I scavenged until I had every last one, and pieced together my multi-colored past.

I found that my story, long before it was mine, belonged to a whole cast of islanders, and to my grandfather above them all. Raoul Orlean lived his whole life in black and white; whispers of magic granddaughters implied areas of gray to which he simply could not subscribe. Nor could he allow me to.

Still, I wonder: had he imagined the truths to be discovered, would he have bothered to do all that he did? I've never asked him, and doubt that I ever will. He's entitled to harbor his private regrets, as I am mine. Even on Oh, where secrets, like mangoes, seem to fall from the sky.

1

If my story has taught me anything, it's that nothing is for certain. Not the palm trees or the tides. Or even the weight of these pages in your hand. Acres of pineapple can disappear under the trickster moon at night. Your favorite book can drive you nearly mad. One day your black eyes might turn out to be red. Such, in fact, was the case, in the place—my place—called Oh.

When you arrive at Oh, they don't stamp your passport. You make your way bovinely through zigs and zags of blue plastic rope that navigate the gritty concrete of the airport floor, a sandpaper sea emptying into the river of Raoul. Behind the Formica counter from which he draws his authority, Raoul is an impressive sight. Flanked and backed by wooden cratefuls of pineapple, his black skin shines with subtle sweat against the pallor of the plywood slats, while the dull metal of his rounded specs vaguely obtrudes, like an artist's signature on still life. His close-cropped hair and pronounced but gentle features foreshadow his demeanor, pointedly official, but given to flights of unofficial tolerance.

You reach his post, dulled by the sight, the scent, the oddity of the scene, and extend your passport with the trepidation of one who desires what another has the power to refuse. Raoul takes the document and thumbs the pages. He glances at you, at your picture, and back at you again. This he does less to verify your identity than to ponder how it is you came to be from where you're from. Were it only as simple as a passport!

When he's satisfied, he types your name on a carbon-paper form in his typewriter that records your arrival, date of birth, and eye color in triplicate, which he prises from the roller's grip with an impatient "aaah." He removes the dry end of an ink stamp from between his teeth and expels a "huh, huh" as he pounds it first onto his inkpad and then onto your triplicate form one time. Then in a single, masterful sleight of hand, Raoul completes the transaction, and you find yourself, passport and creased copy three in your left palm, a pineapple in your right. And so to the rhythmic aaah-huh-huhs of Raoul the line slowly scrapes forward, his airy triads punctuated with a My word! or a What's this? or a hesitant Thank you very much (*Merci beaucoup*, *Muito obrigado*, or *Kiitoksia paljon*, depending on the traveler's provenance).

You can no more escape Raoul's sweet and prickly offering than you can his pondering eye or sticky digits. You can try to refuse it, tell him your hands are full, you aren't hungry, you're allergic, but you won't get through without a pineapple. Oh was blessed with more of them than any tiny island knew what to do with and the inhabitants were torn between their pride in the island's fertility, in its sexy fruits, and their desire to dispose of as many of these same as possible.

Right past Customs and Excise Officer Raoul, who alone represents Border Control on most days, sits the baggage. The daily plane to (and from) Oh usually accommodates only a dozen people, which is fortunate in that the dozen or so arriving passengers need then only sift through the dozen or so more departing bags to find their own. Bags coming and going are heaped into one big pile, you see. (Not to worry, what goes out by mistake will make it back the next day.) So in the cool shade of three concrete walls, concrete floor and concrete ceiling, the twelve or so newly arrived bend over some twenty-odd bags and suitcases until each finds his (or her) own.

The view here is really best at ground level, since the ground is where most of the pineapples end up. Some travelers set them down reverently, four or five feet away from the maelstrom of bare knees and Samsonite. Others rest them on their sides, where they roll round and round themselves, like dogs chasing their tails. Still others hang on to them by the tops of the leaves and swing them back and forth while walking round the pile of luggage. Some tuck them into their bags, where the spiky leaves seem to sprout from the concrete floor up through the lining of a resting tote, or, as your gaze moves upward, from the armpits and elbows of travelers hugging the fruits to their sides. Farther upward still, the sun creeps across the travelers' damp faces as they collect their packs and piñas and head toward the airport's gaping exit, where it's not uncommon, amid ouches and curses, to hear a "Madam, mind your fruit!" or a "Sir, would you kindly stop poking that thing in my eye?"

The exit spills out onto more concrete and sand, the square, chunky sidewalks of the former dusted not-so-lightly with the latter. During the windy season a grainy breeze rolls over the island like a wave slipping over shore. It advances and recedes, quietly, seductively, invades and retreats, its gritty deposits the only reminder that it's been there at all. The sand it leaves behind hugs the convex surface of the road that carries you away from the airport and out to sea; it merges with the rubber tires of taxis and bicycles, presses itself against windshields and windows; it sticks to mailboxes and public phones and spreads itself over rusting Toyotas and corrugated roofs and inner tube swings tied to branches; it rubs your cheeks, touches your lips, licks your batting eyelids; it whispers in your ears, climbs under your fingernails and in between your naked toes in their sandals; it hides deep in your pockets, where, back home months and washings later, your naive fingers plunge into the grit and you are reminded of your visit to Oh. Of your lodgings with the pale blue sheets and smell of coffee, of the aloe sweat on your sun-darkened skin, of the white mariposa, and the man outside the airport selling pineapple knives. It will seem very far away. Your memories advance and recede, invade and retreat, until only the gritty deposit convinces you that you were ever really there at all.

The man outside the airport selling pineapple knives is Bang. The mystery of his name is a tile my mosaic still lacks, but he's one of Raoul's closest friends and godfather to my mother Edda, Raoul's only daughter. As much a character as any in the story that will one day be mine, Bang sells pen-knives to arriving tourists, that they might slice their inconveniences into cubes or rondelles and digest them more easily. The knives have wooden handles in which Bang carves a capital B that he transforms into a pineapple figure by scratching diamond shapes into the letter's cavities and pointed leaves sprouting from its top. He displays the knives on a card table whose padded top was once bright yellow but is now faded in spots and torn in others, where dirty white matting peeks through. To attract customers Bang tosses whole pineapples in the air above the table and filets them on their way down, the slices landing with a wet smack onto paper plates strategically placed near the merchandise. Onlookers rarely have free hands to applaud, but they praise him with their oohs and ahs and eyes, attentive pupils reflecting the flying fruit that dances in the mirrors of Bang's sunglasses. Those unenticed by the performance he lures with the sweet smell of the freshly sliced pulp, which he happily gives away. So through those two most common channels to the heart, the eye and the stomach, Bang wins over the tiny crowd and empties his table daily.

What you remember when you leave Bang's sidewalk display are his long, thick braids, his shiny sunglasses, and his even shinier tooth. He has a gold one, right in front, that returns the sun's hard glare, affording him the impression of one endowed with light, and not exposed by it like the rest of us. You might also remember his voice if you happened to speak to him (though there may not have been need if you had exact change). For the islanders, in fact, it is precisely this melodic attribute with which Bang is most associated. When he isn't carving or selling pineapple knives, he's singing, in soft tones, thick and sharp at once, that rival those of the rolling marimba. He sang lullabies to my mother when she was a child, but now performs exclusively at the Buddha's Belly Bar and Lounge, where almost every night from eight to two he regales the audience with love songs and dance songs and traditional ballads his grandfather taught him.

Bang's grandfather wrote many of the island's ballads himself, to commemorate its struggles with colonialism, communism, capitalism, Catholicism, and the crippling, some 50 years ago, of the pineapple trade. The pineapples of Oh were famous then, and the demand for them so great that the island governors taxed the island growers, who were becoming too rich. The growers in turn cut the wages of the pickers, who quit, leaving the growers to pick the heavy fruits themselves, for sums that hardly made the effort worthwhile. Eventually the growers gave up, certain that sooner or later the windy season would deposit sand in the gears of government, forcing a substitution. So, indeed, it came to pass and soon the plantations were producing the sweet un-taxed Oh variety once more. But like a reader who abandons his (or her) cushion for a cup of tea, the growers could never again find the comfortable position they enjoyed before. The hole they left in the market had been plugged, by Oh's island neighbor, whose fruits and governors were sweeter. Oh's growers would have given up again, but feared even more bad luck. So for superstition's sake, they grew (and still grow) untold and unwanted pineapples, sweet reminders of their bitter past.

But Bang's grandfather did more than write songs about Oh. He was mostly a marimbist. On a marimba he fashioned out of sanded mahogany and polished gourds that he attached beneath the wooden keys, he hammered his way to first place in the island's annual marimba competition ten years running. He could hold six mallets at once, three in each hand, and he maneuvered their woolen heads across two octaves with even more dexterity than that required by Bang's mid-air pineapple chopping. From his grandfather Bang inherited his legerdemain, along with the old man's marimba and mallets when he died.

And Bang too became a gifted marimbist, though eventually his granddad's gourds cracked, forcing him to modernize. He bought a marimba with both mahogany keys and mahogany pipes that hung below them, and upgraded from woolen mallets to silken ones.

Now almost every night at the Buddha's Belly from eight to two, when Bang's voice gets tired, he plays the marimba so it can rest. He has a small back-up band, and sometimes even Raoul is coaxed to join in, on maracas, tambourine, triangle, or all three at once. They play on a low stage near the back of the lounge, a dark, cool gathering-place with ceiling fans that distribute the smoke from the patrons' cigars and cigarettes. In front of the stage sit twenty round tables of wood, thatched chairs tucked beneath them, and behind the tables, at the opposite end of the room, a bar accommodates a dozen imbibers easily. Over the bar hangs a wooden canopy with cubbies for rum and for whiskey, and from its edge, cloudy beer mugs dangle on hooks.

There are two entrances to the Belly, where much of my story—or rather Raoul's part in it—plays out. One leads to the lobby of the Hotel Sincero. The other, to the strip of shore reserved for the hotel's guests. On a crowded night the hotel's owner, Cougar Zanne, drags the tables and chairs onto the beach and props open the door, freeing the inside for dancing, and extending his property and profits by fifty yards. Last year he put loudspeakers on the side of the building, so now Bang's percussion and song can be heard equally within and without.

Our Mr. Zanne has been known as Cougar for so long, that few of the islanders remember his real name anymore. He came up with the feline moniker himself and insisted on its adoption, claiming rights to it because his grandfather rid the island of the scourge of cougars that used to run wild there. Cougar's friends and neighbors (myself included, I might add) don't believe there ever were such beasts on Oh, for surely some evidence of them (hunting spears or pelts, perhaps) would have survived in the Parliamentary Museum for the Preservation of Artistic and Historical Sciences. To such protests, Cougar replies, "Well of course there's no evidence. Grandpa got rid of the cougars' every last trace!"

The grandson dedicates himself to more genteel arts, namely the running of the Hotel Sincero, a locale popular in no small part because of its popular owner. Tall and handsome by island standards, and with a *je ne sais quoi* that straddles smart and smarm,

Cougar reeks of tender allure. He likes to dress himself up—his bold dinner jackets, silk foulards, and calfskin shoes are flown in—and might look pimpish were it not for his innate and genuine sense of style. He's the sort of chap who'd do anything for you, really, so long as he has nothing else to do. He's a problem-solver, icebreaker, cheerleader, pinch-hitter, heartthrob, legal advisor and last resort. It was he who taught my mother Edda to dance.

In the hotel lobby he's quick to fill your hands with maps and brochures, and your head with the local lore, while at the Belly he refills every glass (never taking no for an answer) and adds on to every tab. Upstairs, in the rooms, it's the ambitious island girls he fills, first their bodies, then their minds with poetry to salve their broken hearts: "Silly thing! What's all this talk of love?" He charges money to swim with dolphins lest the creatures be exploited, and lets you carry your own bags lest they get lost. In short, Cougar never means ill.

His Hotel Sincero isn't Oh's poshest, but for two-star accommodations and rates, you get four-star atmosphere. The beach, like all the beaches of Oh, is so smooth and white and wide that any description of it waxes banal. Same for the sea, whose blue distinguishes itself from that of the sky by just the subtlest suggestion of green. Half the rooms overlook this view, and half survey a courtyard of concentric circles in bricks of various shades, the outer edge of which is enclosed by sandstone benches that imitate Italian marble.

Inside the flaxen-colored walls of the two-story hotel, the guest rooms are high-ceilinged and clean. On their tiled floors of cobalt and gray rest low, smallish beds hugged by white headboards and footboards, the wood repainted annually to hide wear. Same for each room's wardrobe, coffee table, and pair of rocking chairs, whose patinas are likewise pristine. And from every room a grand window stretching floor to ceiling opens onto a three-inch ledge with wrought-iron faux-balcony railing, each pane equipped with a wooden shutter to let in light when the window is closed, a positioning the climate forbids.

The biggest attraction at the hotel is the Buddha's Belly Bar and Lounge. Its local celebrity presence, in the guise of Bang and Cougar, and its islander clientele draw not only the Sincero's lodgers, but guests from the more exclusive resorts, too, who return to their air-conditioned suites just after midnight, their appetites for local flavor satisfied. The lodgers regard the visiting resorters with dismissal (though you might expect it the other way round), silently condemning their shallow testing of the deep local waters. All of them, lodgers and resorters alike, clink their murky mugs and rub elbows with Cougar's fine suits, charmed by the sometimes-bare feet of the liming islanders, whose nakedness they mistakenly deem of choice, not of circumstance.

I've introduced you to the crooner and the charmer. The third significant *joueur* in Raoul's workaday world is Nat, the cabbie. Nat taught my mother Edda to drive—and to smoke a cigarette. Trim and quiet, innately dignified, Nat can't sing or play the marimba, and he cares little for habiliments. He wears colored t-shirts he buys from a stand at the market. He has no wife and no girl. They tell him it's because he doesn't try, but when he asks, "Try what?" they don't know what to say. Sometimes he drives an American van, or a Japanese one, sometimes an Italian four-door, or a Japanese one. The cars that come to Oh are mostly used, and then presently used up on the pot-holed inland roads. There's no point telling you what Nat drives now. He'll surely be driving something else the next time you visit.

Nat grew up on a pineapple plantation, running and hiding

in acres of leaves taller than he, knocking his tiny body against the ready fruits. The plantation belonged to his grandfather, and was at the height of production when the trouble started with the pineapple tax. Among the growers immortalized in the ballads of Bang's grandfather was none other than Nat's own. When the winds blew out the old administration, Nat's grandfather tried to make another go of it, but the winds had deposited sand in his own gears, too, and he gave up. The land, undisturbed by the gusts and tariffs, was fertile. It garnered a healthy profit when Nat's grandfather sold it, a profit that fed both his own generation and the next. But by the time Nat was a young man, there was not so much as a song left for him, let alone enough to buy a marimba.

Nat's birthright boiled down to unemployment. He had no livelihood, or rather, any livelihood he might want to entertain the thought of, and at the end of the day considered himself a terribly rich and lucky man. He could be a doctor, or a lawyer, or a cook, or a painter—not an artist, but a man who hung his weight on ropes and pulleys and painted church steeples and schoolhouses. In the end he decided simply to earn a modest living.

With the failure of the pineapple industry, the rest of the island decided the same. A negligible amount of pineapple exportation went on, but the cost of picking, packing, and shipping the small cargoes became too expensive to make it worthwhile. The tourism industry boomed in the meantime, and most of the islanders sought their tiny fortunes there. They taught island dances, sold island dishes, embroidered island cloth, and drove taxis. Nat didn't know many dances or recipes, and had never threaded a needle in his life. So taxi driving it was.

His first car was a van, a Volkswagen that appeared to him

both round and square at the same time. It was noticeably succumbing to the early ravages of rust, but the interior was nicely intact, and Nat kept it washed both inside and out. No small feat, this, transporting wet and sandy beach-goers, or sweaty tourists carrying dusty suitcases and pineapples. Yes, the pineapple custom at Customs existed even then, though it would become a much messier affair some three years later, when Bang would set up his pen-knife table, and passengers began peeling and slicing right in the back seat.

In no time at all Nat had just what he wanted, or what he fooled himself into thinking he wanted: a simple and modest living. Driving his taxi paid for fish and vegetables and gasoline, and a sensible place to live. He could afford almost any t-shirt from the stand at the market and the almost daily nip at the Buddha's Belly. He collected and deposited passengers every day at the airport and the Sincero, and by virtue of daily sightings became friends with Raoul and Cougar, and eventually Bang.

Now on the road that borders the stretch of sidewalk outside the airport, Nat leans against his Volkswagen, or his Toyota, or his Fiat and watches as the travelers file out, juggling their loads, swabbing their brows, glancing from the sun to Bang's gesticulations and back in disbelief. Staggered by the heat and by the spectacle, you don't even notice when Nat approaches and asks, "Where to?" He rounds up a couple more passengers headed to the same destination, shouts a word at Bang (who acknowledges it with a shrug of one shoulder), and completes the transaction with a shove on your posterior that plunges you into the car. You find yourself stuck to vinyl upholstery, an Albanian on your left, a sprouting duffel on your right, and a pineapple on the floor between your knees.

Except, of course, on Tuesday. On Tuesdays at Oh the airport is closed. There is no flight in and no flight out, no triplicate forms to stamp and crease and slip inside your passport, no gratuitous fruit to negotiate. Raoul doesn't size up passengers with his aaah-huh-huhs, and passengers don't hop over rolling pineapples to claim their baggage. Bang doesn't set up his table, or sell knives or perform. Nat won't be waiting in his clean Chevrolet to take you over the gritty roads to Cougar's hotel. Sometimes on Tuesdays even the wind hardly stirs, and the sand keeps clear of your mailbox, your ears, your pockets and toes. Always on Tuesdays, Raoul lies in until 10:25, wakes to his breakfast of coffee and milk and oatmeal, dons his favorite blue shirt with the stripes, and goes to the library, where he spends almost the entire day. (I'll get to his business there later.)

This is how it's been as long as anyone can remember.

That is, on every Tuesday but one. One very distinct Tuesday some 20 years ago, Raoul woke up early, and troubled, at 8:25. He had tea with honey and whipped eggs for breakfast, and wore a white shirt with no stripes at all. He thought about his daughter—his daughter Edda Orlean, who never told a lie and only ever slept with her husband—and he did not go to the library. He went to the grimy-windowed office of the *Morning Crier*, and he placed a classified ad.

Someone on Oh must know how Edda got pregnant!

And so while other baby girls are heralded with cigars or balloons or pale pink ribbons on the front door, my unusual, even magical, birth was from the first denoted in black and white. Not *announced*, exactly, not in glossy black ink on sturdy white stock with a photo of my newborn self tucked lovingly into the envelope, heavens no! My birth was to be *inferred*, from a want ad in the morning edition, the black of the ink flat and impermanent, the paper flimsy and white-*ish* at best.

2

Bad things are supposed to happen in threes. When they're *really* bad, even the bad things themselves know enough to stop at two. Why, on Oh, they don't know any better than to splash themselves across the pages of the newspaper, I couldn't say. Poor Raoul found himself sandwiched between two such cases in point. As if I (his white granddaughter) weren't bad enough, he was faced with a real humdinger of a Customs affair. So he did what he always did, when he wasn't quite sure what to do. He went to the Belly, ordered a beer, and waited for his three best mates to show, which (sooner or later) they always did.

"Bastard!" Raoul whispered loudly to himself. He crumpled the *Crier*'s front page in his fist and slid it from the table to his knee. His little Almondine the talk of Oh and now this? He needed a pineapple-smuggler to worry about like he needed, well, pineapples. He had crumpled and smoothed the paper so many times that day, it was covered in thumb-prints and the newsprint was smudged.

"Aye, matey!" Bang bounded into the chair next to Raoul's, straddling it the wrong way round. He propped his chin on the chair's back, cocked his sailor's cap with one finger, and winked.

Raoul responded with a tilt of the head and reached for his sweating mug of beer. "Popeye?" he asked, surveying Bang's deck-hand whites.

Bang feigned indignation and ripped the newspaper from Raoul's grip. With a menacing crease in his brow, he moved in close to Raoul's troubled face, where a lopsided smile was reluctantly taking shape. "Part of the act," Bang said. He swept his arm toward the Belly's beach exit and, aping a Frenchman, announced, "Songs of zee sea."

Raoul's smile filled itself out and he downed his beer. "Aha." He took back the newspaper and ironed it with his palm, small print mountains flattened into rippled prairies of words that he read again. He shook his head.

Bang straightened and let his arms fall in defeat. When Raoul shook his head it meant trouble. It meant Raoul had something in there that wouldn't leave him alone. Something that like a fly in a lidded jar would knock about inside his brain until it was freed into the clarity beyond the glass, or until it suffocated and died. Raoul had flies of every size. There were gnats he got rid of quickly, say, a crossword clue or that actress who looks so familiar—what was her name? There were garden-variety houseflies, not big, not small: fixing the washing machine, finding the perfect birthday gift for Edda. And then there were the bluebottles, the blowflies big enough to make the morning paper.

"Make it a double, will you?" Nat had arrived, shouting his order over his shoulder as he squeezed between the tables on his way to Raoul's. "You saw?" he asked, and nicked Raoul's newspaper.

"Mm."

"The wonders of Oh. So what do you think? What's buzzing in there?" Nat knocked on Raoul's forehead and sat down.

"I think it's rubbish. It's not true."

Bang looked at Nat but spoke to Raoul. "What do you mean it's not true? It's right there in black and white. Puymute Plantation. Two acres. Vanished. Evaporated."

"What are you, Bang, an idiot? You believe every word you read in the paper?"

Nat came to Bang's defense. "Well, something's going on. I saw Gustave and he says every black-and-white word's true. He ought to know."

"Black magic, if you ask me," Bang continued. "Everyone says so. They say it's been here all the time, right below the topsoil, festering, simmering, waiting. And then... *Voilà*! When you least expect it..." (Bang spread his hands into starbursts that he circled in front of his face.) "...black magical manifestation."

He slurped what was left of Raoul's beer and stood up. "Should have planned on mystical melodies tonight," he sighed. "Let that be a lesson to you boys." (He bent over the two, a hand on each one's shoulder.) "Never listen to Cougar. Steer you wrong every time." He slapped them amiably on the back, clicked his tongue, and was gone, drawn by the noise of shins bumping against microphone stands on stage and the flat-sharp ululations of guitars being tuned.

"So where did you see him?" Raoul reclaimed his newspaper for the second time and looked Nat in the eye.

"Who?"

"Gustave. You said you saw him."

"Took a tourist up to Puymute's this morning. Some artist. Paints fruits and vegetables. Said she once so captured the essence of tomatoes that her real life models turned to pulp before her very eyes. Guess she's onto pineapples now. She heard Puymute's were the best. What's left of them, anyway. *Rotund*, she said they were."

Before we go any further, there are a few things I should explain. I too am a painter, did I tell you that? I suppose it was only natural that I should seek refuge from my black-and-white world in a palette of colors that I could arrange as I see fit. And I can attest to the fact that the pineapples on Cyrus Puymute's property were indeed worthy of the most discerning canvas. Not only were they Oh's plumpest and brightest, but owing to the plantation's fertility (which, I discovered, rivaled only that of a secluded beach to which my mother was partial), they were by far the most...the *most* per square meter. If enough of them had disappeared to put a noticeable—and newsworthy—dent in such bounty, then something was surely afoot.

It may have been the wind playing tricks. Or Gustave Vilder playing his. Perhaps a combination of the two. Gustave Vilder worked for Puymute, and could have pulled off an inside job easily. He dabbled in magic, too, and was very possibly in cahoots with the moon herself. I'll tell you more about him after Bang's song.

Me, I never actually met Gustave, though he figures in my mosaic. He died when I was a baby. The only white man on Oh, at the time, or since.

"Gentlemen!" Cougar said, and nodded in greeting. He dragged along a chair, with which he annexed himself to Raoul's table. He gave Nat a tall shot glass (yellow rum), and snapped his fingers in the air over Raoul's empty beer mug, so that a waiter might replace it with a full one. Raoul raised his eyes from the paper in acknowledgement and Nat raised his rum. A long arpeggio leapt from the piano as if to welcome Cougar as well, and the room fell silent.

"Ladies and gentlemen. Good evening and welcome to the Buddha's Belly. My name is Bang and tonight we're gonna to do some numbers for you inspired by the waters that surround this pretty little island of Oh. So order yourselves something to wet your whistle." (He winked into the audience at Cougar.) "And if you feel like making waves on the dance floor, that's why we put it there!"

You don't need me to tell you that when Bang opens his mouth, it's sometimes hard to take him seriously. Other times, when he opens it in song, he commands the respect of a president or a prince, at least for a little while. So when the music started and Bang began to sing, Raoul shushed the bluebottle buzzing in his brain, Nat put down his rum, Cougar forgot about selling drinks, and the customers stopped shuffling their feet on the floor. The Belly's insides stilled.

You and me by the moonlit sea, our love our only company.

To the soft accompaniment of sparse piano, solemn bass, and tenuous brushes on drum, Bang's sounds left his chest, a vague conjunction of heart, soul, and lung, found shape in his throat, and slid past his lips in an audible, airborne kiss. A kiss that expanded and encompassed the crowd until it was a lover's tongue lapping every listener's ear. They closed their eyes and leaned into the ticklish pleasure of the notes, smiles of anticipation snaking across their faces.

Still, dark sky, you and I, I will give myself to thee.

They listened until the kiss became happily predictable, until they could determine when the tongue's melody would turn up, or down, and ready themselves.

When you miss my loving kiss, I want you to remember this—

But the happily predictable is easily overlooked, and before long, the bartender again noisily shook the shaker in his hand. Cougar got distracted by a low-slung sarong, Nat drank, and Raoul let the bluebottle buzz. Soon Bang's voice was pleasant background noise to the Belly's rumblings, a lover's tongue grown familiar, relegated to that realm of comfort and assuredness where it can be sought at will, but robbed of its ability to catch you unawares.

By the sea, look for me, look for me by the moonlit sea.

Cougar re-focused his attention on Raoul. He knew what was in the newspaper that morning, and he knew it meant a headache that Raoul hadn't dreamed of. "Figures Gustave is at the center of all this. He's always been trouble. His whole family since they came to Oh, even before Grandpa's day. What do you plan to do?"

"Get to the bottom of it, I suppose."

"Raoul, be careful, man. Don't get mixed up with this guy's magic or voodoo or whatever the hell it is. What happened, happened. You don't know what Gustave's capable of. And it's not like anybody's hurt or anything."

Nat piped in. "You think he...you know, *did* it? Or you think things just...happen whenever he's around."

"Of course things don't happen just because he's around," Raoul snapped. "Of course he did it."

"But how, man? All that heavy fruit? I don't see how." Cougar lit himself a cigar.

"He gives me the creeps," Nat said, finishing off his double.

Your eyes are like the sea, full of mystery.

"Speak of the devil." Cougar let his tilted chair fall onto its legs with a thud. He watched Gustave walk in from the beach and make his way to the bar.

"The creeps," Nat reiterated. "Just look at him."

"Nat's right, Raoul. He seems weirder than usual. Look!" Cougar poked Raoul. "I bet this front-page business is getting to him."

"His people are used to attention," Raoul said. "Bruce at the *Crier* told me Gustave called the paper himself with the story."

Whenever you look at me, I forget my misery.

The song Bang was singing that night was an old island love song and one, I'm told, my mother Edda sang to me often. When Gustave walked in, as if by magic, the song carried Raoul from his cozy table at the Belly to the cushions of Edda's sofa a few weeks before. I was less than a week old then and had yet to meet the harsh sun of Oh. I *had* met most of the neighbors (or, rather, they had met me), and more of them were turning up every day. My complexion, it seemed, had become a matter that Raoul could no longer ignore.

Whenever you look at me, I forget my misery.

Edda cooed gently into my newborn ear. I was enraptured by her song, awakened, and I peered up at her, my eyes two roses in the snowy whiteness of my tiny, expectant face.

"Isn't she beautiful, Daddy?" Edda asked.

Raoul sat balancing a cup of tea on a saucer on his knee. He had been dipping cookies into it and was studying the crumbs floating on the bottom, hoping that like tea leaves they would tell him what he should say. It's not that I wasn't beautiful. What baby isn't? "She's very beautiful, dear. Very beautiful," he said.

I just didn't look one iota like my mother Edda or my father Wilbur. "It's just that, well, Edda dear, she doesn't look a bit like you or Wilbur," he told her.

"Doesn't she?" Edda laughed. "But she's so small, daddy, how can you tell?"

What's more, I looked very much like someone else on Oh. "She doesn't remind you of anyone?" Raoul persisted.

"Daddy, don't be silly." Edda rubbed her thumb over my cheeks, one of which was nearly completely covered by a mole. It was (and still is) dark brown, an upside-down teardrop covered in soft blond down.

"Edda, you can tell me. I won't be mad. All I want is to know the truth—and to know you're happy of course—and I can see that you are. Do you have anything to tell me? I won't breathe a word to Wilbur. You can trust me."

"Look at this birthmark, Daddy. It's like a broken heart, like only half of a heart. Do you know who has the other half?"

Oh, thank God! Raoul thought, jerking his body and nearly sending the cup, saucer, and prognosticative cookie crumbs to the floor. An answer at last. "Who? Who has it? How did this happen?"

"I do. Her heart and mine will always be connected, Daddy. I'll always be with her, for as long as she lives."

Raoul's muscles relaxed and he fell back into the sofa. His own heart felt broken just then, for he knew that Edda wanted to be for me what her own mother hadn't been for her.

Poor Raoul. He had always done his best to fill the void that Edda's mother—my grandmother—left behind: he taught Edda to cook and to sew (after teaching himself with books he got at the library); he taught her manners and good posture (they spent hours in the garden with his library books on their heads); he even taught her to braid her hair (he and Bang stole a horse for a whole afternoon once so they could practice on its tail); she had three of the most doting uncles a young girl on Oh could want, too. And Edda loved all of them dearly for it. But it hadn't been enough. That was the truth Raoul finally saw, and the realization of it pained him.

My grandmother, Emma Patrice, disappeared when Edda was less than three. The family was on their first real holiday, a ski holiday in Switzerland, and Raoul and Emma Patrice had decided to descend the tallest slope at the resort. Raoul skied with Edda in a pack on his back, and Emma Patrice skied alone. They all descended the hill together, but Emma Patrice soon picked up speed and gained an advantage over Raoul. It wasn't long before he couldn't see her in front of him at all, and when he got to the bottom there was no sign of her either. He searched for hours with the help of a dozen skiers and a handful of Saint Bernards with barrels of brandy around their necks, but no one ever found a trace of Emma Patrice. Perhaps she picked up so much speed she lost control of her skis and crashed deep in the snow. Or perhaps she picked up just enough, enough to elude Raoul and Edda and a lifetime of laundry and pineapple preserves. Either way, Raoul returned to the resort with Edda, fed her mugfuls of steaming hot chocolate, and told her her mother was gone.

It was a long time before Raoul could stop looking for Emma Patrice in his line at the airport, stop hoping for her handwriting when he picked up the day's mail. And it was a very long time before Edda could drink hot chocolate again, a sweet reminder of her bitter past.

Your eyes are like the sea, full of mystery.

Edda sang to me. My eyes were full of mystery, indeed. They were a purple shade of red, and there was only one man on Oh with the same red eyes. One man with red eyes and white skin marred by a broken-hearted mole. But Edda seemed not to notice the way my skin paled against her own. Raoul watched her and felt re-open in his heart the lacerations from so many years before, when instead of letters from Emma Patrice that he could give to his daughter, he received only catalogues and electricity bills and coupons for free shampoos at the Stairway to Beauty salon. Poor Edda, he thought. Starved for a maternal bond and blinded by maternal love. But even starved and blinded, his daughter wouldn't lie. This, Raoul knew for certain.

"Edda." He looked to the cookie crumbs again. "Edda this isn't easy for me to say, but tell me, please. I won't be angry. Have you shared your bed with anybody besides Wilbur?" he asked.

"Daddy, I most certainly have not."

"And no one has touched you besides Wilbur?"

"No one."

Raoul believed Edda had told him the truth, which made him all the more confused and frustrated. He put his teacup on the coffee table and stood. He paced in front of her, his hands flat on his lower back, his elbows out behind him. "Then how do you explain the mole?"

"I told you what it means, Daddy."

"And the eyes?"

"What about them? They're endless. Like looking into the sea."

Raoul looked at the floor and at the ceiling and at the floor again, trying to come up with an answer to the riddle. Maybe she just *thought* she hadn't slept with anybody else, Raoul reasoned.

Maybe she thought she was with Wilbur, but it was really *him*. He must have tricked her—tricked all of them. Bastard.

"*He's* the one I should be talking to," Raoul muttered, while Edda sang.

When I look in your eyes so blue and so green,

Back at the Belly, Cougar snapped his fingers in front of Raoul's face three times. "Raoul! You want a cigar or not? Hey, man!"

"What? Yeah. Thanks." Raoul took the cigar and leaned into Cougar's lighter.

"So now Gustave's in it knee-deep," Nat was saying, "Puymute's out a boatload of money, and the pickers are scared to death." He blew smoke out of his mouth and looked at the cigar between his fingers, as if trying to understand how the one came from the other.

"What does Gustave say about the pineapples?" Cougar wanted to know. "How did he lose two acres' worth overnight?"

"Shh! Keep your voice down. He's right over there." Nat motioned with his hand in the direction of the bar. He looked like he was swatting a fly. "Gustave says he's cursed. Says he has no idea what happened to two acres of fruit and that someone put a spell on him."

I can't believe I've seen what I've seen.

"I think he put a spell on himself," Nat went on. "The guy's creepy."

"When I was a kid Grandpa used to tell me all kinds of stories about Gustave's family. Nobody really knows where they came from, or even when exactly they came to Oh. I can't believe Puymute ever hired him to run the place," Cougar said.

"And the best part is the government wants export duty on the missing goods," Nat added.

"Yeah, I saw that in the newspaper. That's where our mild-mannered friend here comes in. He'll get back at Gustave *now*." Cougar reached across the table and patted Raoul's upper arm. From under the table Nat gave Cougar a kick.

"Hey! The jacket, man! You almost spilled my drink! Raoul knows he's on the case. It's all over the papers."

You are the one who's meant for me.

Cougar took Raoul's newspaper back from him again and read aloud. "'Customs and Excise officer Raoul Orlean will head up the investigation into the mysterious disappearance of the Puymute pineapples.'"

"I know he *knows*. That's not what I *meant*." Nat said to Cougar, under his breath.

"Would you two stop?" Raoul re-claimed his newspaper again. "I'm going to Puymute's in the morning to get this straightened out."

"Good luck getting answers out there. Everyone's afraid to talk about it. Afraid the curse will get them next," Nat said.

"Might have two more acres missing by tomorrow."

Raoul pointed his cigar at Cougar. "I don't know what your grandpa told you, or what Gustave told *you*..." (He turned to Nat.) "...but there's no magic on Oh. There's an explanation for everything, for pineapples and for...for everything. And I'll find it."

Cougar looked at Nat and shrugged. "Just be careful. Like I said, you don't know what old Red Eyes is capable of."

You and your eyes as deep as the sea.

A hollow, uneven applause clucked inside the Belly, reflective in no way of the audience's scant appreciation of the performance, but of the locals' embarrassment in the face of such formal displays.

"Thank you, ladies and gentlemen. Short break and we'll be right back. Good time for a refill," he winked. "See you at the bar!" Bang pointed an affectionate index finger at the crowd, then bounced down the two steps that led off the stage. He filched a tumbler of water from the tray a passing waitress held up over her head and joined his circle of friends. He seemed unable or unwilling to stand still, like a boxer ready to spring from his corner. "Coug! Great call on those sea songs!" Bang set down the water and showed Cougar two thumbs up. "So what are we talking about?"

"What else? Black magical manifestation," Nat mocked, hand motions and all.

"Says the man who was shaking when he got back from Puymute's this morning," Bang countered. "You two should have seen him at the airport—'curses' this and 'creepy' that. So when's the investigation start?"

"I'm going over in the morning," Raoul announced.

"Here." Bang reached into his pocket. "Take my lucky harmonica. Just keep it on you."

"What am I? Jack and the bloody beanstalk?" Raoul was serious, but Cougar and Nat sniggered.

"What makes it so lucky?" Cougar asked, chuckling.

"A traveling musician gave it to Granddad about sixty years ago, told him to play it when he got in trouble. So one day Granddad's out in his boat and he falls asleep. When he wakes up, he's so far from shore he has no idea where he is. He starts playing." (Bang blew into the harmonica for effect.) "And you know what? A pair of dolphins appear."

"Dolphins? Not right out of the sea! Did they say anything to him?" Nat interrupted. Cougar laughed and even Raoul was amused.

Bang was unshaken: "So Granddad keeps playing, and the two dolphins gently nudge the boat, all the way back home. Saved his life. Not only is it good luck, I think it might be magic, too. Take it." He slid the harmonica toward Raoul.

"I don't play."

"You blow on that thing, Raoul, and the dolphins will capsize you to shut you up," Cougar roared.

"Don't you have a lucky tambourine you can give him, Bang?" Nat suggested, and snapped his fingers in the air. "Rum!"

"Laugh if you will, but humor me." Bang slipped the harmonica into Raoul's shirt pocket and patted him on the chest. "Showtime." And he was gone.

There's an old story that I want to tell.

Raoul let the conversation between Cougar and Nat fade into the distance and looked at the paper again.

PARANORMAL PILFERING OF PUYMUTE PINEAPPLES

Why was Oh so quick to jump to alchemical conclusions? So prone to believe in charms? They just can't be bothered to look for the truth, that's all, he thought. Not a mystery anywhere on the island that couldn't be explained by a book from the Pritchard T. Lullo Public Library. The people of Oh were hungry for magic, always had been. Hungry for something to hope for, something to blame, something to make them feel like they weren't so alone after all, like they weren't just a floating pineapple patch forsaken by anyone who mattered.

The moon on the water cast a spell

Gustave? He was clever. Knew they'd buy right into it, didn't he? He might fool Puymute and the *Morning Crier*, but he wouldn't fool Raoul.

Like it knows how to do so well.

Called out the devil straight from hell.

Gustave sat at the bar. He faced forward and watched his liquid reflection in the glass he held. He could feel people staring at him, could almost hear their whispers. His pineapples the talk of Oh and now this! He needed a baby to worry about like he needed, well, a baby. It got everybody talking again, stirred up the old dusty stories he thought were long buried and forgotten, the legends he'd tried to shake since he was a boy. It was a curse alright. A real chip-your-tooth-on-it curse. And Gustave didn't know what to do next. His elbow on the bar, he leaned into his fist and let his thumb caress the talisman he had carried his whole life, like you or I might rub a rabbit's foot or a lucky penny, or a wise man his long white beard. In downward strokes he smoothed the soft blond down that blanketed the blotch on his cheek.

Called out the devil straight from hell.

"How the hell should *I* know how Edda Orlean got pregnant," Gustave muttered. And Bang sang.

3

Every leaf has two sides. One shiny and smooth. One faded, rough. The existence of one defines the other, though that they exist at all depends on the life-giving veins they share, the convex and the concave conjoined.

On Oh, the leaves sing. You can hear them when the wind is up, a *shhhhhhh shh!* of sides knocking against sides. Bang has a bamboo cylinder with soft chips in it that mimics their song. The leaves' violent lullabies coax the butterfly jasmine and the pineapple fruit. Their sides' coupled hum, the little almond.

My father Wilbur used to listen to the leaves for hours, a fascination he instilled in me from the time I was just a toddler. When I visit him now—not nearly as often as I should—we still spend our evenings on the verandah at home, where the leaves tell their very best stories. My favorite is one about a school-aged Wilbur, who fell in love to their shiver and tremble.

Wilbur's fascination with leafy melodies began when he was a boy. He would hide, cross-legged, under a mango tree in the soft green brush a stone's throw from the edge of the sea, and lose himself in the leaves' sighs. It wasn't just their sighs, however, that drew him to his favorite hiding spot one particular warm and windy afternoon when his school day was done. What drew him that day was a simple—soundless—white ribbon. A white ribbon that danced entangled in what he knew must be the softest black hair that ever was.

It was draped around a petite, plain face adorned with eyes equally as black—eyes unremarkable on Oh, where everyone's eyes are as black as his (or her) skin. But to Wilbur they shone like the gelatinous bulbs of the iguana that slunk around his front porch every morning and in which he had once seen his whole face reflected. Below the eyes a similarly unremarkable nose was positioned some inch or so above duly pinkish lips and a perfectly average chin.

The column on which this capital sat was narrow and smooth under flared cotton dresses that anticipated curves but revealed in the meantime two straight sticks of leg. Edda's legs. Wilbur watched her with her friends as they threw shoes, socks, grammar books and pencil cases into a pile in the sand and ran parallel to the slippery tide, careful not to get their school clothes wet. Not so wet, at least, that they wouldn't dry before the girls reached their homes and began their adverb exercises to the accompaniment of sweetened goat's milk and pineapple tartlets. Wilbur fingered the corner of his own grammar book, mauve with black gridlines on the front, "GRAMMAR IS FUN" mathematically distributed in block letters between them, and imagined it there, on the pile, where hers was, mingled with her thin knee-socks, or pressed against shoe buckles that had touched her fingers.

Sometimes the girls would just sit and draw pictures in the sand, and talk. On those occasions Wilbur would strain to hear their words over the leaves' rhythms. (Usually he was forced to content himself with little more than mumbles and rustling.) At first

Wilbur didn't know why he watched Edda after school, just that he wanted to—and for as long as he could remember. So watch her he did, from the time she wore empty cotton dresses to the time her body began pressing itself against her taut clothing. From the time he didn't know why he watched, to the time he sensed it had something to do with what was under Edda's tightening skirts and blouses.

Before we go any further with my father's story, though, you should know something more about the infamous Gustave Vilder. For me, the lives of these two men go hand in hand—ever since one moonlit night, close to that very spot where we leave Wilbur to contemplate his Edda.

While Wilbur stumbled dumbly through adolescence from his hiding place under the mango near the beach, and Edda tiptoed through hers to keep her schoolclothes dry, Gustave Vilder just tried to grow up. It wasn't easy being a Vilder on Oh, especially not a small one. Like all children, Gustave just wanted to fit in. He wanted invitations to birthday parties and someone to swap sandwich halves with him at lunchtime on the wooden benches outside the school, his fresh purpled octopus for slices of wild pig, or his mother's peanut butter and pineapple jam for papaya and soft cheese. Ambrose Jou made a trade every day. But then Ambrose Jou was dark, like all the natives of Oh: dark skin, dark hair, dark eyes. And more than that, there wasn't a magical hair to be found on his head. (I too would have liked invitations, and *my* Ambrose Jou was an ebony Olinda Berch, who collected balls of bubble gum from every boy in class.)

Gustave, on the other hand, was as pale as the goat cheese on a papaya sandwich. His whole family was. And though you'd be sorely pressed to find a group of elementary-schoolers requiring more than that to alienate a classmate, imagine what the likes of a young Gustave must have endured: stuck in his doughy face were two Vilder eyes of an otherworldly red and the very same distinctive hairy birthmark that branded every Vilder cheek. Gustave tried a slew of remedies to get rid of the mark, so desperately did he wish to narrow the gap that separated him from the others. He scrubbed it with seawater and steel-wool pads. He shaved it and plucked it. For a while he even covered it with a bandage. But he couldn't hide who he was. No one can, especially not here.

I still don't know exactly how or when the Vilders came to Oh, how many of them there were, or why so few were left right about the time that Gustave was scrubbing his birthmark and eating octopus sandwiches alone. I don't think anybody does. The rumors are rampant and purport such actors as a lost Nordic fishing god with forty fairy wives, and such theories as inbreeding and devil worship. I can tell you some of them later, if you want, but they don't change anything. What life isn't a composite of the deaths and sins that preceded it, of tales twisted by time? For now, just know that the stories, perpetuated through island lore and island lay, entangled to create a hazy legend of evildoing and distrust that the Vilders' frightening appearance only served to cement.

How evil or powerful the Vilders' evil powers really were remains as mysterious as their origin. The Vilders didn't chant or poke pins into voodoo dolls. But if a Vilder was cheated or poked fun at, the cheater or poker almost always lost his job or his wife or his money or his fishing rod. Except of course when he simply fell ill and died. For his part, Gustave never believed in his family's magic. Had they really possessed any, surely they would have used it to clean up their moles and their eyes, made themselves just like everybody else, undetectable, and even more powerful. He tried to compose incantations to the effect, in the gridded pages of his own copy of "GRAMMAR IS FUN", but they worked no better than the steel-wool pads. He guessed that once he got old enough his mother would tell him how to tap his evil, magic energies, and when she did, his first feat would be to remove the telltale mole. In the meantime, he waited.

It was a shiny day when Wilbur first decided to speak to Edda alone. The light fell from the sun onto the water that rippled and refracted it in every direction, and from his hiding place in the brush under the mango tree, Wilbur saw the beach laid out before him, a series of wavy golden reflections. They bounced off the sea, the sand, and Edda's black hair. Edda wasn't a girl anymore (nor Wilbur a boy), though she maintained many of her girlhood habits, like her afternoon walks in the tide. Her hair was no longer restrained by the white ribbon that had first lured Wilbur to watch her from the brush. It fell loose over her bare shoulders and over her arms, naked and defined and bent at her sides as she cradled some blossom or seashell or tiny orange crab in her palms. Her skirts were longer, barely revealing the bones of Edda's ankles, but they were gauzy and transparent, and Wilbur preferred them to the short, thicker ones of her youth.

Edda walked alone now. Her friends preferred the tourist beaches and hotel bars where they could flirt with men wearing gold rings and clean shoes. She walked and dug her toes in the sand, wet gray globs of it clumping onto the tops of her feet as she dragged them along. It wasn't the first time Wilbur had seen Edda on the beach alone, but he had never before this time found the courage to speak to her. He waited until she had passed the spot in the brush where he hid, then he crept from under the mango, removed his shoes, and walked behind her in the water.

"Edda!" He called out to her, but the singing leaves swallowed up his shy, hesitant voice. "Edda!" again, louder. She turned toward the sound of her name. She remembered this face from school. This quiet, polite boy.

"Wilbur. What are you doing here?"

"May I walk with you?"

Edda didn't say yes or no. She just looked at him, her hand in a lax salute to block the sun, one of her unremarkable eyes half-closed, and finally resumed her stroll. They walked in silence, though not uncomfortably so, until Wilbur broke it. "Not many people know about this place."

"No," she smiled. "Thank heavens for that." Wilbur let Edda walk straight on while he turned and moved a bit into the sea. He bent down and filled his cupped hands with water. He emptied and filled them twice more, then he finally stood and grinned.

"Edda! Wait! Look!" He rushed to catch up with her, his hands out in front of him, water oozing from between his fingers. She put her face over them and saw a tiny silver fish darting between his palms. It was no bigger than one of Edda's slight fingernails. She smiled again, not just out of politeness this time, and they laughed, looking alternately from each other to the glittering little swimmer. Edda poked her finger into the water in Wilbur's hands, watched the fish swim round and round it. In Edda's black eyes, Wilbur watched the fish's shiny, darting image.

Wilbur and Edda met often on the beach after that day. They walked barefoot and told each other secrets. Wilbur caught her butterflies and Edda let her hips drift nearer to his as she sashayed alongside him. Sometimes they sat in the sand and played tic-tac-toe with their fingers or built lazy, crooked castles. Soon they began to hold hands. One day, Edda let Wilbur kiss her cheek. Before long he had discovered what was under her blouse.

They were a perfect match, Wilbur and Edda. Though she didn't know it exactly, in so many words, all Edda ever really wanted was a family of her own. And all Wilbur had ever really wanted was Edda. So when on that same beach one day Wilbur asked her to marry him, Edda said yes at once, not knowing why, knowing only that it was the right thing to do. They were married at the Town Hall on a late Saturday morning, from where Uncle Nat accompanied them in his washed and waxed Renault to the Sincero, hooting the horn all the way. There, Uncle Cougar offered a lavish wedding lunch, "seeing as how there are just a few of us," and Uncle Bang entertained.

At dusk, as the daylight and Cougar's largesse began to wane, Edda pecked her father Raoul on the cheek, squeezed him in a tight hug and left with her new husband. She took him to the empty beach where they had met and courted, and as the moon bathed the cool damp sand with its light, on a white crocheted coverlet Wilbur would at last discover what lay past Edda's hem.

During *his* schooldays Gustave's only companions were the Vilder legends that flew around the island like hummingbirds—those, and perhaps the hummingbirds themselves. Like the rest of his family he was forced to keep to himself, and he hated it. And them. He often wished his parents dead. They kept their magic from him, forcing him to suffer the insults and the whispers of the other kids. They wouldn't teach him to hide his birthmark or to ruin with rain all the football matches he was excluded from, or to make the air seep slowly out of the tires on Ambrose Jou's bike. Gustave urged his mother every morning at breakfast, "Today, can I learn something magic, Ma, can I?"

But every morning the response was the same, "How can I tell you what you already know? All the magic you need is right here." And she would poke at his heart with her worn and shiny pink fingertip, until he yelled out in discomfort, if not exactly pain.

"There's nothing in there! I want the magic the kids whisper about so I can play tricks on everybody who hates me."

"Mind your tongue. Anybody hates you, they have enough bad magic in their veins. It'll poison their blood soon enough. Now get to school and stop talking that way."

Gustave got up and went, willfully leaving two big spoonfuls of oatmeal in the bottom of his bowl, the lumpy stodge a monument to his angry independence, his flagrant infraction of mother's rule that he must always clean his plate. "She hates me most of all!" he decided, swinging his bag of books so hard that the corner of his maths book poked clean through the cloth. "I wish she would die!"

This scene played out more or less every morning at the Vilder household. The setting was almost always the kitchen, biggest room in the comfortable shack where Gustave lived with his mother and father, yellow curtains with daffodils embroidered in cross-stitching bustled by the breeze from off the water. The props changed sometimes, toasted bread with egg on top or spicy sausages instead of oatmeal. Sometimes his father joined the cast, affecting the disposition of the other actors with his slow bulk and supporting the lead female with nods and listen-to-your-mother-nows. But the lines and gestures were otherwise nearly imperceptible variations on a theme, and Gustave had the bruises in the flesh over his heart to prove it.

The morning the scene played out for the last time, Gustave ran out with a particularly vehement delivery of the wish for his mother's death, his mother who, as Gustave would discover, was perhaps not so wrong about the magic he harbored in his heart. For surely it was his own impassioned wishing, he decided, that did his mother in that day. When he returned from school, she was dead.

"Snakebite," his father said and jostled his head from side to side. The old man survived long enough after that to see Gustave through his early teens, frying him sausages for breakfast and turtle steaks for dinner, though he said and did little more after his wife died than "snakebite" and jostle his head.

As Gustave grew, so did his loneliness, which he hid beneath an armor of hubris and cockiness that, coupled with his reputation and looks, made him even scarier to most of his schoolmates than he otherwise would have been. In truth, most suspected he wasn't too powerful at all if he couldn't save his mother from a snake. But others suspected it was Gustave who had sent the snake to get her. Gustave was among these, as I said, and when his father finally died, he forgot his exaggerated pride and accepted his family's legacy of separation and slouched shoulders, not genetic, but instilled by years of solitude.

A proclaimed pococurante, the one thing Gustave couldn't ignore was his hormones. A young man with no friends or guidance, he couldn't ease into love the way Wilbur did, in the sun's rays with a kind but unremarkable girl. No, Gustave made his discoveries under the shade of night at the island brothel, with Miss Lulu Peacock. He had to pay double, on account of who he was, but a Vilder always knows where to find money when he (or she) needs it. At least there's that.

Miss Peacock introduced Gustave a number of times to what Wilbur would find out about for free. But she did so much more than that! In her embrace Gustave discovered a familiar, beastly energy that lay hidden inside him. He let it surge, a homecoming somewhere in his gut. It crushed his guilt and puffed his chest, sloughed off the droop his shoulders had assumed. After that he didn't sit alone so much in the shack his parents had left him. He was an islander like all the others, he told himself, born and raised there, and had as much a right as they did to fit in. Which he did, nicely, at least in a seedy bar near the port where the girls were too drunk or too desperate—for money, rum, or attention—to care a tinker's damn about who or what he might be.

Soon after is when Wilbur's life found itself connected to Gustave's, or vice versa, though neither would know it until over nine months had passed, and only one of them would ever know how to explain exactly what happened.

It was at dusk on Wilbur's wedding day, the day he'd lift Edda's gauzy and transparent skirt on their secluded strip of sand, that Gustave would end up under Wilbur's mango tree, in the soft, green brush a stone's throw from the edge of the sea, with a girl from the seedy port bar.

The leaves cooed softly as Wilbur spread the white coverlet on the cold damp sand and the moon began to spread its light across it. Edda sat down and reached to remove her sandals, but Wilbur stopped her and guided her head to the ground. He kicked off his shoes and knelt down to remove hers for her. He stroked her shins and kissed her knees, exploring her inner thighs with his fingers. Edda's heart thumped a beat that was unfamiliar but comfortable, and the leaves hummed in her ears. Her legs fell open as his fingers found hers and their hands interlocked. She squeezed until her knuckles felt white, while Wilbur licked the soft skin that finished in her hidden and pale something-blue wedding satin. She was afraid, impatient, and reluctant at once and steadied herself for Wilbur's hands on the elastic, wishing him to free her hips so she might know what would follow. But his hands tricked her and fell onto the opalescent buttons of her dress instead.

Gustave meanwhile heard hummingbirds as he left the dusky beach behind him and entered the darkness of the soft green wood. His hand was wrapped around a girl, her neck in the crook of his elbow, and their bodies bumped awkwardly against each other as they walked out of step, owing to the excess of alcohol they had swallowed. Gustave kicked off his shoes and pushed the girl onto the ground, nearly collapsing next to her. "You alright?" she giggled, competing with the leaves to be heard. Gustave didn't say yes or no. He put his hands on her waist and with grunts and jerks pushed down the tight jeans the girl wore, rolling them into an inside-out bundle at her ankles, unable to pull them past her complicated strappy sandals. The girl's heart thumped a drunken din that echoed from her chest to her ears. Her legs fell open as Gustave's hand found hers and pulled it to his middle, while his other hand guided her head. Her hands fell onto the zipper with which she'd come face to face, and she maneuvered his pants down his body. She was afraid, impatient, and reluctant at once, suddenly and acutely aware of who her companion was, and steadied herself for the taste of Gustave in her mouth.

Wilbur, somehow freed now of his pleated matrimonial trousers, finished with the buttons of Edda's dress. His tongue found her breasts but the cicadas' vibrations kept her low moan a secret. He licked her neck and her ears. His warm breath on the wet saliva made her shudder. They kissed finally and Edda thought she would suffocate when his mouth overwhelmed hers. She closed her hands around his neck and her legs around his waist, still separated from him by her satin of pale blue.

Both the beach and the brush had fallen into darkness by this time, though the evening's curtain was thinned by the moon. It had risen up fully now, exerting its pull and release on the waves that crashed loudly and rolled to shore. Gustave pulled the girl's head to his face and kissed her, rolling her over so that he lay on top of her. Wilbur ripped the pale blue material, removing the last barrier between him and his wife, and climbed onto Edda.

The couples grappled, Gustave and the girl under the mango, and Wilbur and Edda in the sand just far enough away, or so they thought. Mouths gasped for air and lips covered lips. Gustave pushed inside the girl. Edda, startled, eased into Wilbur's rhythms, frightened and aroused. Edda's hair mingled with the damp sand, the girl's with the dry twigs of the brush. Hands caressed faces and thighs. Feet caressed feet.

The mischievous moon smiled down on them all and sent the sea into a violent, enchanted rush, guiding the female contractions that mimicked the waves. Spurred by the sea's urgency and assisted by the wind, the leaves sang even louder suddenly, in harmony with the cicadas and the hummingbirds who didn't know if it was night or day. The song crescendoed to a frantic, fevered buzz; it fell on top of the naked lovers, like a thick blanket that might smother them all.

They could hear nothing for the noise that filled their ears, the living sound that seemed to populate the air around them. They tried to ignore it, to escape it by closing their eyes. The girl focused on Gustave's body. Edda rocked hers in time to Wilbur's, which moved in unison with the island's quiver.

The magic moon laughed at the lovers' struggle. The waves were too agitated, the wind too strong. It ripped the leaves from the very trees that bore them.

The fracas finally culminated in a guttural human cry that confirmed a superhuman deed, and the moon silenced the waves, calmed the cicadas, and finally closed her eyes. She was placid, the mighty moon, and pleased. Her finger had poked a hole in the soil of an earthly womb and dropped an almond seed into it, stitched together as if from two stolen sides of leaf.

In the dark, the lovers slept. Tired, sticky-skinned, spent heavy limb on spent heavy limb. The leaves were sleepy, too. They trembled still, and shuddered a broken lullaby, while their shiny sides awaited the sun.

4

My grandfather Raoul once read a book with just a line on every page. He thought, maybe one line was enough, enough for the reader to fill in what was missing and write between the lines, as it were, on the blank pages in his (or her) head. Raoul didn't mind the book. He found it rather bold. But then Raoul knows how to hold his own with fancy raconteurs, even one so clever as to write a whole book without writing a whole book.

This wasn't always the case. Time *was* when Raoul had little patience for know-all volumes (and littler still for the folly of fiction) and took things at face value—meaning that what wasn't as clear as a nose on a face didn't much interest him. While he simply had no use for books, his wife Emma Patrice devoured them. Every night when he crawled into bed he found her there, rustling pages and shushing him. She told him it was her way of escaping, though he could never imagine what a modern housewife with the market place a hundred meters away and a pearl-handled sewing basket could have to escape from. Even less could he imagine how one could escape from whatever there was needed escaping from into the brittle world of those colorless pages. It smacked somewhat of magic, and if there's one thing a man who takes things at face value the way Raoul did cannot tolerate, it's that. Which is why, when Emma Patrice skied off that day and Raoul was left to raise Edda alone, he quietly removed his missing wife's books from the house, stirred by the strange but sure sensation that the bound nuisances had in some way contributed to her disappearance.

But don't infer from Raoul's boycotting of books that he wasn't smart or clever. In an old-fashioned sort of way he was. He worked hard, had a headful of common sense, followed complicated orders with ease and efficiency, and kept matters in pineapple-pie order, or at least looking like they were, which is sometimes even more important. In fact, he built quite a Customs career for himself with this handful of bricks, a feat smacking somewhat of magic itself.

All the same, there came a time when Raoul's disdain for the less-than-obvious gave way. There were things his daughter Edda wanted him to teach her. And though Raoul had seen his wife bake a million cakes and pies, when he showed Edda how to mix the sugar and the butter and the eggs, what they drew out of the oven at the end of the lesson was lumpy or greasy or crumbly. So it was that Raoul set out one day for the Pritchard T. Lullo Public Library on the island's east end to find a recipe for fritters. He would work his way up to cake.

The library was housed in a square stuccoed building of lime green. An open, welcoming porch with two low steps and thin white columns wrapped in bud-dotted vines announced double wooden doors, whose colored panes gave a reverential glow to the single room on the other side. There, bathed in natural light, dark wooden bookshelves lined the four white walls and kept watch over the six-drawered altar of Miss Lila Partridge, head librarian, positioned squarely in the center. A book-fearing man with no knowledge of card catalogs or Dewey decimals, Raoul couldn't ease his way into a hardback the way Emma Patrice could, the secrets between the covers urging every page that was turned. No, he needed help, and thus his first discoveries—in the shade of the Cookery shelf—were under the guidance of Miss Lila. Miss Lila showed Raoul all the ways to fry and manipulate dough, from fritters to crullers to buns. But she did so much more than that! Her offerings lured him back to the library again and again, and from behind her eyeglasses she watched the slow process of seduction the demanding pages exerted on him. From cookbooks to almanacs to memoirs and more, he set about exploring every fold in the library's soft skins and found what he needed there to fill the void in his head and his heart. He found solace and science and knowledge and, yes, escape. Before he knew it (or maybe without ever really knowing it at all) he had become something of a philosopher, one who takes things at face value, but backs up what he sees with books.

Typically Raoul did his exploring on Tuesdays. Miss Lila would show him the week's new arrivals, if there were any, and he would acquaint himself with them at a table in the corner, with whodunnits, biologies, biographies, tragicomedies, and poems. On the Tuesday that I'm going to tell you about, however, he wasn't reading for philosophy or fun. He was far too pressed for that. *This* Tuesday Raoul was there on business, the business of debunking his least favorite thing.

Magic.

Raoul's atypical Tuesday (the second in as many weeks) had started off badly. Seeing as how it *was* Tuesday, he should have slept in until 10:25, awoken to his breakfast of coffee-milk-and-oatmeal, donned his favorite blue shirt with the stripes, and gone to the library. But duty called, and the recent hullabaloo at Puymute's, namely the mysterious disappearance of two acres' worth of ripe pineapple, required the attention of the Excise Office, day of the week notwithstanding. So Raoul awoke at 9, rushed through a breakfast of espresso and bread that he didn't fancy at all, and forwent his favorite blue shirt for a less worn and less comfortable yellow one. Then muttering under his breath about "that damn Vilder" and the newly-arrived *New Modern History of the Silent Stage* that he wouldn't get to read at the library that morning, Raoul set off on the two-mile walk to the plantation.

It was a warm day, as they all are on Oh, but the cotton of his shirt kept him cool. The porous fabric, a bit tighter than he'd have liked, was dampened slightly with his sweat and felt cold against his skin as the wind blew on it. It was a windy day, too, as they almost all are on Oh, and Raoul wore sunglasses to shield his eyes from both the blowing sand and the scrutiny of Puymute's neighbors, should he run into any on the way. He had decided to take the tight path that led up Dante's Mountain (it's really a big hill at best), from the top of which he'd be able to survey all of Puymute's property and possibly find some clue. It mightn't be a bad idea, after all, to get a view of the whole situation before he took himself wading around in the muck of it.

Halfway up, Raoul stopped to smoke a cigarette and to catch his breath. He wouldn't be able to see Puymute's place until he got to the top, but from the side of the mountain on which he stood he could see the island's far end. Buildings of pink and yellow and beige dotted the landscape, themselves dotted with roofs of red and brown and orange. Here the bushy green head of a palm, there the humble gray spire of a church. All of it wrapped in a white-sand ribbon tugged at by the sea, whose water looked more silver than blue in the early sun. It was a mosaic fashioned by man and god, as perfectly imperfect as any Raoul had seen in photograph at the library. A trompe l'oeil in which the sharp edges of the rainbow buildings cut out the dirt and the dust from which they sprang. The air was filled with salt and sand and the two mingled with the sweet taste of the tobacco Raoul drew into his lungs, as if his very cigarettes were made of the tide.

Sometimes at the airport he couldn't help but wonder about all the visitors to Oh, what it was they could possibly wish to see here. But on this Tuesday morning when he should have been reading about shaded actresses and newsreels and was instead climbing a makeshift mountain for clues that might lead him to a pineapple smuggler, Oh's beauty fell upon him like one of the island's weighty fruits. How easy not to see the air you breathe! He wondered if it was a blindness that struck everywhere, or only there, where the constant sun played tricks on the eyes. On the faraway shore the tide slithered inland. Raoul listened to its marvelous silence and watched as he exhaled and blew it back to sea in white smoky wisps.

His reveries, alas, were short-lived.

"Oy! Mr. Orlean! Oy there!"

Along with sun and sea and tide and trees, Oh is full of pests. Mosquitoes, mice, gnats, fleas. And Pedros. Or, rather, one Pedro Bunch, though his company is as exhausting as if you were caught in a whole swarm of him. Pedro Bunch means well enough. The trouble is that he lives on his own, and off the beaten path, and suffers from an incurable desire to be heard, a condition exacerbated by his encounter with any creature who can hear. Even the goats hide when they know Pedro is coming, for fear of some long and futile conversation that it would be impolite to run away from.

Panting, Pedro rushed toward Raoul, as much as a man of a certain age on a mountainside and carrying walking-stick and sack of cassava can do. "Oy there, I say. This is a treat to find yourself here."

"Yes, well, felt like a day for a walk."

"Didn't look to me like you were walking."

"Just taking a breather." Raoul crushed his cigarette out against a rock and dusted his hands against each other elaborately, hoping that to Pedro the gesture would indicate some sort of business awaited. "Forgot about the view from up here."

"Ah, yes. Finer, they don't come." Pedro had positioned himself in Raoul's path. "So where's this walk of yours headed, then, Mr. Orlean?"

"Oh, I don't know. Thought maybe I'd finish the climb and go down the other side. I see you've got your hands full. Don't let me keep you." With that, Raoul patted the man on the back and squeezed past him.

"Don't mind a climb up top myself, now you mention it. Mind you, I'm not as quick as you are, I expect, but you can hardly hurry past a view fine as this one, then, can you?"

Certainly not today, Raoul thought, annoyed that his sentimental musings may now well cost him a good half-hour. There was little use in protesting. The quicker he got Pedro moving, the quicker he'd get where he wanted to be. So he took up the old man's plastic sack and nudged him on. To the rhythm, as sure and regular as a military cadence, of Pedro's observations on subjects as diverse as trout with lemon, telephone listings, and eyebrow tweezers, they made their way up. Pedro was nothing if not indefatigable.

When they got to the top, three-quarters of an hour later, Raoul's patience was wearing thin. Puymute's plantation stretched out before him, as much a sea as the one made of water on the mountain's other side. Its waves of tall stalks rippled their long, thin leaves into pointy crests of green and gold that stretched off into the horizon, peppered with the bobbing heads of sweaty, black-haired pickers. At intervals the sun-baked sea was divided into smaller bodies by pathways cut into its thickness to ease navigation. Raoul let his view relax and fall over the undulating activity of the scene below him, hoping some irregularity might catch his eye.

"Ah, yes. Finer, they don't come." Pedro moved close to Raoul, helping himself to a portion of the panorama and warming Raoul's neck with his hot-pepper breath. Clearly, it would be impossible to concentrate with Pedro's chatter—Heavens, he's worse than Bang! Raoul thought to himself—so he thanked Pedro for his company, pointed out that Pedro's house was on the opposite side of the mountain from that on which Raoul planned to descend, gave back the old man's plastic sack of cassava and nudged him on again.

"Well, if that's that, I'll just be on my way, then, won't I?" With the help of his walking-stick Pedro straightened his curved back into a stretch and turned to go back down the mountain. "Now don't linger, Mr. Orlean. No telling what might befall a fellow finds himself hanging round here. No telling."

Raoul, intent on surveying the plantation below, took a moment to register the words and detect something of a threat therein. He looked behind him, from where the words had come, but Pedro was gone. "Pedro!" Raoul shouted. "Pedro!"

Odd, this.

Raoul looked all around him, but there was nothing to see. He strained to hear his companion's receding steps and for a moment was sure Pedro's voice rang out it's warning again. "No telling, Mr. Orlean. No telling."

Perhaps it was just the clever wind.

Bothered by the echo of Pedro's words, Raoul finished the climb down Dante's Mountain. He decided finally that the misgiving he sensed in the old man's tone was on account of the rumors that some supernatural swindler was responsible for Puymute's missing crops. It was neighborly concern and nothing more.

Pedro needn't have troubled himself. Raoul didn't believe in anything he couldn't explain, so a supernatural solution was out of the question. And even had he been inclined to consider such a hypothesis, it didn't make sense to him that whatever cosmic prankster had punished the island with all those pineapples would someday simply up and steal them back. Even a phantom must submit to some fundamental logic, surely.

"Listen to me!" Raoul said to himself and shook his head. "Phantom talk!" Another reason, along with his rushed breakfast, too-tight shirt, and climb with Pedro, that he hated this particular day so far.

And he expected it would only get worse.

Raoul was cranky and thirsty when he reached the manor house from which Puymute managed his estate. His long walk had been useless. Nothing on the plantation looked amiss from on high, and on the ground it would be easy enough for Puymute or Gustave Vilder to camouflage the truth. Raoul was hoping to speak to Puymute himself, but he had a nagging suspicion, based on the tenor of the day and on Gustave's General Manager title, that Gustave would be the one waiting to see him.

Imagine. It would be their first meeting since Raoul placed the ad about my mother's pregnancy. They had glanced at each other the night before during Bang's show at the Belly, but they hadn't spoken. They had only *ever* spoken once, in fact, just a week or so earlier, right after I was born—which is what led to the ad in the first place. I'll tell you about that time, too, but right now let's finish our trip to Puymute's, and get Raoul back to the library and to his research.

The manor house was a welcoming shade of salmon that set off the green-gold sea below it and the light blue sky above, disappearing entirely at dusk and at dawn, like a chameleon on the branch of a tree. Tall potted plants dressed the portico, where in lieu of a visible door, sheer white curtains billowed from an opening eight feet high and eight feet wide. Raoul pushed them aside and entered a lavish foyer, lavish by Oh standards, with white tile flooring and a garish chandelier of gold leaf that had only just begun to flake. To the left of the entrance a young woman, legs crossed, sat at a table with pad, pencil, and telephone, its dangling cord gripped between the first two toes of her sandaled foot. "Are you looking for someone, sir?"

"Raoul Orlean. Customs and Excise. I'm here to see Mr. Puymute."

"Mr. Puymute's in the patch, but the General Manager's here. Should I get him for you?"

"Fine."

The girl dialed a number on the phone, mumbled something Raoul couldn't make out, then hung up and escorted him to an office one flight up. Gustave wasn't there yet, but he would be momentarily, and in the meantime would Mr. Orlean like some tea? Raoul didn't fancy the idea of sharing tea with any Vilder, and with Gustave least of all, but the climb up and down Dante's Mountain had made him too thirsty to refuse. "Yes, thank you. With milk."

Gustave arrived a few minutes later, the sandaled secretary trailing behind him with a tray of tea accoutrements. She put the tray on the desk that separated the two men and left.

"Mr. Orlean," Gustave nodded. He had just come from outside, his face still damp with perspiration. His shirt was tucked and buttoned and his manner polite and official. If he didn't extend his hand to Raoul for a shake, it was only because he wondered what he would do with it, should Raoul leave it hovering there, unmet. (His last meeting with Raoul, the one right after I was born, did not end well at all.)

"It's *Officer* Orlean today. May I?" Raoul poured himself a cup of tea, barely watching or waiting for Gustave's consent. He swallowed a whole cupful and felt refreshed and almost cheerful, until, setting his cup on the tray again, he remembered where he was and why.

"Let's get this over with, Vilder. State your name for the record please." Raoul pulled a notepad and ballpoint from the pocket of his shirt. He could barely look Gustave in the face.

"Gustave Vilder, General Manager."

"Mr. Vilder, I am here in the name of the Office of Customs and Excise to investigate the matter of two acres' worth of pineapple that seems to have gone missing from the estate of Mr. Cyrus Puymute. As you are aware, any such merchandise leaving the island is subject to excise, and I am here to collect."

"That's true, any such merchandise leaving the island is certainly subject to excise. But if I'm not mistaken, the tax should be paid by the one who sent the merchandise away. That was not myself, nor was it Mr. Puymute." Gustave sipped his tea and replaced the cup on the saucer in a tremolo of ceramic that belied his complacent demeanor.

In the meantime, Raoul's patience had worn as thin as the favorite blue shirt he had been forced to leave at home that morning. He emphasized every syllable of his response: "Then – who – was – it?"

"I – don't – know."

"Damn it, Vilder!" Raoul pounded his fist on the desk and the tea tray clattered. "You expect me to believe that you have no idea where all that fruit ended up, nor how it got there? What kind of fool do you take me for? You as near as confessed to me before the crime was ever committed! You think I forgot about your little proposition?"

"Proposition? Crime?" Gustave repeated blankly, and with a hint of satisfaction. "Now, now, Officer Orlean. You read the paper. You must have seen the story in the *Crier* yesterday." Gustave produced a copy of the newspaper from the day before, though where it came from Raoul couldn't see just then, and tossed it on the desk. "Mr. Puymute seems to be the victim of...a curse...magic...the wizardry that we all take for granted around here—that is, until we wake up one morning to two empty pineapple patches and realize that we ought to pay it a bit more mind."

"I know all about the story, Vilder. It's as phony as you are. You tipped off the paper and fed them *your* version of the facts. You and I both know exactly where those pineapples went."

Now it was Gustave's turn to be angry. "I know I'm to blame for most of the things that go wrong on this floating little shard of Oh, but sometimes there simply isn't an explanation. Looking for one might only bring more trouble."

"What's that supposed to mean?" Raoul remembered Pedro's strange farewell.

"Only that whatever mystical force is at play here might not take kindly to being questioned too much. Or doubted. No telling what it might do if that were the case." Gustave was standing now, his palms flat on the desk, his fiery eyes looking down on Raoul in his chair. "No telling."

The conversation ended there, at least in the conventional sense. For although it was cut short by Raoul's sudden and silent departure (Gustave had so angered him he'd gone momentarily mute and left), each continued talking to himself in mumbled threats and half-whispers.

"I – will – get – him. I will prove what he's got up to. Somehow. And he – will – pay," spat Raoul. "Babies? Pineapples? Who does he think he is?"

"He can't prove a thing!" countered Gustave. "No one can prove anything on this island! Things happen all by themselves and then everyone looks at *me*."

"A curse! Magic! I should have known a Vilder would stoop to something like this. Scaring up the whole bloody island. He's nothing but a liar and a thief."

"Why not a curse at Puymute's? Or anywhere else for that matter? Should I be the only one bent by the powers of this place?"

There's no telling how long the conversation would have gone on had it not been for Nat, who pulled alongside Raoul as he was walking back to town and offered him a lift. They drove in silence, Raoul still thinking about what he and Gustave hadn't said to each other. The truth is that, though they ostensibly talked about taxes, both men had much more on their minds: that "proposition" for one (which you'll hear about next), and me. It was mostly *me* they had on the brain. Pineapples are a dime a dozen on Oh, but a rare and red-eyed almond? That's worth fighting over, and definitely worth figuring out.

Finally back at the library, seated at his table in the corner, Raoul felt relieved. Despite the daunting research that lay before him, he was comfortable for the first time that day, a pearl nestled in the oyster of all those shelves lined with books. He breathed in, relishing the scent of the library air in his nose, a mélange of paper stock, lead pencil, and Miss Partridge's honey-flavored eau de toilette. He closed his eyes, but soon the crinkles of his worried forehead tugged upward on his brow. Somewhere behind it, a bluebottle buzzed. Raoul opened his eyes and listened a minute. Then he sighed a honey dew onto his reading glasses, polished them up, and got to work.

5

Promises aren't contracts to be entered into lightly. Not anywhere. And especially not on Oh. They imply a pledge, which in turn implies some measure of honor, and an expectation, some rightful return on an investment of trust. Promises on Oh, like in many places, are the currency on which the economy was built. Once, you could promise your day's catch of mahi mahi to the widow Corinna and she would wash and iron your three shirts. A bushel of spinach could get you hair tonic and a bobbin of thread, and a boon of butter would buy you a nice scrap of leather or a wooden chair for your little one. A chair of your own would cost you some cream and cake as well.

But unlike in many places, where currencies of gold and silver, or rainbow notes with profiled presidents or kings, replaced the devalued promise, on Oh it's still legal tender—just about, for there never seem to be quite enough of those rainbow bills to go around. Many of the islanders, when they do get their hands on one, prefer to save it for a rainy day. So a promise on Oh is always taken very seriously—by the islanders blessed with all the rainbow bills they need, by those without, and by the characters in our story, most of whom fall somewhere in between—even when the promise is for promise's sake, and for nothing in return.

So far, Raoul has promised to find an explanation for missing pineapples (and for anything else that smells of magic); Pedro and Gustave have promised possible trouble if he tries; Wilbur has pledged his heart to Edda; Edda has pledged hers to a red-eyed, cheek-stained baby girl; Bang, his lucky harmonica to Raoul; and I, I have said you would hear the story of Raoul's first meeting with Gustave, the one that inspired the ad in the *Morning Crier*.

It happened about a week before Puymute's pineapples disappeared. I was just a few days old and had yet to venture outside the house where I was born, but the steady stream of visitors continued. They came with jams and jellies and bedcovers, and they left with theories and verdicts, and some nice, juicy fat to chew while they strung up their washing and peeled their potatoes. It was clear to everyone but my mother ("blind little dumpling," the islanders said) that I was a Vilder. It was also common knowledge that up to then Gustave was the only Vilder left on Oh, and thus the only one who could be my father. But the science behind my mother's pregnancy was a matter that divided the islanders into two factions.

Some accepted Edda's denials (Why *did* they keep asking her who had shared her bed?) and admitted to an indefinable magic, some trickery on the part of Gustave. Among these were my father Wilbur ("poor little dumpling, too"), who wasn't so bothered as long as his wife was happy, and Gustave himself. Gustave was as certain that he hadn't fathered me as he was uncertain about his own magic powers. He had mustered enough to kill his mother, that's true, and Miss Peacock had unleashed something inside him, that was true, too. But magic-wise he hadn't really accomplished much since then.

Had he?

Others denied Edda's acceptance (Did she *really* expect them to believe she didn't see the truth?) and admitted to only the unmentionable (though they mentioned little else), some trickery on the part of Edda. Among these were Bang, Cougar, and Nat, believe it or not. They believed in Gustave's magic, too, they certainly did; but they knew Edda, they practically raised her after all, and suspected that in this case their little dumpling might be hiding some spice between the folds. They would never have fessed up to such feelings in front of Raoul, of course. As far as he knew, they were staunch supporters of the magic faction and defenders of his little dumpling's honor.

Raoul's sympathies lay somewhere in between. He didn't for a minute doubt his daughter's word. But magic? Raoul couldn't stomach such a shady truth as that. He wanted an answer that was as clear as a nose on a face. And when he looked *this* matter square in the face, nothing was clear at all. I was his grandchild, and I was an Orlean, there was no doubting that. Raoul had watched my mother swell and bloat and pucker in the months preceding my arrival, and Abigail, the island's most practiced midwife, had herself delivered me—Miss Almondine Orlean (I was given my mother's family name, which she kept after marriage, Oh not being completely devoid of modern tendencies). Yet when Raoul looked into my eyes, his own didn't stare back at him the way they did when he looked into Edda's. In place of Raoul's dark, black Orlean eyes, I ("pale little creature") had red Vilder globes.

The first time Raoul peered into my face, he forgot where he was and what he was doing, like the first thick seconds that cloud a still-sleepy mind as the body awakes from a nap. When his mind caught up with his limbs and tried to verify the surroundings, the bedroom window's darned curtain and the mint-green coverlet on the mattress, it recognized nothing at all. My face should have been a mirror to Raoul's heart, but in it his reflection was haunted, at once familiar and foreign—an abrupt and glowing consciousness that we are more, or less, than we think we are.

So Raoul decided then and there that, if no answers were to be found in my face, then perhaps one as clear as a nose could be gleaned or gotten from Gustave's. Gustave had twice left word for Raoul in the week before my birth that the two men needed to talk. Once at the airport and once at the Belly. But Raoul, who had little regard for Gustave Vilder, had been too busy to bother with either message. Gustave must have wanted to come clean all along! So days after I came into the world, Raoul finally left for Gustave's dwelling, and a chat.

Gustave lived on the westernmost shore of the island, on the land where the comfortable shack with the daffodil curtains and his heart-poking mother once stood. A small, simple villa stood there now, for thanks to Miss Peacock and the girls of the seedy port bar, Gustave had found the power to make something more of himself than the slouch-shouldered family legacy had dictated he should be. He had gotten himself hired by Puymute, who paid well, and finagled himself a loan from the bank, where the manager feared him too much to refuse. And he had built himself a house with indoor plumbing.

A house, but not quite a home. For it lacked a woman's touch, or at least the touch of someone other than Gustave Vilder. Despite its bright colors, its wispy fabrics, and the sun that pounded it most of the day, the small, simple villa was a thick and shaded place, where even the welcoming froth of the sugared coffee proffered in the most expensive cups to be had at the market was disagreeable.

When Raoul reached the jagged fence of thick twigs that wrapped itself around the house, he could barely hear for all the noise in his head.

Flies.

The whole way there he had pondered what Gustave would say to him, what explanation Gustave would give, and every hypothesis was a buzz in his brain. They mingled in there and clashed and hummed. Had he tricked her in her sleep? Did he creep into the house while Wilbur delivered the mail (that's what my father does on Oh) and Edda lay napping? Did he hide in her bed one night while Wilbur dozed in the breezy hammock on the porch? (He does that sometimes, too.) Did he sneak up on her from behind and slink away before Edda realized he wasn't her husband? All troubling theories, these, but less troubling than magic-talk, Raoul said to himself, and far less troubling than a mystery.

Though the common buzz of all those flies fired and bounced in his head, the thought that it would soon be silenced, that the riddle would soon be solved, was enough to make the commotion not only tolerable, but enticing. Raoul was almost giggling by the time he knocked at Gustave's door.

Inside the house, Gustave sat with his feet up, sipping pineapple wine. He was soon to embark on what would likely be a lucrative business venture and he was celebrating. There was still much to do, dozens of details to be ironed out, but Gustave had a heavy hand and felt sure he was up to the task. He was cheerily ticking the details off in his head when Raoul's knock cracked his satisfied smile. "Oy! Vilder! Are you in there?"

Gustave looked at the closed door as if it might identify this unknown, familiar voice.

"I say, are you in there? It's Raoul Orlean. You wanted to talk to me."

Gustave smiled again, ticked off yet one more detail, and invited Raoul to come in. "Why, just the man I wanted to see!"

"I should think so. You have something to say for yourself, Vilder?"

"Yes, sir, I do! But call me Gustave. Sit down. I was just sampling Puymute's finest."

Raoul sat and accepted a glass. His giddiness had faded, supplanted by a mixture of puzzlement and unease. How was it so dark and hot in this place? The windows were open but the island gusts seemed to pass them right by, as did the light of the sun. Its heat, on the other hand, was focused squarely on the roof (it must have been), for inside, the villa was a brightly-colored, wispy-fabricked stove. Raoul stuffed into his pocket the handkerchief now wet from his brow and looked up to find Gustave with awaiting eyes, his glass perched in the air.

How is it that this fool is so hospitable? Raoul wondered, his puzzlement poised on the verge of offense. He looked Gustave close up and square in the nose. Their glasses clinked. "Now say your piece."

"I have just one word for you, Raoul. May I call you Raoul?" Gustave was practically bursting at the seams, but with delight. Not confession. Raoul's puzzlement resisted. He wrinkled his forehead and silenced the now not-so-happy hum in his head.

A weak and raspy "Well?" was all he could spit out.

"'Well' what?"

"Your one word. What is it?" The hum awoke again with ricocheted suggestions: Sorry. Trickery. Apology. Betrayal. Deceit.

"Mealybugs."

Raoul rattled his head and smacked one ear with the palm of his hand. He examined the fizzy wine in his glass then set the glass on the table, pushing it away with the tip of his finger. "What's that you say?"

"Mealybugs."

Again. How much wine had he drunk? Mealybugs? "What do mealybugs have to bloody do with anything?" he finally managed.

More delight from Gustave. "They have to do with everything!" He refilled his glass and tried to top off Raoul's but Raoul's hand lashed out to protect it. "There's mealybugs on Killig. The island's overrun and this year's crop has wilted away to nothing." (Killig is the island neighbor that Bang's grandfather sang about, the one with sweet fruits and sweet governors that plugged the hole in the pineapple market during the tax trouble on Oh.)

Gustave continued. "You'll be getting the official word eventually, soon as the mayor over there talks to the governor and the governor goes to Parliament and Parliament makes a proclamation for the prime minister to put to referendum. Then they have to vote, you know. Shouldn't take more than three or four months."

"Referendum?" That certainly wasn't one of Raoul's fly-theories, which had all gone instantly quiet at the mention of mealybugs.

"Referendum. They got obligations to meet. Companies all over the world with exclusive contracts for Killig pineapples. And Killig's got pests. They'll be coming to desperate little Oh just begging to buy our precious piñas so they can sell 'em off as their own and cut their losses."

Raoul still didn't see how any of this had anything to do with *me*, his baby Almondine. Had Edda swallowed a mealybug with her fruited morning yogurt? "What are you saying, Gustave?"

"I'm saying we wait for mayors, governors, and ministers and sell Oh's pineapples to Killig minus the big chunk of profits that you excisemen will nibble—worse than those mealybugs you are—or you and I join forces and move now. Put all the profits straight in our own pockets. I've been in touch with some growers on Killig, and I got it all worked out for moving the fruit, everything but Customs. That's where you come in. You type us some phony forms for a fifty-fifty split. Can't pass up a deal like that. We'd be ready to go in less than a week."

Raoul was so angry that he went momentarily mute. (Gustave had that effect on him.) He huffed and sputtered and ah-huh-huhhed until the indignation choking his throat finally leaped out. Or so it seemed to Raoul. In reality the leap was more of a clumsy stumble, a tumbleweed of tongue and retort, for Raoul didn't know where to begin. He was pretty sure his honor had been insulted, he thought perhaps his wine had been drugged, he wondered if he shouldn't call the police, and then there were the bugs. Raoul had come expecting apologies and amends, but had been offered insects instead. White, powdery, leaf-wilting insects and hot, pineapple wine.

The flies were really stirring now, and Raoul let them out all at once. How dare Gustave even suggest such an incriminating collaboration? Cheating the governments of Killig and Oh in one fell swoop, pineapple-trafficking with crooked growers, why, Raoul would have nothing to do with such flimflammery and had half a mind to call the police. Phony forms indeed! Who was Gustave to meddle in the affairs of mayors and ministers? To bungle referendums and jeopardize honest excisemen? To barter behind the square-shouldered back of the Customs Office and to benefit from blight while Edda sat tricked, swindled, sneaked up on, and Wilbur, a respected officer of the Island Post, bamboozled in his breezy hammock on the porch? What about poor Edda, whose black eyes couldn't hear, and baby Almondine, whose red ones said so much, poor baby Almondine with her blotched and haunted face and her dubious genes that awaited explanation and retribution, but mostly explanation, so that Raoul could get a good's night sleep, without the flies buzzing in his bed? What about that? he said. What about the flies?!

Now it was Gustave's turn to be puzzled. He was speaking mealybugs and Raoul answered bedbugs and flies. Funny, Gustave had drunk more wine than Raoul, yet Raoul seemed far more drunk.

Mind you, it didn't come as a complete surprise that Raoul shouldn't go along. Gustave almost expected as much and had a back-up plan for that—assuming he could reason with this fellow spouting nonsense about sleeping mailmen and eyes that were hard of hearing. Though Gustave had some idea of what genes were, he couldn't for the life of him imagine them awaiting an explanation, to say nothing of the fact that he didn't know how or why he should be the person to provide one, nor how, if he did, it might keep the insects out of Raoul's bed.

In the end, genes and mailmen weren't really his concern, so Gustave tried to steer Raoul's racing thoughts back to the matter at hand. "Now, why don't I just let you mull this over for a few days. You might change your mind when your head's clearer and you've thought things through."

"Clearer? Clearer?" Raoul sputtered before his indignation leaped again. "Why, you'd have to feed me a barrelful of that swill before my head would be clear enough to be in cahoots with the likes of you."

"Very well." Gustave was standing now, pacing in front of Raoul, his hands clasped behind him, his flip-flops smacking the floor's terracotta tiles in between his slow, deliberate words. "I understand. You're a respected officer of the law, don't want to get your hands dirty. Fair enough."

Back-up plan: "Maybe you'd be interested in dipping your fingers in the pie just long enough to keep your head turned while those pineapples ship off to Killig. I can't promise you fifty-fifty, in that case, but you turn a blind eye if something should look fishy at Customs and I'll make it worth your while."

Raoul went mute again. He was so angered now that even his flies were speechless. He stood and pounded his fist on the table (Gustave had that effect on him, too) so hard that the half-emptied glass of Puymute's finest toppled over, its contents dripping into a shallow, sticky puddle. Gustave bent to wipe away the mess with a dishcloth that had somehow appeared in his hand. By the time he stood back up, Raoul had found his voice.

"Now you listen here, Vilder. Let it be as clear as the nose on my face that I want nothing to do with this scheme of yours. And I'd advise you to forgo it as well. You can't likely get away with it now, anyway, can you? Now that you've gone and spouted off about it?"

"No. I guess it won't work now, will it?" But Gustave was bursting at the seams again, again in delight. Not defeat. For he had a back-up plan for the back-up plan, and the back-up's back-up put all the profits straight in Gustave's pockets alone. He would have to stir up a little magic, which was perhaps not as easy or proper as proper phony customs forms, but how was Gustave to blame if Officer Orlean refused to cooperate?

Refuse to cooperate, he did, for Raoul was upstanding. His instincts told him to have no part in the plan, and instinctively he had said no. Right then and there, though, as he was refusing, Raoul wasn't thinking about upstandingness or about his Customs career. He had gone to Gustave's to find out the truth, to solve a riddle, resolve a mystery. To explain those dubious genes swimming inside the blood he shared with his granddaughter. And no amount of mealybugs or money was going to tell him who she was.

It was time to ask Gustave flat out about Edda.

In the seconds while Gustave contemplated the magic he'd have to stir and Raoul deliberated dubious genes, the sun set, quieting the humors of both the island and the islanders alike. As if in agreement, the two men calmly sat back down and Raoul uprighted the glass that had tumbled over and spun on its edge.

Calmly, my grandfather began: "Let's have no more talk of bugs and governors. That's not what I came here for. I came to find out about Edda."

Even more certain now of Raoul's inebriation, for he really was making little sense, Gustave exhaled a cautious, "Edda, your daughter, Edda?"

"That's right."

"What about her?"

"Now don't be funny, Gustave. I think you know something about Almondine."

"Something like what?" Set sun or no, Gustave was feeling prickly-necked now.

"You must have heard what people are saying."

"I heard some crazy lie about how this baby looks like me."

Raoul was feeling a little prickly-necked now, too. "Well how do you explain it?"

"How should I know? A coincidence. How much like me could the child possibly look, if I haven't ever been within two inches of your daughter?" Gustave was bursting again, with feigned nonchalance, but underneath the casual coating he was worried. He hadn't said it, the word, but it was there in the room with both of them—"magic"—as loudly as if he had. His whole life Gustave hated the terrible word almost as much as Raoul did, if for different reasons, and never more so than now. On Oh, Gustave *wielded* magic, he didn't succumb to it. But he was beginning to have his doubts in that regard.

On the other side of Gustave's indifferent shell, Raoul heard it too—"magic"—and although he didn't believe Gustave's assertion about Edda, although he didn't understand the exact relationship between Gustave and the terrible word, a hint of Gustave's doubts reached Raoul's nose, a faint scent, but terrible enough to send Raoul home in a fog of worried disappointment and pity (was it?), resignedly aware that this particular night had held no answers for him.

As he opened the jagged gate of thick twigs to take his leave, he heard Gustave's voice behind him."Raoul! Listen, if you change your mind..."

Raoul hollered over his shoulder, "Call me 'Mr. Orlean'!"

Poor Gustave.

Inside his head, yet one more detail came *un*-ticked.

In his bedroom, Raoul sat at the desk by the window, where he usually read. The walk from Gustave's house had cleared his head, but it hadn't changed his mind. He wasn't a smuggler, or about to become one, and he still needed answers, or at least one answer as clear as a nose on a face. Why had he let Gustave off so easily? Was it the wine? He didn't really believe Gustave knew nothing about the baby, did he? And yet...

And yet.

Another fly hatched right then, still small enough that when Raoul shook his head—no, there's more to this than Gustave's telling—he shook it away. Perhaps somebody had seen Gustave creep into the house while Wilbur delivered the mail or dozed on the porch. Perhaps Gustave had bragged of his coup. Just possibly there was a witness, or someone who had heard something. Raoul would have to advertise to find out.

He pulled a lined sheet of paper from the desk drawer and sharpened a pencil. Staring out into the night, he composed the words with silent lips, his eyes fixed on the moon. She had followed him home, watching and winking, and now as he bent his head to write, she splashed her light over the desk and the paper before him. The impertinent moon, full and high and blue, a promise of the gifts wrapped up in the still, dark sky.

6

When Raoul's ad finally appeared in the paper, it caused quite a stir on the island, as you might imagine. It had the unfortunate effect of getting people talking, about all the wrong things. No one dared implicate Gustave—most were as content as ever to simply accept that he'd had a hand (or worse) in the matter—and no one had any information to share about *me*. Not a witness came forth.

The islanders did have plenty to say about some of the *other* Orleans, my mother to start. She was far too kind and gentle for them to accuse her outright, but their suspicions niggled and eventually made themselves heard. Mainly, though, they talked about Raoul. All of Oh was sure my grandfather was losing his mind. While Raoul was sure he wasn't, he did know he was stressed (and to think that at that point not a pineapple as yet had disappeared). So as was his usual, he sought solace at the Belly. Alas, there wasn't much there to be found, as you'll see.

I know I'm jumping around a bit, in place as well as time. Stories on Oh are rarely straightforward. The wind has a way of tossing them about and mixing them up—and our lives along with them—so that often we find ourselves right where we started and sorting our way back to where we've already been. Like the tide that claws its way inland every time it's dragged back to sea.

Just now the wind is blowing us back to the Belly with Raoul. The ad has caused its trouble, Edda's name is on the tip of every tongue, and half the island (at least) thinks Raoul is wholly mad. For *his* part, all he wants is a quiet evening and a little cheering up.

"Bastard! He's making Raoul look like a real fool. Have you seen this?" Cougar stood, elbow propped on the bar's edge, wide-brimmed whitish straw hat propped on his head, and thrust the *Morning Crier* into Bang's hand.

"Seen it? It's all anybody's talking about." Bang knocked his knuckles on the bar and the bartender brought him water. "I know Raoul likes to get to the bottom of things, but this! He's gonna get himself killed."

"Killed? What do you mean?"

"Gustave, what else? If he had a hand in this..." (Bang lowered his voice.) "...and we know he must have, then Raoul's just made himself a nasty little enemy, calling attention to the situation like he did. I told him to mind his business and to keep quiet, I told him."

"No one's killing anybody." Cougar began to light his nightly cigar and paused. "Are they? You don't really think...?"

Bang leaned close into Cougar's chest. "Well, if he can magically impregnate a person, I don't see why he can't kill one."

"I guess." Cougar lit the cigar now and tilted his head upward in reflection. "'Course, he really doesn't have to. The whole island thinks Raoul's mad. He keeps this up, no one will listen to a word he says, about Gustave or otherwise. We need to talk some sense into him."

"Well don't look at me. I tried. I told him. Mind your business. Keep. Quiet." Bang gargled softly and warmed his vocal chords with deep hums that rose and fell in pitch and volume.

"There is always the possibility that Raoul knows what he's doing and that someone will answer the ad," Cougar suggested.

Bang gargle-hum-choked an "Are you serious?!" He spat the water back into the glass and over a good portion of the bar. "Even if someone knows something..." (He lowered his voice again.) "... and I don't think they do, who's going to point a finger at someone like Vilder and maybe lose his job or his wife or his money or his fishing rod, or even fall down and die? Would you? If you knew something about Edda, would you tell Raoul?"

"No. No I don't suppose I would." Cougar sent out a cloud of perfumed smoke and caught sight of Nat, who had just walked into the Belly.

"Over here, Nat," Cougar shouted. "Two doubles," he told the bartender. "Yellow rum."

"'Evening," Nat said and slid onto a barstool. "I just brought you a hotel guest. Lady from Belgium. Had a suitcase full of hazelnuts."

"No need for those around here. There's plenty of nuts on Oh already," Cougar said.

Bang handed Nat the newspaper. "Poor Raoul has gone a little mad, I'm afraid."

Nat put the paper on the bar and sighed. "Raoul says there's an explanation for everything. Says there must be a witness. I told him to mind his own business—"

"That's exactly what I said!" Bang interrupted.

"You know what I think of Gustave," Nat went on. "Creepy. But I told Raoul to leave well enough alone. Almondine's healthy,

Edda's happy, Wilbur's too in love to know the difference. Funny things happen around here. It's nothing new. But you know Raoul."

They did, of course, know Raoul, and they also knew that nothing they could say or do would dissuade him from ruffling feathers or looking foolish or doing whatever else might be required to find the explanation he was certain must exist. *That* was nothing new either. It's true that Raoul had never resorted to newspaper ads before now, so the particulars were a bit out of the ordinary, but in general he had long been known to noodle. There was no matter on Oh too trivial, no minutia too minute, to escape elucidation by Raoul.

This time, though, the noodling was different. It was public. Normally, Bang, Cougar, and Nat were the extent of the audience to Raoul's follies, and his three pals preferred it that way. They could affectionately chuckle behind his back (There he goes again, man!), pat him on it when he was around (You'll get to the bottom of it, mate, no worries!), and all in the privacy of a dark corner table at the Buddha's Belly Bar and Lounge, where their loyalty was no less true for its discretion.

But Raoul's latest stunt had flung them from the peaceful anonymity of the audience into the spotlight center-stage. The ad had only just appeared in the morning's paper and by the end of the day they already felt the burden of their allegiance. Distracted by the questions of the local passersby, Bang had badly butchered almost half a dozen pineapples. Cougar caught his cooks and his chambermaids gossiping instead of chopping and cleaning. And Nat, Nat only had peace when he was locked in his taxi with a tourist who was none the wiser, and *that*, that only until noontime, by when even the visitors had heard of the ad: say, you don't know this fellow wanting to know where babies come from, do you? As a matter of fact he did, Nat defended, and of course this fellow knew where babies came from, generally, just not this particular one.

Raoul's three friends were troubled. They were tired of being hassled (though secretly Cougar hoped his association with Raoul would bring in curious customers). They were embarrassed (even love and loyalty have their boundaries). And they were scared, though none would have admitted it to either of the other two. All three loved Raoul, I'm sure of that, if each in his own bumbling and selfish way, but none wanted an inadvertent enemy in Gustave Vilder.

And besides being troubled, tired, embarrassed, and scared, they were worried and sorry, worried because Raoul might be putting himself in danger, and sorry because Raoul had become the butt of the islanders' jokes. Had Raoul kept quiet, the rumors about little Almondine would eventually have needled their way into the fabric of the history and lore with which the islanders inveterately cloaked themselves, the individual threads (Edda's transgression, or Gustave's) lost in the weave. Leave it to Raoul, they thought, to tug a loose end and unravel time-honored tradition.

There was little that Bang, Cougar, or Nat could think to do just then to alleviate their symptoms. In fact there was little to be done. So, like many before them and many to come, with no idea of how to solve their problem, they ignored it. At least in front of Raoul. At least for now.

"Alright, that's settled. Not a word when Raoul gets here." Cougar raised his glass and the others knocked theirs into it. (Rum. Water. Rum.)

Raoul joined them just then—"Beer, please," he said—and was greeted with enough superfluous enthusiasm to raise his eyebrows and arouse his suspicion. "What's the occasion?" he asked, his nose pointed at their glasses, still hanging in the air.

Cougar looked at Bang, who looked at Nat, who somehow managed to salvage their secret. "No occasion," he said. "Just wishing Bang a bit of luck before the show."

Raoul didn't believe them, but he had bigger problems than their antics to concern himself with. "Cheers, then. Good luck." He clinked his mug against Bang's tumbler (Beer. Water.) and asked about the show. "What's on the menu this evening? Pineapple polkas? Jellyfish jazz?"

"Tribute to the night," Bang replied, unfazed. "Don't you see I'm dressed in black?" Indeed he was. Pleated crepe trousers, black t-shirt, secondhand tuxedo coat to cover the tiny holes that dotted the t-shirt's back like freckles.

"Aha." Raoul smiled. (Bang had that effect on him.)

By this time the Belly was full and the band could be heard tuning up and plugging in and sending random chords into the regular din of the drinkers and discussants at the Belly's round tables that night. Bang made his way to the stage and in the shadow of his presence, the room fell silent.

"Ladies and gentlemen. Good evening and welcome to the Buddha's Belly. My name is Bang and tonight we're gonna do some numbers for you inspired by the deep, black night that blankets this pretty little island of Oh. So get yourselves something to wet your whistle," he winked. "And if you feel like blanketing the dance floor, that's what it's there for!"

Silly Bang.

Who knows what goes on in the night?

Bang began his song, his voice coating the Belly and soothing it, his notes illuminating the speckled sky that succumbed to the invasion of the loudspeakers Cougar had affixed to the Belly's outside walls. The tide advanced and receded, but more quietly now, and the leaves of the two thin sentinel palms that overlooked Cougar's beach-front tables paused in their rustling, not wanting to overshadow the singer. The moon glowed and bristled, Bang's tongue tickling her ears.

What you'll find in the morning light?

Raoul, Cougar, and Nat looked from Bang to each other to their drinks. Each was reluctant to break the silence that inevitably fell at the start of Bang's show, but tonight they were equally reluctant to allow the uncomfortable pause in their conversation to last a moment longer. They all knew exactly what it was they weren't talking about, and knew that talking about something else, anything else (fishing, storm drains, the price of gasoline), would make their not-talking less trying.

What forces there that play in the dark?

Cougar wished to speak, to say something safe and reassuring to Raoul, but for all his efforts to think of any topic other than the ad, the ad was the very (and only) thing that came to mind. Nat, for all his discomfort, felt that their common distress and the silence were preferable to the singular distress of speaking up. So he, too, held his tongue. The unwitting bad intentions of the very best of friends.

Who hides behind the mango's bark?

All Raoul wanted was for them to say something, anything, to him. He wanted to hear his friends' opinions, their assurances, even their barbs. It didn't matter if they thought he was crazy. It didn't matter if anybody did. Raoul could handle that. A man who took things at face value the way he did was used to it. A man who respected his principles and pursued truths as plain as noses on faces almost came to expect it. But amidst his principles and his pursuits, at least he had never felt alone. Well, not up to now.

Who knows what goes on in the night?

Bang's song was an old one. Cougar remembered when it first reached the island; my mother was just a child and his hotel Sincero only just getting on its feet; the memory of Emma Patrice had finally begun to fade, Raoul looking less and less for her face in his line at the airport, for her handwriting when he picked up the day's mail. He would take Edda to the hotel with him every day after work, partly because entertaining her on his own was too exhausting, and partly because he didn't know what else to do with her.

While the men sat in the Belly smoking cigarettes (they considered themselves too young then for cigars) and sipping pineapple punch (their drinks grew stiffer as their bodies did), Uncle Cougar let little Edda roam freely on the hotel property. A warrior in the courtyard, she sparred with a garden statuette of Mars, his sandstone shield no match for her twig-sword's blows. In the rooms, a princess, whose dainty feet must only touch the gray tiles, never the blue, on their way to the three-inch ledge with wrought-iron, faux-balcony railing beyond which her prince awaited. And peckish, purring feline in the kitchen, where her favorite of the two cooks, a tall, toothless chap called Tripper, fed her bowls of flavored milk that tasted of berries and daisies and slices of ginger.

While the men sat in the Belly smoking cigarettes and sipping pineapple punch, rating and berating the tourists—the lookers, the talkers, the tippers, the snobs—the feline princess warrior turned into a girl.

If in the morning it will be alright?

Cougar remembered this, too, when it first happened, or rather, when he first noticed that it had. A Saturday, and Edda off from school. Raoul was at the airport thumbing passports and passing out pineapples, Bang was filleting them onto paper plates outside, and Nat was transporting them, on the floor of his Renault between pairs of pale Romanian knees. Cougar, left alone with the feline princess warrior who had clearly had her fill of flowery milk, pretend princes, and still statues, suggested a hike to the Crater.

It seems that Oh once had a volcano ("seems" because no one knows for sure), a volcano that supposedly tired of Oh's sandy winds and sticky scents and meddling moons, so much so that it shut itself off, burned itself out, and settled into silence. The crater it left behind in reproof of the island's affronts was too much for the islanders to bear. They, too, tired, so much so that they submerged it, drowned it, and turned it into a lake. The lake, as it so happened, loved the winds and scents and moons and decided to stay, to stay and to get comfortable. It adorned itself with grassy shores and stubby trees that were a perfect fit and insisted, rightly so, on a respectable name, Lake George, perhaps, or Lake Burl; but as respectable a lake as it was, no islander had ever called it anything but the Crater, for deep inside that's what it really was. And even the prickliest islander on prickly, pineappled Oh would figure out, sooner or later, that the deep insides mattered more than a rippled surface.

So you wait for the sun in your bed.

To the Crater, then, for Uncle Cougar and Edda, who found themselves alone on a sunny Saturday afternoon at the Sincero. Armed with a picnic lunch prepared by Tripper, tuna steak on triangles of toasted wheat bread, a salad of olive-sized capers and pear, and cream with honeyed peach, they began their walk. Cougar asked Edda about her schoolwork and her teachers, about her friends and her plans. Her studies were going well enough, she said, though she was never in the top of the class. She simply didn't like books, not since her missing mother's volumes had been removed from the house by Raoul, and the teachers expected her to read all the time, even when she studied science or history or mathematics, imagine! But she liked her teachers nonetheless and often brought them oleander and poinsettias from the garden behind her house. She had friends at school, yes, the other girls, but they weren't interested in gardening. She walked with them after school every day on the beach, where the other girls talked only of boys, and, while Edda didn't mind this (or the boys themselves, for that matter), she didn't much see the point of it. And her plans? Plans for what?

Cougar laughed. Such a child she was still, he thought to himself. A sweet child. He turned to look at her and, laughing, put his arm around her shoulders as they continued on, past the market and the bank and the grimy-windowed office of the *Morning Crier*. Tucked under his arm, Edda turned her head to meet his eyes and his laughter, and the meeting left Cougar chilled, as if a breath had blown on the warm, musky sweat that till then rested shiny and ignored on his neck and his dark brown arms, on his dark brown arm wrapped around Edda's dark brown shoulders.

Odd, this.

Cougar pulled himself away. He looked all around him, expecting to observe the source of the breath that had kissed his skin, but there was nothing to see. Nothing except the wet mark on Edda's back that still betrayed the sweaty trespassing of Cougar's skin on hers. Surely it hadn't been Edda who provoked such a reaction in him? She was just a child, he told himself, Raoul's child no less, and even Cougar, who was fond of a fresh can of worms now and then, knew better than to stick his hand in this one. He was mistaken about the breeze that Edda's body had blown through him. He must have been, for he thought he still felt it now, though their bodies no longer touched.

Perhaps it was just the clever wind.

So you wait for some light in your head.

As Edda and Cougar neared the Crater, the landscape steepened and the path became more rocky. Cougar sent Edda ahead of him, so that he could catch her should her dainty feet find difficulty navigating the path. But the path was short, if sharp, and it wasn't long before Edda reached the low summit and stopped to peer down at the lake in front of her. The sun, hanging midway between zenith and horizon, transformed the lake's blues into flickering diamonds of silver, white, and purple, against the background of which Edda was an aubergine cut-out, flat and curved at once. Cougar, following behind, admired the silhouette that lay decidedly at the end of his path. The feline princess warrior had not only turned into a girl, but one whose outlines harbingered the woman deep inside.

He joined her at the Crater's edge and they made their way to a shaded spot nearby. In the diamond light of the lake they ate, tuna, capers, pear, peach, Cougar all the while tossed by Edda's (or someone's) invisible breeze. He noticed parts of her he had never noticed before, her ankle, her heels, her calf, her wrist, the pink moons on her even pinker round fingernails. To her remarks about Tripper's recipes, the capers, the cream, he nodded and emitted gentle grunts, avoiding her glance and wondering if from this harbinger girl yet flowed a woman's blood. It wasn't a question he could pose to Raoul, and why exactly he wished to know he couldn't decide.

Who knows what goes on in the night?

"Mr. Zanne? Do you want another?" a waitress asked, tossing him suddenly from the edge of the Crater to the heart of the Belly. "Mr. Zanne?"

"Cougar! Hey! Don't you hear your waitress talking to you?" Nat jabbed his elbow into Cougar's ribcage. "He'll have another and I will, too, if you don't mind. How about you, Raoul? Another beer?"

"Thanks," Raoul said.

The girl busied herself behind the bar and the men resumed their silence.

Figures, Bang's on stage when you need him, Nat thought to himself. He'd have some nonsense or other to tell Raoul right about now. Some story about a lucky trumpet or a daft old relative of his. What could Nat possibly say to make him feel better? Nat had never owned a lucky charm in his life, and he had no family left. What little of it preceded him had used up the family fortunes and fables, leaving Nat empty-handed. Raoul already knew that story anyway. He could tell Raoul about the lady with the hazelnuts in her suitcase, but unusual as that was, it wouldn't do to cheer him up proper.

You try to see but you've lost your sight,

Why was Raoul so stubborn anyway? Other people managed to get the flies out of their heads. Why couldn't he? Wasn't Almondine all that mattered? She looked to be doing well enough. Nat had been one of the first to visit Edda's house after the birth. (He brought her roasted corncobs, and for me, a rattle shaped like a butterfly.) He didn't know firsthand what new mothers said or did, but Edda seemed to know. Nat had never seen her so happy. Not on her wedding day, or after her wedding night. A daughter's happiness was all that a father should care about, wasn't it? If Nat could figure out that much, than certainly so should Raoul.

Then there was Cougar. What about him in all this? Why should Nat assume the burden of breaking the silence or not, of comforting Raoul or reprimanding him. Why was Cougar so distracted this evening? Maybe Nat would tell Raoul about the hazelnuts after all.

Until dawn and then you look around,

Little did Nat know, as he debated about Edda and about the Belgian woman's baggage, that Bang's song had triggered in Cougar reminiscences he was loath to renounce. Cougar was stuck in the Crater. Stuck on the checkered tablecloth that Tripper had packed for a blanket, stuck on the grassy shores of the lake that sparkled white behind Edda's now sitting silhouette, stuck on a sunny Saturday afternoon a long long time ago, with Edda, the daughter of his very best friend.

But Nat was firmly at the Belly, where he could bear his friend's silence no longer. He took a deep breath, and before he could change his mind about opening his mouth, exhaled "Raoul, guess who I picked up today?"

"Who?"

"A lady from Belgium, with a suitcase full of hazelnuts. She's staying right here at the Sincero, too. What do you suppose she plans to do with them?"

"With what?"

"With the nuts? What do you think she'll do with all those nuts?"

Raoul took a long, slow drink of his beer, and Nat elbowed Cougar again, his jabs saying, See? He's thinking about nuts now, which is better than thinking about babies and ads.

"I don't know," Raoul finally said. "I don't know what she'll do with all those nuts." But after that he said nothing more, so Cougar jabbed Nat to say, The nuts just weren't enough.

Indeed they weren't. As Nat had suspected, it wasn't a cheer-up proper, and it wasn't the reassurance that Raoul had hoped for. But it helped, if only a little. Raoul knew what Nat was trying to do and it helped.

And you see the tracks betrayed by the ground.

Raoul sat, silent, at the bar. He faced forward and watched his reflection in the glass he held. He could feel people staring at him, could almost hear their whispers. He knew they were laughing at him, and at his ad, but he was confident something would come of it. There was an explanation for everything on Oh, and, that being the case, Raoul had no intention of renouncing the one for his granddaughter's Vilder looks. It was Almondine he thought of, Almondine for whom he sought the truth. What almond could flower on uncertain roots?

And you see the tracks betrayed by the ground.

"If Gustave won't explain it, then maybe the ad will tell us all how Edda got pregnant," Raoul muttered to himself. And Bang sang.

7

At the Pritchard T. Lullo Public Library, Raoul once read a book about dangling dead bodies that oozed a deadly poison. He read about a man who loved sheep, girls who hid in cupboards, and a country where everything broke. He read about cheaters, gardeners, pilots and poets, and a nun who collected clocks. He read thousand-page books by a doctor, and short ones by a preacher named Glen. Raoul read about whales and rain forests, about dinosaurs, engines, and pumps, and lands where it always snowed. He read about stomachache, heartbreak, and lust. And sometimes he read about joy.

Raoul was always delighted to stumble into a joyful book, for he had a nasty habit of pretending that he was every character he read about. And while it was thrilling to find a dinosaur bone in the dust or invent a pump that could take water to a village atop a hill, collecting clocks and swinging limp from a tree were no fun to imagine at all. But any time, after pages of suffered black-and-white meanderings, Raoul realized he was in for a happy ending (requited love, retrieved treasures, a truth like a nose on a face), well, it was all he could do to keep himself from skipping right to the very last page. Not that he ever did, of course. Raoul had long learned the lesson of anticipation's sweetness.

Raoul's favorite book was a joyful book, and one that was to become very important in his search for my true identity. It was a book about a man who woke up one day and didn't know who he was. He knew his name, of course, that's not what I mean. He was Mr. Stan Kalpi, mathematics teacher at the Sacred Heart School for Boys. He liked to drink beer on hot days (they were all hot where Mr. Stan Kalpi lived), ate meat almost every night, played golf when he could afford the visitor's fee at the club, and was learning to play an instrument he had fashioned himself, not quite guitar but more than mandolin. This so that he might serenade his bride, if and when he found her. The book said Mr. Stan Kalpi had brown eyes, brown eyes that looked green if he tilted his head toward the sun in the late afternoon. Raoul thought maybe the author was wrong about that; surely, Mr. Stan Kalpi's eyes were black.

His story goes something like this. One morning dressed up like every other morning (cloudless blue sky, matins and coffee-steam wafting from next-door Betty's), Mr. Stan Kalpi awoke and decided there must be more to him than long-division and his penchant for pork and for ale. Who was he really? More than maths teacher. Not quite musician. He was like the polynomials he taught his students at school, a string of undefined variables that together equaled himself. That's a good start, he thought, perhaps more maths teacher than he was willing to admit. Now it was just a matter of defining the variables, of assigning a value to each and adding them up.

His mother would be a variable, and his father, too, but those were dead ends, for both mother and father were dead. He remembered what his mother looked like, at least he was pretty sure he did, but when he tried to picture his father, the face that showed itself to his mind was that of a kindly old man he often spotted smoking in front of the station. Mr. Stan Kalpi could not be blamed for his faulty recollections. Adult inaccuracies in the telling of a child's story must be forgiven, and especially in his case. He spent just a few sparse years with his parents, who had little money, little food, and little time to devote to their toddler. Only work was granted them in abundance, blistered hands and stringy muscle under sun-hardened skin.

When their son was five years old, the parents of the dark, skinny youth who would grow to be Mr. Stan Kalpi sent their son away. On a cool night, with his newest shoes and the still, dark sky for a cloak, their burden and their hope was led off by the richer and more capable hand of a city-dwelling aunt. In her house Mr. Stan Kalpi grew tall and immune to the marvels that he surveyed from her windows, tallish buildings and taxicabs that his parents would never know the likes of. He wore clean clothes and attended school, where he displayed an early aptitude for maths, fond of the absolutes that governed geometrical shapes and soothed by the precision of deductive algebraic processes. It made perfect sense to Raoul that Mr. Stan Kalpi should harbor such inclinations toward order, product of the disordered infancy that he was, but whether Mr. Stan Kalpi himself saw it like this, the author doesn't say.

A teaching position at the local school for boys and a small house purchased largely by his aunt completed Mr. Stan Kalpi's formal education. He was on his own now, to make of life what he would. Though he didn't seem able to find himself a wife, he did work hard, gaining the respect of his superiors and his students alike, and he carefully managed his money, allowing himself, in addition to fresh meat daily and the occasional round of golf, a once-a-month trip to the cinema. This too made perfect sense to Raoul, that a man who was careful with his money should allow himself such an indulgence, for my grandfather was a bit of a cinema buff himself and not a little annoyed that on a certain Tuesday to which we will soon return, he was researching magic instead of perusing the library's newly-arrived *New Modern History of the Silent Stage.*

But back to Raoul's favorite book.

Despite his job and his balanced accounts and his monthly movies, Mr. Stan Kalpi experienced moments of puzzlement and unease. Sometimes a sound (the crackle of a fire, a snippet of song on the wind) or a smell (oniony stew; the dusty, wet leather of his sandals when he wore them in the rain) would jar him and he didn't know why. As if the crackles and snippets and the onions and the shoes wished to remind him of something, a person, a place, a time that he hadn't ever really known well enough to recall. The only people, places, and times he couldn't recall were those of his early childhood. So these, too, he deduced, must be undefined variables in the polynomial that was he. Mr. Stan Kalpi could smell and hear his past, or at least the echoes of it, but the time had come to see it.

From his rich and capable aunt he learned the name of the village he left that night with his new shoes and his dark-sky cloak. She reminded him of his parents' names (Isla and Matik) and told him that these would be a sufficient means of identifying himself to the villagers once he arrived (everyone in Mr. Stan Kalpi's native village was known as the son—or the daughter—of someone). The aunt hadn't been to the village since that same night, so her memory of the road that would take him there was sketchy. But this didn't worry Mr. Stan. He was at least a mathematics teacher and almost a musician, and was confident that he could find his way. He thanked the aunt for her help and renewed his gratitude for the love and resources she had invested in his upbringing. Then he wrote a letter to the headmaster. He was very sorry, it said, but he must take a leave to attend to his past.

One morning like every other morning, then, cloudless blue sky, more matins and coffee-steam wafting from next-door Betty's, Mr. Stan Kalpi locked up his small house and set off.

"Take care, Betty. I may be away for a while."

"Where to, Mr. Stan?"

"I'm going to look for my past," he told her.

"What for, Mr. Stan?"

"Betty, do you know what a polynomial is?"

Betty shook her head. "Is that what you're looking for?"

"Not exactly. Some parts of one, maybe."

Betty stood leaning on a rake in the middle of her garden, her head tilted upward to meet his, her eyes locked on his eyes while she waited for an answer. "What for, Mr. Stan?" she repeated.

"I hear songs on the wind, Betty. Songs from my past and I'm going to find them."

Betty laughed. She laughed so hard that from each of her eyes seeped two large droplets that she wiped away with the hem of her long, tattered, berry-stained apron. When she recovered her composure she said to him, smiling still, "It's the leaves, Mr. Stan. What you hear are just the leaves."

Mr. Stan Kalpi croaked an "Aah!" and gave her a dismissive wave, as if he were batting a tsetse fly. Then he left. What did silly old Betty know?

In fact, silly old Betty knew her fair share. She was old after all and had spent years amassing the kind of knowledge a woman of her lowly position and means could amass. She didn't know about polynomials, but she did know about things like turnips and tea leaves and trees. And she was right about the leaves. Almost. The leaves were responsible for what Mr. Stan Kalpi heard, true, but for him they sang a special song, a song for which lucky old Betty had no need (she knew her past like she knew the crevices of her tired hands and feet), a song that Mr. Stan Kalpi was right to seek out.

The sketchy directions supplied by his aunt proved too skeletal even for Mr. Stan Kalpi's mathematical, musical mind. They turned a weeks-long trip into a months-long trip, leading him on an elaborate series of wild-goose chases in the process. But the road that burrows into the heart of one's past is never immediate or well paved, I can assure you. It climbs and plunges, pulls first in one direction and then another, each zig and zag a hope to be dashed, a theory to be undone. It prods the pilgrim along its gritty surface, deposits its sand between the traveler's toes, then steers him (or her) at last homeward, a fortified soul on broken heel. So it was with Mr. Stan Kalpi.

En route to his native village he crossed a desert, a river, and went up a mountain and down. He met chiefs and fools, the wise, the sick, the weary. He learned the medicine man's cures and the wiles of the wanton. He found adventure at every detour, detours too numerous and too great for me to report them all here. It is enough to tell you that he was still Mr. Stan Kalpi by the time he arrived, but a much richer and more sapient one indeed.

The road to his past deposited him finally at the village gates on the morning after a long night's rain. Spilled out before him, the moist flora shone in brilliant hues of purple and green, in tones of yellow and blue that had escaped him his whole life, but that now appeared before him familiar as the color of his own skin. He had acquired an air of importance and wisdom on his journey, a visible testament to his trials, that sent word of his presence coursing like fire and brought the villagers from their dwellings, bowed over in respect. But despite his lessons and his triumphs, Mr. Stan Kalpi remained a humble man, a humble mathematician-musician who simply had yet a few more variables to define. He bowed in reciprocated respect and begged the villagers to rise, then introduced himself, son of Isla and Matik.

Though the couple was long dead, there were aunts and uncles and cousins who ran to embrace him. One lit a fire, another fetched wine, and soon the air bristled with the crackle and tease of a roasting goat stuffed with onions and herbs, and snippets of laughter and song. They ate, they drank, they danced. In thanks, Mr. Stan Kalpi serenaded them on his mandolin-guitar, his voice and his strings a perfect fit among the other sounds and scents that filled the space around them. The variables had been defined and totaled and Mr. Stan Kalpi was a polynomial no more. He was a sum, of his schooling and his aunt and old Betty's coffee, of Isla and Matik, of the gritty zig-zagged road, of the faces and the speech that from every direction now set upon his eyes and his ears. He was he.

Mr. Stan Kalpi never returned to the small house his aunt had largely purchased, and he never returned to the Sacred Heart School for Boys. He stayed in the land where the songs and the onions spoke to him, where he recognized his past clearly enough to understand his future. He married seven wives and had seventeen children to whom he taught mathematics and mandolin-guitar. He lived out his life as the wisest man in the village, considered so for his knowledge of polynomials and for the extravagant experiences of his journey, which he would happily discuss with any who would listen.

Raoul liked the book of Mr. Stan Kalpi so much that he read it at least once a month. Everything about it pleased him, the author's style and the story's detail and even the book jacket's front, a stark white background on which the dark, faceless silhouette of, presumably, Mr. Stan Kalpi, with pointed chin and prominent nose, hovered. But mostly the character of Mr. Stan Kalpi himself pleased Raoul, that and the happy ending. Not that Raoul wanted seven wives and seventeen children. One wife had proved too much to keep under his roof, and one child was proving just as challenging, if in different ways. Raoul admired Mr. Stan Kalpi's accumulated wisdom, envied the lessons he had derived from his adventures with wayfarers and women, with tribesmen and thieves. Surely it was only by keeping such company that one could really hope to learn about life.

Secretly, the humble Raoul indulged in but a single vanity: to be as worthy of some author's time and trouble as the formidable Mr. Stan Kalpi had been. Raoul had confessed as much to me when I was a baby, or so I'm told, every time he read to me from the mathematician-musician's story at bedtime. But then I grew old enough to talk, and the humble Raoul, who resignedly saw in himself an unlikely Mr. Stan, silenced his vain confidences lest I should repeat them and his secret be revealed.

But that was a long way off. I had yet to utter my first words on that Tuesday that found Raoul in the library polishing his specs and feeling a bit like Mr. Stan Kalpi on the day he awoke and didn't know who he was. Things were out of sorts. Raoul's shirt was tight, his breakfast strange in his stomach, and echoes of threats (from both Pedro and Gustave) vied with the bluebottle inside his head. It was a decidedly different Tuesday from the kind Raoul relished at the end of a long week's work.

Miss Lila, too, saw that things were out of sorts. It wasn't like Raoul to dirty his hands on the Sorcery shelf, or to get to his corner table so late in the day. But she had read the article about Puymute's pineapples in the *Morning Crier* and suspected Raoul was shaken by the prospect of demystifying the mystery of the disappearing fruit. It never dawned on the librarian that Raoul might be researching a magical matter of a different sort.

It wasn't the missing pineapples that had Raoul so upset. He knew that the only mystery surrounding their disappearance was how Gustave had pulled it off, a feat that Raoul would get to the bottom of, sooner or later. The real reason for Raoul's dismay, in addition to his ruined Tuesday routine, his tedious trek with Pedro, and his unpleasant exchange at Puymute's, was still me. Nat had summed it up nicely: of course Raoul knew where babies came from, generally, just not this particular one. Where had *I* come from? I belonged to Edda and Wilbur as near as Raoul could tell, but I looked just exactly like Gustave. And Raoul's now week-old ad had yet to produce a witness who could place Gustave at the scene of the crime or implicate him in any way in Edda's pregnancy.

Gustave had still not even seen me then, the baby that allegedly resembled him so. Maybe if he had, he would have been as interested as Raoul in bringing the truth to light. Or maybe not. Gustave and Raoul were different men. Raoul needed answers to the questions that crossed his path, while Gustave, well, his past had taught him how unfair and unyielding both questions and questioners could be, and he had learned it best to turn his back on both. The questioners would believe what they wanted. They always did. And Gustave found lonely truth more painful than persistent mystery.

Poor Gustave. Raoul almost (almost) felt sorry for him. He was a victim of sorts, not of the magic of Oh (the existence of which Raoul still intended to disprove), but of the islanders who chose to see in Gustave the proof that appeased their superstitious curiosity and satisfied their magical appetites. And they discriminated against him accordingly.

Raoul couldn't shake the feeling he'd felt that day at Gustave's house. Could it have been the pineapple wine that dulled his senses? Or had he really smelled fear and befuddlement in Gustave's not-so-nonchalant denials about my mother? Raoul tried to remember. He had definitely smelled something, yes. He had heard something, too, that unspoken awful word. It couldn't really exist, could it?

"Aah!" Raoul pounded his fist on the library's corner table in response to a tsetse fly that droned inside his head. From her altar in the center of the hall, Miss Lila looked at him crossly, her gaze a cocktail of rebuke and surprise. Raoul was out of sorts, he was. She wondered if he was drunk.

Miss Lila Partridge was a clever chickadee, but she couldn't have been more wrong. Raoul was as sober as she. (She did slip into the Belly for a tipple from time to time—vodka tonic—but was sober as a librarian that day, as was Raoul.) His malaise had nothing to do with bourbon or beer. And he wasn't drunk on Puymute's finest the night he confronted Gustave at his home. His senses, olfactory and auditory, had functioned as they should. Possibly, they said, Gustave had been duped along with the rest of them.

And yet.

How innocent could Gustave Vilder be, Raoul asked himself, if he had swiped two acres of pineapple and pinned it on a phantom in the press? Phony magic existed on Oh, but how to distinguish it from the real thing, if there was a real thing? How to prove which kind was responsible for me, his mysterious granddaughter, and Gustave responsible for the bogus burglary at the plantation?

Raoul was mixing up his flies. He had started this unfortunate Tuesday investigating one crime and now he found himself contemplating another. The mathematical Mr. Stan Kalpi would never have approved of this. One polynomial at a time was all that Raoul should ponder. His process must be logical and his calculations orderly, if he was to harbor any hope of defining his undefined variables. Would Mr. Stan Kalpi have found his native land had he wandered willy-nilly on the road to his past, and navigated its contours in random dribs and drabs?

Certainly not. When the detours confounded him and the curves cut too sharp, he stopped to line up his variables. With a stick in the sand, his toe in the mud, or even a finger in the air, he marked them down, and then he stepped back to have a look. He closed his right eye and looked with his left, then he tried it the other way round. He guarded his eyes from the rain or shaded them from the sun, then rubbed his chin and started all over again. Always it would surface, in the sand or the mud or the sky: an error in his arithmetic or the solution's next logical step. "I see it now," he would say. "I see it very clearly." Then Mr. Stan Kalpi would put down his stick or put on his shoe and continue on his way.

"Well, there you have it," Raoul concluded. "Easy as pineapple pie. I just have to line up my variables." He was talking to himself, or to Mr. Stan, or maybe even to his tsetse fly. Miss Lila shook her finger at him, sending another stiff glance his way. He pretended not to see her and busied himself lining up the articles that lay collected on the table. There was the notebook in which he had noted Gustave's story and the ballpoint with which he had done so, the honey-dewed hanky he had used to wipe off his specs. Nat had given him hard candy en route to the library in the cab, and he aligned the shiny transparent yellow rocks with everything else. From the Sorcery shelf he had extracted a number of works, on witchcraft and voodoo and telekinesis, and a dictionary of spells with a meaty Appendix on potions and herbs, from Agrimony to Zinnia. These too he put in a row.

Hmm.

Raoul closed his right eye and looked with his left, then he tried it the other way round. He guarded his eyes from Miss Partridge's reign and shaded them from the afternoon sun, then rubbed his chin and started all over again. No error surfaced, no suggestions sallied forth. Had he forgotten a variable when he lined them up? He patted his thighs and felt the contents of his pockets: cigarettes, house key, a few rainbow bills and some coins. Chewing gum, paper clip, pencil, and a tiny plastic shoe (a doll's, presumably, and rescued from the gritty airport floor). Stopwatch, lip balm, bookmark, plum. Can't hurt, he said to himself, and arranged the items with the others. He looked again, right, left, reign, sun, chin. Still nothing. Raoul drummed his fingers on the wooden tabletop and wondered if he hadn't gotten Mr. Stan Kalpi all wrong. His mathematics worked in books, but not in real life. On Oh, Mr. Stan probably couldn't find his way from the Crater to the Post. And if *Bang* had never come up with a mandolin-guitar, then no one had. Raoul's favorite book was a bunch of lies.

Now what?

He felt the puzzled stare of Miss Partridge on the line-up of trinkets he had constructed, and he sniffed the storm brooding beneath her eyelids. "What a fool I am," he whispered. There was no advice from Mr. Stan Kalpi on what to do in a case like this, but Raoul figured full retreat was as good a tactic as any. He stood and hiked up his trousers. Before he left he would return the volumes to their holes in the Sorcery shelf, to spare Miss Lila the climb on the stepladder and to curb her speculations as to what he was doing. Now, where had the stepladder got to?

Raoul stepped back from the table, about to turn away from it, and stopped. Something in the linear junkyard on its surface caught his eye. An arithmetic error, announced by the plum or the paperclip. Or the solution's next logical step, suggested by the stopwatch or the tiny plastic shoe.

"I see it now," he said. "I see it very clearly."

8

The only dead bodies Gustave knew anything about were his parents' and (unlike the ones in Raoul's library book) those hadn't dangled or oozed their deadly poison into pots. Theirs, rather, was a slow and subtle process of contamination that death had fettered, not unleashed: the Vilders' poison wasn't measured in droplets after the fact, but in a soft and terrible fog that had quietly deposited its mold into their growing son's every pore, camouflaged cleverly though it was in loving pokes to the heart and turtle steaks for dinner.

Whether or not the poison determined those likes and dislikes specific to Gustave, no one could say for sure, though most of the islanders tried. Little matter, what they said. His likes and his dislikes were what they were. Among the former, the spicy fried sausages of his youth and an especially good vintage of pineapple wine; among the latter, calypso night at the Buddha's Belly, and books.

Gustave hated to read. Ever since the days of "GRAMMAR IS FUN" and the fruitless spells he composed underneath its covers. No book had ever done for him what it had done for Raoul, filled the void in his heart or his head, furnished solace or escape or even a recipe for fritters. There was nothing Miss Lila Partridge could show him in the shade of the Cookery shelf. And he most certainly had no use for the likes of Mr. Stan Kalpi and his variables, or for next-door Betty's matins. Gustave's maths were simple and his religion absolute, their sum total no less than his ultimate and exclusive salvation.

So the last thing he would have done that day, when Puymute was in the patch and Raoul drank tea with milk and accused Gustave of knowing about all those missing pineapples—the very last thing—was to run off to the library looking for answers and clues. Not that a clue wouldn't have soon come in handy, for, like Raoul, Gustave was about to face a mystery of his own.

Oh, he knew what had happened to the pineapples. That was magic pure and simple, and he had cooked it up himself. The islanders were hungry for magic, always had been. Hungry for something to hope for or to blame, and the temptation to satisfy their cravings once in a while was one to which Gustave periodically succumbed, his seasonal sins a bitter tribute to his sweet, snake-bitten mum.

It wasn't the pineapples that would pester Gustave. It was a white ribbon. A white ribbon that danced entangled in what he knew must be the softest yellow hair that ever was.

After Raoul left Gustave's office at Puymute's that day the two spoke, Gustave walked from the plantation to town, continuing in his head his argument with Officer Orlean. "Get *me*? Figure out what *I've* been up to? I'd like to see him try, damn fool that he is! Fed *my* version of the facts to the paper, did I? Whilst he's putting adverts in the bloody *Morning Crier* about that brat of his? Puh!

That's a cargo-shipful of nerve right there, it is." His discourse and his path rambled, climbing and plunging, pulling first in one direction and then another, zigging and zagging their way over the holes and humps of the gritty surface that finally deposited Gustave in sight of the market square. He propped his palm against an almond tree, resting his case, and looked down at two stray dogs who sniffed at him in agreement. "That's right," he told them, adding a firm "humph" for emphasis.

Below, the market beckoned, a susurrus of flapping batiks, clanking balances, and tumbling melons whose hollow voices were lost in the rustle of the wind. Gustave kicked the dogs aside and as he neared the noisy space, the rustle sharpened into hello's and how-much's and have-a-breadfruit-won't-you's, two-for-ten. Its voice shattered, the wind wafted angry scents through the crowd of shoppers—cocoa, saffron, swordfish, sweat—who were used to such tantrums and paid the scents no mind. Their eyes, though, never did grow accustomed to the market's assault, and they flitted from sandals, baskets, bananas, and drums, to carrots, squash, potatoes, brooms, and jars, from the shiny sun that pierced their pockets to the faded canopy of blue-green-yellow-red umbrellas under which their rainbow bills changed hands.

Among those accosted eyes that chased round the market square that day were my very own glassy rosebuds, for while Gustave puh-humph-ed his way to town and Raoul ahh-huh-huh-ed at the library under Miss Lila's scrutinizing glare, my mother decided it was high time to take me for a walk. The islanders had all been so kind, making special trips to see me at home and bringing all those jams and jellies and blankets, but now the island itself awaited, Oh with its sandy wind and singing leaves, with its mangoes and its manchineel, to welcome its newest citizen.

At just two weeks old, quite a respectable citizen I had become, despite my Vilder eyeballs and the fuzzy blotch on my cheek. I was long and plump and quiet and smooth, with a soft disposition and a generous portion of velvety blond hair that had already grown well past the rim of the sunbonnet sewn for me by midwife Abigail Davies. The excess was gathered into a tiny ponytail tied with a long white ribbon, which the nimble wind twisted through my hair each time my mother lifted me from the pram. It was this windy maneuver that caught Gustave Vilder's eye as he approached the market collage of greens and gourds.

He had almost reached Cordelia's table of spices and marmalade, where Nat was telling Cordelia about a lady passenger who had lost her typewriter keys, when a flicker on the market's other side jumped into Gustave's view. The sun had somehow mixed itself up in the wind's coiffing of my velvety locks, and the shine from one had entwined with that of the other. Like a spark before a fire, this familiar glint ignited in Gustave a flame that lay hidden inside him, a homecoming somewhere in his soul that crushed his guilt and puffed his chest, sloughed off the droop his shoulders still sometimes assumed. Only Miss Peacock ever made him feel this way, or close to it, but she was nowhere near. And this urge, though as primal as the ones she inspired, was to protect, not to procure.

Gustave's eyes moved from the shiny light at the tip of my ponytail to my fresh, white doughy face. My mouth was agape in a laugh, the inside of it as deeply red as both his eyes and mine. Gustave's mouth gaped, then, too and he stumbled backward. Only a step or two, but enough to topple a pyramid of pale green coconuts that Harold Ticker had assembled at his feet next to a faded and illegible hand-painted sign.

To the music of Harold's angry shouts, the coconuts danced from one end of the square to the other. They waltzed under Cordelia's table of spices and marmalade, which overturned when Harold dashed under it to recover his wares. They tangoed over the toes of brothers Jake and Stu Mutter, who mistook them for scurrying rats and scurried themselves. They merengued with old Sonia Susa, who jumped to avoid them, giggling like a girl at her first marimba-contest dance. Everyone else stood and scratched their heads, wondering what the scurrying and giggling and shouting was about, and how on earth the cautious Cordelia had managed to overturn her table.

It was bound to happen, small as Oh is—not that Cordelia should overturn her table (though long had it wobbled), but that Gustave should spot Edda with me in her arms. When Gustave's eyes moved from mine to hers, he instantly appreciated the weight of Raoul's ad and the heights that the island gossip must have reached.

He tried to reassure himself. So Edda's baby looked like him. So what? He knew he had never touched her. The islanders just needed a helping of magic stew and they had served up Almondine. Soon enough their silly talk would cease. Unfortunate, Gustave thought, that they should satisfy their craving just then, though. Too much magic meant a bellyache and left a bitter taste, and what he had yet cooked up for Puymute's pineapples could not be postponed. Once certain forces were in motion, it was impossible to stop them.

Gustave could no more undo all he had done than Raoul could un-place his ad or un-see what he saw when he lined up his variables at the library. And Edda could no more take back her baby than I could undo who I was, or un-tell you what you know of my story.

Likewise, the "silly talk" turned out to be as unstoppable a force as the one Gustave had cooked up, for it did not cease as he predicted. The islanders' bellyache grew, as Edda's belly had some ten months before. It was proving to be too much. On Oh they tolerated, even savored, Gustave's poison, but only in small doses. Any more than that and their tolerance, even approval, turned into indignant hatred. Which Gustave had learned to accept, when he was at fault. But to suffer their rebuffs for something he hadn't done, well that was too much, too.

Up to then, he hadn't understood the islanders' readiness to blame him for Edda's baby, but after seeing me in my mother's arms, he saw why they couldn't do otherwise, and was soon part of the island faction that accepted Edda's puzzled denials of the events leading up to her pregnancy, for puzzling they were indeed. Had Gustave seen Edda somewhere, admired her, and imagined himself in her arms? Had he wished himself inside her like he had wished his mother dead? Had she stumbled into the seedy port bar unrecognized and fallen under his spell, landed in his bed? Perhaps he had dreamed Almondine into being.

Wherever the truth lay, it was perhaps unfair before to suggest that Gustave would not have been interested in bringing it to light, that he and Raoul should have differed on the matter of looking for answers and clues. The mystery of *me* is most definitely one that Gustave would have wished to solve. That I belonged to the Vilder family tree, and he was convinced that I did, bothered him little. What worried him was that he had no recollection of planting any such seed. Either the forces he commanded were greater than even he had ever dreamed, or he found himself at odds with forces over which he had no command whatsoever. Both prospects frightened him. So, too, did the idea that his every move now was under the islanders' scrutiny: not *all* mysteries were meant to be solved.

At the plantation, meanwhile, Cyrus Puymute stomped around, looking for clues in the patch. They were in high demand that day on Oh, clues were. Had any of the islanders had a few to sell, it would have meant a handsome bundle of rainbow bills.

"And you don't recall seeing anything out of order?" Puymute asked, hands on hips and head tipped upward to meet the blank faces of three of his pickers. "Anything at all?"

"No sir."

"Nope."

"Not a thing, sir."

Puymute shaded his eyes from the sun and looked from one member of the trio to the next and back again. "Fine kettle of something *this* is," he said and continued his stomping. He had been scouring that part of his property from which the pineapples went missing ever since the day before, when the police had appeared, found not a single clue, formulated not a single theory, and deduced that Puymute was a pineapple smuggler. They would have arrested him on the spot had they been able to unearth a shred of evidence, but lacking as much, they settled for shaking their index fingers at him and called in Customs and Excise.

The shred of evidence the police had overlooked must surely still be there, Puymute decided, so he had single-handedly, or footedly, undertaken an inspection of the two acres in question, hoping his shoes might land on some rock-hard evidence that could clear his name. What the clue would point to, a pineapple pincher or a poltergeist, Puymute didn't know. And he didn't care. Crime didn't bother him, and neither did magic. But paying the tax on those missing goods sure did. So he would stomp from sun-up to sundown, if necessary, until he found something that would save him his money.

Precisely because magic didn't bother Puymute, who concerned himself as exclusively and as passionately with his humble collection of rainbow notes as Raoul did with his plain-as-noses-on-faces philosophies, he never thought twice about making Gustave Vilder his general manager. Gustave could mix up all the potions and cook up all the spells he wanted on his own time, as long as he kept the plantation up and running. But, Puymute now realized, stomping every square inch of two acres from sun-up to sundown was about as far from up-and-running as you could get.

"Shoulda listened," he said, and shook his head. "Shoulda listened."

The islanders had tried to warn him that hiring Gustave to manage his affairs and his fruit was unwise, but Puymute hadn't paid attention. And, he had to admit, up to now—and a good ten years had passed so far—Gustave had done as decent a job as anyone could have.

"Barely get a car on this island that'll run you that long," Puymute stomped. "Guess a breakdown was due."

At ten years and two days, quite a respectable breakdown it was. Not only did Puymute (like the other growers on Oh) grow pineapples for pitiful profits, which was bad enough, but now he had trouble with the law, too. Or maybe with a swindling ghost.

He shook his head again. "Shoulda listened."

In Mr. Puymute's defense, that was easier said than done. Gustave had acted cleverly when he sought the plantation post, calling on the owner at just the right time, when his general manager, Agustín Boe, was dead.

"Snakebite," Puymute told him, and jostled his head from side to side.

Not one to dodge the benefits of another's misfortune, Gustave had presented himself at the salmon-colored manor house that set off the green-gold sea below it and the light blue sky above. He told Puymute that the pickers were drinking beer in the patch, that a new manager must be installed straight away. He didn't tell Puymute that he himself had delivered the beer, instructing the men—on Puymute's behalf—to drink to the dead general manager's health.

Puymute, anxious for the plantation to be up and running again, and sober, did as Gustave said. So before poor Agustín was even buried, he was replaced, his shoes and his teacup filled. Gustave sipped from it and looked out the first-story window of that same room in which, years later, he would receive the accusing, fist-pounding Officer Orlean. He took his place in the chair behind the desk and propped his feet on top of it, on the cardboard cover of an account book stained with Mr. Boe's inky fingerprints. Then he grinned and lit a celebratory cigar. In the patch below, the bloated pickers tossed aside their empty beer bottles and returned to their work.

Gustave's hiring had been hasty, no question about it. Puymute saw that now.

And yet.

Most of the workers feared Gustave so, and for so long, that they didn't dare turn up late or sleep on the job or argue when their salaries were sliced thinner than the pineapples Bang chopped up at the airport. Not even Edouard, the island's strongest man—who could lift four crates of pineapples at once, and high up over his head—dared to refuse Gustave a favor or to ignore one of his orders. Hmm. (Puymute stomped on an empty bottle that shattered under his weight; no hard evidence there.) Maybe the islanders were wrong, after all, Puymute rebutted. Maybe Gustave Vilder was a fine general manager, who happened to have run into a spot of bad luck.

"Oy! Mr. Puymute. Oy there!" Puymute's rebuttals were interrupted by one Pedro Bunch, still carrying walking-stick and sack of cassava. "Fancy finding yourself here!"

"What? On my own property?" Puymute felt about Pedro the way everybody on Oh did. All you could do was to cross yourself and hope the storm would soon pass.

"What's that you're doing, Mr. Puymute?"

"I'm missing two acres' worth and I'm looking for clues. What's it look like I'm doing?" Puymute stomped with intensified rigor.

"Didn't look to me like you were looking for clues. Looks like you're stomping. You don't have ants in your shoes, do you?"

Puymute turned to stare at Pedro. He opened his mouth to speak and then thought better of it. No slow storm ever blew by faster because you yelled at it. He shut his mouth and turned back to the ground and his search.

"What kind of clue you think you'll find, then, Mr. Puymute?"

"Don't know exactly. Some kind of hard evidence to take to the police so they'll call off their Customs and Excise hounds, I hope. What brings you round here anyway, with such a heavy sack?"

What *had* brought Pedro into Puymute's pineapple patch, onto his plantation, which lay at the bottom of Dante's mountain, on the opposite side from that where his lonely house was situated?

"Felt like a climb up top," Pedro replied. "View from up there don't come any finer."

"But why come down on this side, lugging your supper around?"

"Supper? My, no! This isn't for supper. Have a stew all ready at home for that."

While Puymute stomped, Pedro talked. He talked about his stew, and the pork snout he used to flavor it. He talked about his shoes (they were wearing thin) and about the Island Post (he was awaiting a package). He talked about cotton and cricket. About ginger and gin. Newsprint, nectarines, and nuns. About everything except the reason for which he happened to be on the plantation that day. When he started in on sea turtles, Puymute could take no more. He stopped his stomping and turned around, grappling for some way to break the speaker's stride.

"Say, Pedro, you don't recall seeing anything out of order here lately, do you?"

"Out of order?"

"Yes, you know, anything unusual."

"Oh, no sirree. Nothing unusual around here. Not unless you count...," Pedro paused for dramatic effect before continuing, "... no, that's not so unusual. Hardly worth mentioning."

"What isn't?"

"Well," Pedro started and stopped again. "Nah. Couldn't mean a thing."

"Now, he stops talking," Puymute muttered under his breath. "What is it, Pedro?" he nearly shouted at the old man. "Let me be the judge of what it means."

"Well," Pedro started once more, "it's just that I found Raoul Orlean sneaking around a bit ago. Spying from up top, sneaking his way back down. That's why I—"

"Why you what?"

"Why I...why I...why I got distracted and came down the wrong side of the mountain. He nearly threatened me if I didn't stop walking behind him. I was so scared I ran off and got turned around."

Not hard evidence, but certainly a clue. Why, wondered Puymute, would Raoul Orlean be sneaking around, threatening the likes of Pedro Bunch, instead of conducting a proper up-front investigation? What, exactly, was he hiding?

In an instant the storm was gone and Puymute forgot all about the blathering Pedro. Puymute would have to pose these questions, and others, to his general manager Gustave. Off he went to do so, stomping and running at once, like an angry ostrich crossing a plain.

Back at the manor house, Gustave was just returning from his walk to town and his sighting of my little-more-than-newborn self at the market. He was worried and his head hurt. The mystery of me still weighed heavy on his mind, and even heavier weighed the agitation caused by Raoul's investigation. There was too much magic in the air, even for Oh to handle, too much noise. The waves were too agitated, the wind too strong. Gustave sat behind his desk and propped his feet on top of it, the way he often did.

A cigar. That was what he needed. Something to savor while he mulled over his problems, figured out how he had fathered Almondine and how to stop the spotlight that followed his every move. On Oh it was Gustave who wielded the magic. Not the other way around. Magical deeds couldn't just overlap and interfere with each other. Unknown variables did not belong in Gustave's simple maths. But he seemed to be faced with one now, one that had the islanders (and one taxman) breathing down his neck. How could he get rid of them? How could he cure their bellyaches and sweeten the bitter taste in their mouths?

Gustave, who didn't see how he would ever answer such queries, searched the drawers of his desk for matches to light his cigar. From the first one he pulled a ball of string, a seashell, three marbles and a dead bug. From the second, a walnut, sunglasses, a fishhook, and some keys. And from the third, a bandage and a dirty magazine. Not a single match to light a cigar that he so desperately needed to savor. He was still worried and his head still hurt. He rubbed his temples and the bridge of his nose, closed his eyes and rubbed those, too. He opened them again, first right, then left, and sighed. Perhaps it was best to just call it a day.

Gustave stood and stepped back from the desk, about to turn away from it, and stopped. Something in the linear junkyard on its surface caught his eye. An arithmetic error announced by the string or the seashell. Or the solution's next logical step, suggested by the fishhook or the dirty magazine.

"I see it now," he said. "I see it very clearly."

9

Like a piece of shiny hard candy gnawed and sucked by the mouth of the sea, Oh's sandy shore dissolves. Its contours thin and grow jagged, its edges tear, its heart a plaything for the watery tongue that prods its rent middle then, with healing laps, smoothes the cracks and gashes until the next wave's assault. Harboring no grudge or rancor alongside its few bobbing crafts, the gritty floor yields and folds, compliant and pliable host to the tide that leaves its threshold bare. In turn, the palm and the bougainvillea, the loofah and the lily, bare themselves before the advances of the wind, rain, and sun—the billowing, pelting, and parching—their surrender and resilience witness to the lessons gleaned from the example of the supple shore.

To the forces that prey upon it—meteorological, magical, or otherwise—the island has only ever known surrender, for what sense is there in trying to contain the uncontainable? Hex or hurricane, certain forces once set in motion took on a life of their own and Oh knew better than to resist them. Resistance required energy better spent saved, for when the forces set in motion were done and the island could recover in their wake. After the drought, the banana bears fruit; after the downpour, the almond flowers. After the moon's meddling, the leaves repair their song.

Pliable like the island's almonds or its bananas, and equally resilient, the islanders mimicked the landscape, learning by example and recovering quickly from the bites of the indiscriminate jaws of fate. Droughts and downpours were temporary; tides could not dissolve their desires. When the wind toppled the stand where Raleigh Bello sold fried seaweed, he rebuilt it. When the rain sent Alejandro Creek's motorbike tumbling down a hill in a mudslide, he retrieved it. And when the sun dried up Lullaby Peet's bed of buttercups and orchids, she replanted. The people of Oh would not be gnawed and sucked like shiny candies, and Raleigh, Alejandro, and Lullaby of this were proof positive. As was Abigail Davies, who had perfected the art of withstanding the advances of the elements, and those of the islanders as well.

Abigail is as near a grandmother as I have, on the island, anyway. From the time she delivered me (she was, and still is, Oh's most practiced midwife, as you're about to hear), she took it upon herself to defend my interests, and a fine job of it she did. My real grandmother, Emma Patrice, was Abigail's closest girlhood friend and long gone by the time I was born, already swallowed up by her snowy mountain. In her absence—or because of it—Abigail felt as protective of me as if I were her own.

Her path to midwifery began when her girlhood came to an almost-overnight close at the age of fifteen, as her body began to press itself with more and more insistence against her taut clothing. She was tall and full and quick and smooth, and before long it was all her mother could do to contain Abigail's breasts, which demonstrated a tendency to spill over the top of any frock her mother stitched her. As Abigail blossomed, the rest of the Davies family withered, for the money her father made building small fishing boats was quickly turned into bolts of cloth from the market,

Abigail's mother sewing all the patterns she could think of to try and keep the girl covered. There was little money left for shrimp and cheese and ham, so the family got by on vegetable broth, containing little more than two plump onions that bobbed mockingly in all the salted water the family pot could hold.

When Abigail turned sixteen, the rest of the Davies family, no longer willing to withstand the insult of the bosomy stew, decided to marry her off. She was a catch after all. Any of her father's customers would have attested to it. She had black eyes and black hair (like all the islanders), which she braided and piled on top of her head, and her disposition was spicy. Perhaps a little too much so, for though all the fishermen wanted a taste, no one wanted to marry her. They offered her ice cream or whiskey or lacy socks to entice her onto their bobbing crafts, but when she returned ashore at the end of the day she had not-so-much as a portion of the day's catch to show for herself. Faced nightly with the sight of her thinning parents and siblings, while the fishermen's offerings kept her plump, she often hid in her father's unfinished boats and cried herself to sleep.

When Abigail Davies turned seventeen, her mother told her she best look for a job. If Abigail insisted on not marrying (as if the poor girl had any say in the matter), then the least she could do was to contribute a few rainbow bills for all those bolts of cloth. If she did well for herself, they might add some pigeons or a hen to their onion stew. The rest of the Davies family, which continued to grow in number, seconded the idea, already imagining on their tongues the tiny bones they would gnaw and suck dry. The very next morning Abigail walked to town in search of work.

She was wearing a yellow dress with a rounded white collar that plunged toward her waist and struggled, as all her collars did, to hold her in. The heads of the passers-by, both men and women alike, turned to study her as their paths crossed, their mouths emitting "my-words" and "well-I-nevers," though the men's for one reason and the women's for quite another.

When Abigail reached the center of town she stopped in front of the Island Post and wondered how best to look for the job that her mother told her she best look for. She turned to her right and saw a taxi stand where three drivers waited in line for a passenger to pass. She turned again and saw the distant church, its tower scornfully fixed on her sinful collar. She turned once more and saw a Ministry, whose mint green exterior was spattered with the spittle of what she assumed must be ministers' chewing tobacco on its threshold. She turned and turned, her eyes ready to spot any sign that there might be paid work to be had, until she came full circle and found herself staring once more at the Island Post.

The widow Corinna, who had exited the post office with one eye on the change in her palm and one on the street, where a pick-pocket might be lurking (though Oh had no pickpockets, for the islanders swindled each other openly), found her gaze drawn to the centrifuge of Abigail's rotating décolletage. She clapped both hands to her mouth, to hold in the "well-I-nevers," and sent the change in her palm reeling noisily to the ground. Abigail rushed to her aid, crawling on hand and knee to pick up the scattering coins and straining her struggling collar even further. The widow Corinna stood, gobsmacked, her gaze glued to Abigail's chest, until the girl had collected all the wayward coins and risen to her feet.

"My word," was all she could muster, as she held out her empty palm to reclaim her money.

"Did I get it all?" Abigail asked her. "Have I missed any?" She started to bend over again, but the widow Corinna grabbed her arm and stopped her.

"Thank you, my dear," Corinna said. "I think you've done far more than you should have already. Spinning about like that in the middle of the street! What were you doing?"

Abigail explained to Corinna about her father's fishing boats and her mother's frocks and the onion stew her family ate for dinner every day. She told her about the bolts of cloth and the fishermen's whiskey, and the pigeon bones the rest of the Davies family wanted to gnaw and suck. In short, she said, she needed a job and had literally been looking around for one, when Corinna spotted her and dropped her change.

The widow was touched by Abigail's story and by her efforts to contribute to the family coffers. Perhaps Abigail ought to try Mr. Rousse, the bookkeeper, Corinna suggested. She didn't see how he could possibly keep his accounts straight, as distracted as he always appeared to be, whether pinching melons at the market or smoking on the barber's porch before his daily shave. "A man like that is certain to need the help of a sensible girl," she said. And sent Abigail on her way.

Mr. Rousse had never given much thought to hiring an assistant. He got on fine by himself, despite how distracted Corinna might have considered him. The way a man pinched a melon said nothing about how balanced his accounts were. Most of the time, Mr. Rousse's were in perfect order. But Abigail's pleas and her pouty collar were more than Mr. Rousse could resist and he offered to hire her on a trial basis. He showed her where the accounting books were stored and taught her how they were numbered and catalogued. And he sharpened her a brand new pencil.

Behind the desk he sat close by her side and told her about debits and credits, brushing his arm across her bosom as he stretched to indicate the columns for noting the ones and the others.

"Debits go out, credits come in," he said. "Two sides to every account. The trick is to make them balance." He showed her a long series of examples, brushing his arm against her again, every time he moved his pencil from the left-hand column to the right and back, until he was certain she understood clearly the nature of the help she could provide him. The whole morning she worked, and the afternoon, marking the registers, balancing credits and debits, outs and ins. She had a knack for keeping track of both sides at once.

But at the end of the day, Mr. Rousse terminated her trial employment, for he really did get on fine by himself and had no use for the help of a sensible girl, certainly not full time. Just a taste of Abigail's spicy disposition was all that he had wanted. He paid her for the day's work, but his payment, like the fishermen's before it, fattened only her. Not the rest of the Davies family, which continued to grow in number.

The next time Abigail tried to find a job, she didn't waste her time turning around in the center of town. Instead, she stuck an announcement on the glass pane of the wooden door that opened into the Savings Bank. Though there were never enough rainbow bills to go around on Oh, some of the islanders did have enough of them to warrant their storage within the safe, thick walls of the island's only financial institution. And since those islanders liked to check on their rainbow bills daily, Abigail's announcement was sure to be spotted. In neat black letters it simply declared AVAILABLE FOR HIRE beneath a picture of Abigail in a pale blue blouse that accented her dark complexion and accentuated her daunting cleavage. Abigail put up her sign at eight o'clock in the morning, before the Savings Bank opened for business.

At nine, the widow Corinna, who didn't have any rainbow bills to check on in the Bank but who passed it every morning on her way to church, caught sight of the sign and its boasting blue bodice. She clapped both hands to her mouth, to hold in the "well-I-nevers," and sent the rosary she held in her palm reeling noisily to the ground. Abigail, who had been loitering nearby, ready to present herself should some islander show interest in her sign, rushed to the widow's aid, crawling on the ground to pick up the scattering prayer beads that had sprung free of their cord. The widow Corinna watched her, her gaze again glued to Abigail's chest, until the girl had collected all the wayward beads and risen to her feet.

"My word," was all Corinna could muster as she held out her empty palm to reclaim her holy bits. Then she remembered her manners and added, "Thank you my dear, very kind of you. But can you tell me the meaning of this shameful sign?"

Abigail was puzzled, for she saw nothing shameful about her advertisement. But she ignored the affront and reminded the widow Corinna about the boats and the frocks and the onion stew, the cloth, the whiskey, and the pigeon bones. She added to her tale the episode of Mr. Rousse the bookkeeper, telling Corinna about the movements of his debits and his credits. In short, she said, she still needed a job and had posted a sign to say so.

The widow was again touched by Abigail's story and by her efforts to contribute to her growing family's coffers. Perhaps Abigail ought to try Mr. Kipfer, the painter, Corinna suggested. She didn't see how he could possibly handle a big job alone, for he was a very small man. "A man like that is sure to need the help of a sensible girl," she said. And sent Abigail on her way.

If Mr. Rousse had never given much thought to hiring an assistant, Mr. Kipfer certainly never had. He got on very fine by himself, despite how small Corinna considered him to be, for he had an extensive array of ladders with which he adjusted his height at will. But Abigail's pleas and her boasting bodice were more than Mr. Kipfer could resist and he offered to hire her on a trial basis. He showed her his rollers and taught her how to mix and stir the paint. Then he handed her her very own paintbrush.

Before following her up on the ladder, he helped her into a pair of fresh canvas overalls, which he buttoned up himself. Then standing behind her, one rung below, he stretched past her, spattering her white canvas clothes with streaks of sea green from his brush, which landed on the wall in front of them in dramatic and demonstrative strokes.

"Up and down, nice and even, you see?" he said. "Otherwise you won't get good coverage of what's underneath." He remained one rung below her as he worked, spattering her canvas and stroking the wall, until he was certain she understood clearly the nature of the help she could provide him. The whole morning she worked, and the afternoon, climbing the ladder, mixing paint, applying herself to nice and even strokes. She had a knack for covering up what lay underneath.

But at the end of the day, Mr. Kipfer terminated her trial employment, for he really did get on very fine by himself and had no use for the help of a sensible girl, certainly not full time. Just a taste of Abigail's spicy disposition was all that he had wanted. He paid her for the day's work, but his payment, like the fishermen's and the bookkeeper's before it, fattened only her. Not the rest of the Davies family, which was growing in number now at least once a year.

The next time Abigail tried to find a job, she distributed flyers with her name and address, on market day, when all of Oh would pass through town. She didn't include her picture on them, for that would have been too costly, and she sensed that the picture had something (she wasn't sure what) to do with the widow Corinna's "shameful" classification of her announcement on the Savings Bank door. She positioned herself near the entrance to the market's main square, offering to each passer-by one of her fluttering pages. But the market was a noisy place, with its usual flapping batiks and clanking balances, and Abigail's "pardon-me's" and "may-I-give-you-one-of-my-flyers-please's" were lost in the windy din. The islanders, intent on their shopping and haggling, could neither hear her nor see her, for in the visual assault that was the marketplace, even Abigail's cumbersome chest was camouflaged among the coconuts, calabash, and onions.

Frustrated, the girl, who had long become a woman, stepped up onto the two-foot-high stone wall that encased the marketplace. To the wall's height she added another foot or so to her position by jumping up into the air. The combined effect of gravity, Abigail's propulsions, and the paucity of her polka-dotted dress, shifted the wind in her favor and her flyers were suddenly in great demand.

But, alas, the widow Corinna, who could not seem to escape the taunting of Abigail's top half, chose just then to pass by. She clapped both hands to her mouth, to hold in the "well-I-nevers," and sent the just-acquired cloves and peppercorns she held in her palm reeling to the ground. Abigail, who witnessed Corinna's clumsiness from the vantage point above the wall, felt compelled to relinquish her post and rushed to the helpful widow's aid, crawling on the ground to pick up her purchases. The widow Corinna watched her, her gaze yet again glued to Abigail's chest, until the girl had collected all the wayward spices and risen to her feet.

"My word," was all Corinna could muster as she held out her empty palm to reclaim her cloves and corns. Then she remembered her manners and added, "Thank you my dear, very kind of you. But jumping about like that in the middle of the market! What were you doing?"

Abigail was puzzled again. She considered herself rather clever for outwitting the noisy wind and she didn't know why Corinna should be so bothered by her behavior. But she ignored the remark (Corinna had always been a bit touchy) and again reminded the old woman about the frocks and onions and the growing family who still couldn't afford any pigeons, adding to her tale, right after the part about Mr. Rousse the bookkeeper, the episode of Mr. Kipfer the painter and his nice and even strokes. In short, she said, she still needed a job and had jumped up and down to let the other islanders know it.

The widow was yet again touched by Abigail's story and her efforts. Perhaps she ought to try Mr. Floroseda, the plumber, Corinna suggested. She didn't see how he could keep all the island's pipes clean on his own, for he moved way too slowly when he biked from job to job, stopping often to fill his nose with the scents of whatever flowers he spotted on the side of the road. "A man like that is sure to need the help of a sensible girl," she said. And sent Abigail on her way.

If Mr. Rousse and Mr. Kipfer had never given much thought to hiring an assistant, Mr. Floroseda certainly never had either. He got on very very fine by himself, despite how slow Corinna considered him to be, for the way a man rode a bicycle said little about his pipes. And most of the time, Mr. Floroseda's were in perfect order. But Abigail's pleas and her paltry polka-dots were more than Mr. Floroseda could resist and he offered to hire her on a trial basis. He taught her about plungers and spigots and snakes, about faucets and washers and drains. And he gave her a kit with a handle and some tools.

In the dark damp of the crawlspace under Mrs. Hobbs' wash basin, he showed her how to position herself to accommodate the curves in the pipes she came across. Stretched out on the floor alongside her, he brushed against her with every twist of his spanner.

"Not too loose, not too tight," he said. "Otherwise you'll crack your pipe." He maneuvered his arm around her, working the spanner back and forth, until he was certain she understood clearly the nature of the help she could provide him. The whole morning she worked, and the afternoon, accommodating pipes and silencing the troublesome drip-drip of leaky faucets. She had a knack for keeping things quiet.

But at the end of the day, Mr. Floroseda terminated her trial employment, for he really did get on very, very fine by himself and had no use for the help of a sensible girl, certainly not full time. Just a taste of Abigail's spicy disposition was all that he had wanted. He paid her for the day's work, but his payment, like the fishermen's, the bookkeeper's, and the painter's before it, fattened only her. Not the rest of the Davies family, which grew in number yet again.

Abigail was getting no younger, her family had grown, and still she had found no job, her search inevitably and repeatedly interrupted by her growing belly and her growing brood. She was fed up with trying to find work as someone's assistant, fed up with being plump all the time while her family got thinner and thinner. So Abigail decided to go into business for herself. She had training, didn't she? She had learned to balance both sides of any account, to cover things up nice and even, and to keep troublesome things quiet. And thanks to the positions she had assumed on a trial basis over the years, she knew about having babies.

Why, she should have thought of it sooner! A midwife, that's what she would be. The islanders were always having babies. Business would be good. And if anyone on Oh could manage a pregnancy that needed managing, it was Abigail.

My mother's was to be one of these, though not even Abigail herself could have guessed how much so, until I came along.

"Ouch!" Abigail cried out. She was at home with my mother, sewing the sunbonnet that I would wear on the day I caught Gustave's eye.

"What is it?" A pregnant Edda, frightened suddenly, lowered her feet from the footstool that held them and raised her torso from the cushion of her chair, poised to rush to Abigail's aid.

"Now, now, don't go jumping up in your condition. Just a little poke. My eyes aren't what they used to be." Abigail sucked the drop of blood that pooled on her fingertip and threatened the clean white cotton of my tiny bonnet.

"It's almost night. You should do that stitching in the daylight."

"You're right. Your husband will be home soon." Abigail lifted herself from Edda's sofa with the ease of a woman ten years her junior. She wore a full gray skirt over hips that bore witness to all the children she had had and a pink blouse that still struggled to contain her large top, though the years were slowly granting an advantage to the thinning cloth. "Time for me to go. I'll be back tomorrow." She gave Edda a peck on the forehead.

"Thank you, Abigail. What chance would my baby have without you?"

Abigail collected her things and left. She stepped out into the night that through the windows of Edda's sitting room had announced itself, warm and soft. In the still, dark sky, the moon shone down on Abigail and followed her home, watching and winking. The leaves sang a song of foreboding as she passed them, the moon's light splashed across her face, but Abigail paid them no mind. In shuddering choruses their smooth, shiny sides tried to warn her, while their rough, faded halves told her the tale of the moon's deceit. Of the leaf stitched from two stolen parts and the almond seed sown almost nine moons before. Of the fruit that Abigail's hands were about to reap. In response, the moon just mocked the silly leaves, guiding the waves that drowned their song and crashed on the sandy shore, gnawing it and soothing it in turn.

10

While we've busied ourselves with the story of Abigail Davies, Raoul and Gustave have had their hands full with the solutions' next logical steps. Gustave's step landed him back on the paper's front page, and Raoul's sent him back to the Belly, waiting on a beer and a little black magic.

"Bastard!" Raoul chuckled. He shook his head over the *Morning Crier*, now wrinkled and tired from the long day's wear. He was smiling when he said it again: "Bastard!" With gentle movements he smoothed the creases from the headline and, satisfied that it was sufficiently legible, he turned it wrong way round and shoved it at Cougar, who stood opposite him behind the bar.

PARANORMAL PILFERING OF PUYMUTE PINEAPPLES— TAKE TWO

"I saw," Cougar nodded at him. He glanced at the paper and polished a shiny cocktail shaker with his sleeve. "He got you again," he said, straightening his tie in the reflection that grinned and gleamed at him from the curves of the silver tumbler.

"Got me?" Raoul giggled. "Got *me*?"

Cougar was puzzled. He stopped his grooming and looked Raoul square in the face. "Yeah. Got you. You, Customs and Excise Officer Raoul Orlean who still doesn't know where the first lot of fruit went and now another lot's missing. Got. *You*. Didn't he?"

But Raoul didn't hear Cougar's question. Raoul was off on that road of holes and humps, zigs and zags, obstacle and illumination that Mr. Stan Kalpi had traveled before him. He was defining his variables, adding them up, and sorting out the solution's next logical step.

You remember Raoul's variables lined up on the library table, shaded from the afternoon sun and Miss Partridge's reign? The hanky, the hard candy, the keys, and the coins? The tiny plastic shoe, as small and insignificant as Gustave's denials of dear Almondine, and the plum, soft as Raoul's head when for a moment he believed them? There was a pencil, too, sharp as the buzz from the fly in Raoul's brain that had said to come up with a plan.

The stopwatch suggested that Raoul take his time and wait, wait for Gustave to slip like the ballpoint that slipped and slid across Raoul's notebook during their interview earlier that same day. Gustave had orchestrated the pineapple caper for cash and had even offered Raoul a slice of the profits, that time they talked mealybugs over hot pineapple wine. Raoul's rainbow bills reminded him of that. His cigarettes, side by side in their cellophane pack, those told him that more and more capers would befall Puymute's patches, though like the chewing gum whose flavor fails when it's stretched, Gustave, too, would falter, if he tried to push his luck.

Raoul would let him try to do just that, and, like the bookmark, would follow the actions of the story's antagonist until they grew sloppy and betrayed him. So implied the lip balm that had seeped its gooey wax beyond its cap and onto the inside of Raoul's trouser pocket before landing on the library table. Raoul must watch and wait, and when Gustave inadvertently handed him a clue, a paper-clipped page in the book of pineapple plots, then Raoul could go back to the library and study up on what to do. This final step he deduced from the sorcery books and the dictionary that he suddenly saw as clearly and as plainly as noses on faces. If he managed to catch Gustave smuggling pineapples *in flagrante* then Officer Orlean would have some bargaining power and might just get Gustave to confess the truth about Edda and Almondine.

Which was why it made Raoul giggle with excitement that Gustave had struck again so soon and why he didn't hear a word of Cougar's question.

Cougar, unruffled, went back to his quiet primping, but not before filling one of the mugs that dangled over the Belly's bar with island beer, and pushing it Raoul's way. Raoul, newspaper still in hand, sipped and smirked and studied, shaking his satisfied head from side to side. He knew the story by heart, but he continued to read and re-read it, looking for patterns and clues to measure against what had happened and what was to come, confronting the curves and the detours of his dusty path. Confident that in due time it would deposit him, worn but wiser, home.

"You saw?" Nat asked and declared at the same time, as he slid onto the stool next to Raoul's and swiped his paper. "Just took a lady mountain-climber to Dante's Mountain. Says she's always right about everything and *she* thinks we ought to call it Dante's Hill."

"What did you tell her?" Cougar asked, passing him a shot of yellow rum.

"Thanks." Nat took the rum and downed it in one gulp. "I told her she was mad! You can't go changing a person's name just like that. Or a mountain's either. A name's a legacy. You can't change your legacy. What if I started calling myself Herbert? Or Gene? You wouldn't know who I was." He slammed his empty shot glass onto the bar for emphasis.

"Gene Gentle, huh?" Raoul mused. "That's not so bad, you know." (Gentle was Nat's last name.)

"How about you, Raoul?" Cougar suggested. "Gene Orlean is even better."

Raoul and Cougar laughed and clunked drinks high in the air.

"Have your fun," Nat went on. "All I'm saying is a Gentle is a Gentle and an Orlean is an Orlean. A name grows up with a person. Or a mountain. Give me another rum, will you?"

Cougar poured, Nat pored over the paper, and Raoul drummed his fingers on the bar.

"Where's Bang?" Raoul inquired, his high spirits making him more in want of company and of nonsense than he had been since I first came into the world.

As if in response to Raoul's wishes, Bang appeared in the Belly's doorway. He wore a blue beret and carried a fishing rod and knocked the latter against the former in salutation as he neared his buddies at the bar.

"What's it going to be tonight, then? Songs of zee swordfish?" Raoul teased.

"*You're* in a good mood." Bang maneuvered his pole over the bar and into a corner. "Am I to assume you haven't seen the *Morning Crier* today?" He snatched the paper from Nat and read aloud:

> For the second time in ten days, two acres' worth of pineapples have gone mysteriously missing from the plantation of Cyrus Puymute. The crops disappeared overnight, seemingly without a trace. Police investigations are ongoing, though the earlier case was dismissed for lack of evidence and deemed supernatural. The Office of Customs and Excise will continue to investigate in an attempt to recover lost duty on the apparently-exported fruit.

"You seem too happy to have read *that*," Bang declared. "Not that I'm complaining to find you in a good mood, mind you."

"Oh, I've read it alright. I've read it," Raoul replied.

"And?" Bang looked at him.

"And what?"

"And you aren't upset about all this magic business you can never seem to stomach? This is black magic if ever there was any. That's four acres now that are gone. As if in a puff of smoke." (Bang's hands opened into the starbursts that he always circled in front of his face whenever he discussed Oh's black magical manifestations.)

Raoul just giggled and shook his head.

Bang looked at Cougar, with whom he exchanged a helpless shrug. "Fireflies," they said in unison.

You see, whenever Raoul giggled and shook his head it meant trouble. It meant that his usual flies had transformed themselves into bright ideas, bright ideas that like fireflies in a lidded jar would knock about inside his brain until they were freed into the clarity beyond the glass, or until they burned out and died. Like Raoul's every-day flies, his fireflies, too, came in every size. There were small ones, say, a short-cut that got him faster to work in the mornings or a cup that kept his pencils from rolling off his desk. There were medium-sized ones: a TV antenna fastened to his roof, an irrigation system for the garden in the back of his house. And then there were the biggest and the brightest ideas, like newspaper ads about babies, and now, evidently, a plan to nab a pineapple thief.

"Out with it, Raoul. What have you got in there?" Nat knocked on Raoul's forehead.

Raoul, his high spirits making him more tolerant, too, of company and of nonsense than he had been since I first came into the world, started to explain about Stan Kalpi and the singing wind, about the mandolin-guitar and Stan's toes doing maths in the mud, about his own variables—the notebook, the bookmark, the balm and the shoe—lined up on the table at the Pritchard T. Lullo Public Library. He was barely at the part about the soft plum, when Bang, convinced he had cottoned on to the Stan Kalpi maths, excitedly interjected that the plum must mean someone was hungry. While Bang, Nat, and Cougar debated whether the someone were Raoul or Gustave or the phantom of Puymute's patch, Raoul, somewhat less tolerant than a few minutes before, took back his paper and returned to his quiet sipping, smirking, and study.

The three might have debated all night about the solution's next logical step had Cougar not noticed the filling Belly and the darkening sky and reminded Bang of the time.

"Hey, you never did say what you're singing about tonight," Raoul said, happy to hear that the subject had changed.

Bang bounced onto his feet and raised his waterglass to Raoul, Cougar, and Nat. "Tonight, gentlemen, I sing about friends."

"Friends?" Nat repeated, confused. "What do you mean you sing about friends?"

"Friends. You know. Mates. Chums. Good friends. Bad friends. Honest friends. Cheating friends."

"Cheating friends?" Raoul marveled. "What kind of friends are those?"

But Bang was already on stage and didn't hear Raoul's question.

"Ladies and gentlemen. Good evening and welcome to the Buddha's Belly. My name is Bang and tonight we're going to do some numbers for you inspired by friendship, which we have lots of on this pretty little island of Oh. So find yourselves a friend to sit next to, get yourselves something from the bar..." (He winked his usual wink at Cougar.) "...and enjoy the show."

Who do I turn to when I need to know

Bang's voice, announced by the soft, humid tones of the marimba, was met with the usual reverent, if temporary, silence that it garnered every night when it calmed the Belly's rumblings. Amid whispered orders for tonics and rums (which tasted more forbidden for the sottovoce with which they were requested), the customers tried not to shuffle or cough or scrape their chairs against the floor. Raoul re-read his paper. Cougar tended bar. Nat lit the daily cigar he bummed from Cougar's cache.

Like the bold dinner jackets, silk foulards, and calfskin shoes that Cougar has flown in to the island for himself, so too are his cigars of the choicest quality. Nat could never have afforded them on his own, at least not yet, and as he let the rich perfume fill his mouth, to the accompaniment of Bang's homage to friendship, the full worth of Cougar's friendship—and Nat's dependency on it for good cigars and a second or third or even a fourth round of rum—struck him acutely and painfully.

Someone's there when I'm feeling low?

Normally Nat wasn't bothered by his flimsy financial affairs. For if Bang was born with the gift of gab and song, Cougar with luck and charm, and Raoul with brains and heart, Nat was blessed with that pliability that was the stuff of Oh's Abigail Davies's and its Alejandro Creeks. It mattered not to him that his once-wealthy family had chewed up its fortune without so much as spitting out a few seeds for him to live on, a kerchief of land for him to plant or a marimba fashioned of mahogany and polished gourds. He was happy to be able to pay for fish and vegetables and gasoline, to afford a t-shirt at the market and at least one daily nip. There were many islanders who considered him a rather wealthy man, in fact, for many islanders had never even seen a rainbow bill or eaten a vegetable they hadn't planted and harvested themselves.

Someone who will hold my hand

But lately Nat had grown as restless as the sea that dissolved Oh's sandy shores. He wanted to go to movies and to travel, to take a day off now and then, and to maybe find a wife. A wife, he knew, would never be satisfied with market-day t-shirts and a diet wanting of beef, a fact that added to Nat's malaise. Money matters were something he knew little about, having had such little money all his life, so he found himself faced with a problem whose very solution was contrary to everything he thought or did.

When my eyes are blinded by the blowing sand.

Back to Cougar's fancy cigars. They had special appeal for Nat on this night that was drawing him into melancholy rumination about friendships and hardships and the solution's next logical step. They were the same cigars Nat's grandfather had smoked when Nat was just a little boy, running and hiding in the acres of leaves taller than he that spread across the Gentle plantation like a green-gold sea. Had Cougar changed brands? Surely Nat hadn't been smoking these very same cigars all along, oblivious to the scent of his childhood and his past? Either way, fact of the matter is, on the night in question, like Mr. Stan Kalpi drawn home by the smells of wet leather and oniony stew, Nat let the cigar's perfume and Bang's affectionate songs carry him back to a richer, happier time.

Where would I be without your shoulder

He remembered his grandfather's birthday parties, the one luxury (in addition to expensive cigars) that the plantation owner allowed himself all year. Though his family benefited greatly from his riches, he himself was happiest knee-deep in the foliage that populated his pineapple patches, provided he had taken a morning's bowl of hot porridge and an evening's bowl awaited him on the stove. Except, of course, on April 27th.

On April 27th of any given year, Henry (that was Nat's grandfather's name, Henry) did not don his overalls and breakfast on gooey mush. Rather he wore a dark green jacket with a tie of black and white diagonal stripes, and from early morning, breakfast-less, he supervised the set-up of tents and tables and bandstands and balloons. By noon the guests would start to arrive (practically all of Oh was invited) and while the children played cricket and lawn tennis the adults drank and smoked and discussed the current state of affairs. Late in the afternoon, just before dinner was served, the guests were given kites, which they all flew at once, a tangled explosion of painted and dotted diamonds that lit up the sky in Henry's honor.

To lean upon as I grow older?

Dinner followed the kite-flying: breadfruit roasted over open fires, green pumpkin soup, barrels of pork and swordfish stew, steamed lobsters, crunchy corncobs, salads of papaya and fig, and coconuts full of soft jelly or rum. Music followed the dinner: steel drums and marimba, mandolin and guitar, love songs, dance songs, traditional ballads. Just the sort of party the grown-up Bang would have loved, Nat thought, but like Nat, Bang was just a boy when the money ran out and the tradition of Henry Gentle's birthday parties stopped.

To brace me in my time of need

Bang's accidental intrusion into Nat's reminiscing jerked Nat back to the Belly and away from the confusion of sweating dancers and dragging kite strings and discarded rinds of coconut. Around him the clientele was only just beginning to make noise again, Bang's voice still prevailing over the cheerful, restrained din. Nat closed his eyes and breathed in the smoke that drifted from his cigar and hovered in front of him before climbing to wrap itself around the blades of the ceiling fans that dispersed it. Like a dreamer who wakes from a vague and pleasant dream, and struggles to return to it, Nat tried to get back to the field where the music played and dancers leaned in closer as night fell, where his grandfather's cigar smoke enveloped him as he sat on the old man's lap. But the field was too far away.

Or when I face a mighty deed.

"Hey Raoul, you remember those parties my grandfather had when we were kids?"

Raoul looked up from his paper. "Sure," he said. "Hard to forget those. Once I ended up with a kite as tall as I was."

"What was tall as you were?" Cougar asked. He had just finished preparing a dry martini and joined the conversation late.

"A kite I got once at one of those parties Henry Gentle used to give. Remember those?"

"Yeah, 'course. Haven't thought about old Henry in years," Cougar said.

"Me neither." Raoul motioned for a refill. "Not in years." And back he went to his paper.

Nat turned on his stool to face the stage. When was the last time *he* had thought—*really* thought—about his grandfather? he wondered. Ah, yes! he smiled to himself and nodded his head. Edda's twelfth birthday...so, some eight years ago. At Captain Bowles' beach.

Why should I wake with the sun every day

What Nat refers to as Captain Bowles' beach never really did belong to Captain Bowles; Oh's bays and beaches belong to everybody and anybody who happens to find himself (or herself) on one of them. But Captain Bowles had built the big house on top of the hill overlooking this particular beach, and so "Captain Bowles' beach" it was called. The house, which the captain built almost forty years before this night in which we find ourselves intruding on Nat's private thoughts, was host to some of the greatest and most famous minds of the captain's day, his own being among them. In fact, to call it simply a "big house" is to diminish the grandeur of the once mansion-cum-salon, though it seems a suitable label now, the house long having fallen into abandonment and ruin.

The story of Captain Bowles, who he was and how he arrived on Oh, belongs between covers of its own. Suffice it to say that he was one of the few outsiders, maybe the only one, who managed to easily needle his way into the fabric of the history and lore with which the islanders inadvertently cloaked themselves, despite the fact that his individual thread stood out in the weave. Captain

Bowles put Oh on the map, as they say, at least for a little while, for which the islanders were mostly grateful. But his story has a sad ending, and after it, back off the map Oh quietly fell.

If not so I might see your face?

It was indeed eight years before, at Captain Bowles' beach, or, rather, at the house that Captain Bowles built, where Nat had last thought about his grandfather in the company of a twelve-year old Edda. It was her birthday, and Raoul and Cougar had charged Nat with taking her for a long walk while, along with Tripper the cook, they prepared her a birthday surprise at the Sincero. Nat and Edda had meandered along the beaches of Oh's southern coast when Nat suggested that from Captain Bowles' beach they make the climb up to the big, deserted house. With typical twelve-year old zeal, Edda charged up the hillside, anxious to reach the decrepit building that loomed above her like a haunted house from a fairy tale. Nat, following behind, watched her against the light of the sun, an aubergine cut-out, flat and curved at once. He admired the silhouette that lay decidedly at the end of his path, barely recognizing the feline princess warrior whose outlines were those of a young woman.

My faith and my friend, from now till the end,

When they reached the house, Edda ran through its gutted insides, which were scattered with debris that betrayed the splendor the house once was: chipped and faded moldings along ceilings and floors and windows, a broken chandelier that lay crooked in a corner, rubble of cracked white marble that in younger days must have withstood the tangos and waltzes of only the most fashionable and expensive of shoes. While Edda explored, Nat sat on the rocky edge of the hill and looked down at the buildings of pink and yellow and beige that dotted Oh's landscape, wrapped in a white-sand ribbon that was tugged at by the sea. Just beyond the cluster of pastels that marked the center of town, Nat spotted what used to be his family's land, and knowing that back at the Sincero a birthday fete awaited, he was reminded of the parties that the plantation once saw. When Edda came out of the house, she and Nat sat close together on the precipice, and he told her all about them in the shadow of the withered mansion. Nat didn't realize it then, but now as his mind replayed that birthday of Edda's through the filter of time, it fell upon him like one of the island's weighty fruits: Nat was no different than Captain Bowles' big house, a product of great wealth, but now broke, empty, and abandoned.

Poor Nat. He realized then that in eight years little had changed. Alone at the Belly, with no date, no dance-partner, and no prospect for either, he drank donated rum and puffed on a borrowed cigar.

My comfort, my refuge, my grace.

My faith and my friend, from now till the end,

While Nat brooded, a satisfied Gustave sat at one of the tables that rested in the sand beyond the Belly's propped-open door. Without realizing it, he had been doing a little Stan Kalpi maths of his own, for in the lined-up variables that he pulled from his desk drawers that day he needed a match (you remember: seashell, bandage, walnut, keys), the solution's next logical step had suggested itself. If the islanders and the excisemen wanted to believe that he was responsible for everything on Oh, from Edda's baby to illicit exports, then let them! He would give them a magic show they would never forget, pull out all the stops like he pulled all the junk from his desk. He would see to it that more and more acres disappeared, and worse, if necessary (so said the fishhook), until the islanders were so afraid of him that they would finally leave him alone (like the dead bug did).

My comfort, my refuge, my grace.

His elbow on the small round table that tilted into the beach, Gustave leaned into his fist and let his thumb caress the talisman he had carried his whole life, like you or I might rub a rabbit's foot or a lucky penny, or a wise man his long white beard. With a smug smile, and in higher spirits than he had been since first I came along, Gustave smoothed the soft blond down that blanketed the blotch on his cheek, though he was feeling little in need of luck just then.

My faith and my friend, from now till the end,

For Gustave now had help. The three marbles, two days before, had reminded him of that.

My comfort, my refuge, my grace.

Behind the bar Cougar leaned silently against the wall of bottles, somewhat more ruffled than at the evening's start, though it would seem odd to attribute this to the talk of friendship and pleasant childhood memories. Raoul still leaned over the *Morning Crier* looking for hints and clues, certain that once Gustave was cornered for one crime, he would finally confess to another. (In other words, the only mysterious crop Raoul was really interested in explaining was his own little almond.) Nat, Nat sat melancholy, torn up over and confused about his money problems—and even more torn as to their solution.

My comfort, my refuge, my grace.

"How the hell did I get myself mixed up in this?" Nat muttered to himself. And Bang sang.

II

Gustave Vilder had a vague recollection of my mother's pregnancy. A vague recollection of the way her body bloated, swelled, and puckered under her clothes and inside her sandals, and of the islanders' respectful nods when she passed them by. Vague, because though he saw her counting her rainbow bills at the bank or standing in line at the office of the Island Post, he never thought of her as relevant and therefore paid her little mind. Edda Orlean was simply part of the scenery in front of which Gustave's daily errands and efforts played out, like Cordelia's table of spices and marmalade at the market or the dried-up leaves of the flamboyant tree that crunched under Gustave's feet near the seedy port bar. A silly pregnant girl was just that.

His vague recollection of Edda's burgeoning middle is maybe somewhat like your own recollection of Cyrus Puymute in his patch. You remember, he was stomping the ground for rock-hard evidence when Pedro Bunch let it slip that Raoul had been spying nearby; then he bounded, like an angry ostrich across a plain, toward the manor house for a parley with his General Manager.

A silly stomping plantation owner is just that, you thought, part of Oh's flamboyant scenery and no more relevant than the flamboyant's crunchy leaves.

But like Edda's belly (if perhaps not to the same degree), Cyrus Puymute's clumsy trek was indeed relevant, for it culminated in a tête-à-tête with Gustave that serves a dual purpose: it puts our angry ostrich's head back into the sand, and elucidates the moods of Cougar and Nat in the previous chapter's rendezvous at the Belly, where the two were ruffled and torn up, respectively.

It all started the day the sun entangled itself in my hair, causing Gustave to stumble. It wasn't just my shiny locks that shocked him, but rather the resemblance that my face bore to his own, a resemblance for which the magical Gustave had no explanation. None came to him as he stumbled at the market. None as he walked himself back to the manor house at Puymute's plantation. None as he sat at his desk, feet propped on the dead Mr. Boe's account book, and decided to smoke a cigar. Not even when he lined up his variables, while looking for a match, did he come up with one (all they told him was what magic to do next).

As Gustave tidied his desktop, dropping the variables back into their drawers to cover his tracks, Cyrus Puymute's clumsy bird-ish trek ended, and the latter bounded into Gustave's office without so much as a knock.

"Vilder! Vilder! I've got news!" Puymute's arrival put an end to Gustave's tidying and to his ponderings, which no doubt would have lingered on the still-unexplained subject of Edda's baby Almondine. No matter, he told himself. Almondine would wait. Which she did, for what else could she do?

"Calm down, Cyrus. You're in a state! What news?"

Cyrus proceeded to recount how he had been in the patch stomping for rock-hard evidence of pineapple smugglers (human or superhuman, he didn't care which), evidence that he could take to the police to clear his name and erase his excise fine, when he found Pedro wandering around with a sack. "'What are you doing here?' I said, 'lugging your supper round the wrong side of the mountain?'"

Gustave nodded and Puymute continued.

"Well, you know Pedro. He went on about candles and clippers and lightbulbs and lava, goldfish and jelly and moss. Sea turtles—"

"Cyrus! Please!" Gustave huffed, not nearly as angry as he seemed, for he knew well that an encounter with Pedro could leave the best of men (and goats) out of sorts.

"Yes, yes. Sorry. First, I wondered what Pedro was doing by the patch, but good thing he was there. He caught Raoul Orlean sneaking around while I was stomping."

"Sneaking around? Sneaking around where?"

"Up Dante's Mountain."

That Raoul should be sneaking around in the vicinity of the plantation didn't strike Gustave as odd, for Raoul *was* the Customs Officer assigned to investigate the case. Nor did it strike Gustave as odd that this fact should be lost on Cyrus Puymute, who was often out of sorts, whether Pedro Bunch could be blamed for it or not. It was also obvious to Gustave, though there was no way it could have been to Cyrus, that Pedro was "lugging his supper round the wrong side of the mountain," headed for Gustave and the manor house, so as to report on Raoul's not-so-suspicious sneaking. Gustave had charged Pedro with precisely this function: wandering around the plantation looking for sneaks, and alerting Gustave immediately should he find any. (Gustave had never instructed Pedro to launch any threats; that, Pedro had done of his own overzealous accord.)

The last thing Gustave desired on that late, hot afternoon was a debate with Puymute, but he let the man unburden himself of his theories: conspiracy at Customs and Excise, planted evidence (though neither the police nor Puymute had found any), and, possibly, Pedro in on it all the while, for surely his talk of crabs and silk and electrical sockets was designed to distract attention from the truth. Puymute conjectured and Gustave nodded, until the sun set.

When Gustave was satisfied that Puymute's excitability no longer posed a threat (things were complicated enough without an anxious plantation owner bounding about like an ostrich, stomping and spouting theories), Gustave pointed out that perhaps Raoul's presence was legitimate, seeing as the case was his, and he assured Puymute that Pedro's loyalties lay within the confines of the plantation and immediate vicinity, which were under his constant and secret surveillance. That a chatterer like Pedro made for a dicey sort of spy never dawned on Puymute, so had the sun's setting calmed his temper. He listened to Gustave's reassurances, rose, suddenly hungry after his long day's stomp, and walked out into the dusk, just as the dusk was sneaking into Gustave's open office window.

Though its heat still seeped forth from every beach and hillside, the sun that tormented the island by day was finally gone. It had relinquished Oh to the whims of the gibbous moon that—bloated, swollen, and puckered under the clouds and amidst the stars—presided over the darkening sky. The moon's light invaded Gustave's office and splashed over the desk, illuminating the variables that Puymute's interruption had kept Gustave from putting away.

"Bloody fool," Gustave said, shook his head, and began to tidy again.

A fool, Puymute may well have been; it bears little on Raoul's story, or mine. But the fact that foolish Puymute arrived on that late afternoon in which Gustave would have rather been pondering the roots of one little almond, *that* bears a great deal on Raoul's story—and mine—and on Raoul's journey along the road that burrowed into the heart of my brief past. Had Puymute never presented himself at the manor house that day, Gustave would have tucked away his variables and left, gone off to the seedy port bar where the leaves crunched under his feet and the seedy port girls caved under his stare.

His variables had told him to pull out all the stops. He had seen it very clearly and he was satisfied. He would have strolled beneath the rays that shined from the moon's roundness (as relevant as Edda's, though Gustave paid it as little mind), mulling over his next move. He would never have noticed the marbles.

Three of them shone on the desktop, three leftover and undefined variables, their smooth, loyal surfaces reflecting the moonbeams that trespassed now through Gustave's window. (It's really as much the moon's fault as Puymute's that the marbles caught Gustave's attention.) Mr. Stan Kalpi couldn't have seen their meaning more clearly: Bang, Cougar, Nat. What better way to circumvent Raoul's meddlesome investigation than to make allies of his enemy's best mates? They knew Raoul's patterns and his movements, and they needed money (well, Bang and Nat did, anyway, and Cougar would never turn any down). The solution's next logical step.

Gustave finally did put away all the variables that littered his desktop. He tucked them into the dark musty drawers of the desk, where not even the moon's pervasive gleam could reach them. He did not, however, go off to the seedy port bar, no. He lingered, replaying in his head the day's earlier events: his trip to the market, the glint of my hair, and my eyes that reflected his own, like the marbles reflected the moon.

What would Mr. Stan Kalpi have to say about *those*? Gustave didn't ask himself this question, for he knew nothing of Mr. Stan, despite having stumbled into some Stan Kalpi maths. But Gustave *was* wondering about my eyes. He would have done almost anything to explain them.

And in this, he was not alone.

"Bang!" Nat shouted from the window of a pristine Peugeot, as he pulled up to the airport, Cougar next to him in the car. "Jump in for a minute," he said and jerked his head toward the empty back seat. Bang abandoned his card table of pineapple slices and pineapple knives and obeyed.

"Well," Cougar started, once they had driven past the stretch of sidewalk outside the airport and parked under a tree of what appeared to be giant buttercups (scientifically speaking, they were some other plant entirely), "what are we going to do?"

None of the three was willing to admit how afraid he was of saying no to Gustave, who had approached them all that morning with his marble plan. Furthermore, Gustave had been right. Bang and Nat needed money, and Cougar would never turn any down. But what about Raoul? Were fear and poverty (or in Cougar's case, greed) reasons to turn on a friend? Or might betrayal be justified, if it served a friend's best interests?

Fortunately, the ugliest of actions is rendered palatable by pretty design, which is why when Raoul's three chums were approached by Gustave and asked to take part in the smuggling scam, they ultimately agreed. For, they thought, what better way to circumvent Gustave's denials of Almondine than to make an ally of their best mate's enemy and perhaps find out the truth? The three of them might—single-handedly—solve the mystery of red-eyed, white-faced me! Thus they sliced their inconvenience, like the cubes and rondelles of Bang's airport pineapples, in order to digest it more easily.

So it was that the second pineapple pilfering heralded by the *Morning Crier* took place with their help, which is why, as Bang sang about friendship that night at the Belly, Cougar was ruffled by, and Nat was torn up over, their role in the rotten affair.

If I didn't bother with the particulars of the second pilfering before telling you of their effect on Cougar and Nat, it's because on Oh, as in many places, a deed's repercussions echo farther and louder than the deed itself, often little more than a fistful of stolen minutes under cloak of night. Nat's troubled demeanor after the fact warranted prompter attention than did his participation. He didn't relish cheating his friend. Neither did Cougar, which is why he leaned, ruffled and silent, against the wall of bottles by the bar. Bang spent the evening on stage, as you know, and I'm not sure what he was thinking or why on that, of all nights, he sang of good friends, bad friends, honest friends and cheating friends. But the three of them were grown men, men who should have known better than to steal a fistful of minutes that could never be given back.

That being the case, here's how the fistful unfolded.

It was a shiny night that witnessed the first conspiring of Gustave with Bang, Cougar, and Nat. Against the background of the still, dark sky, the light fell from the growing moon onto the water that rippled and refracted it in every direction. From his hiding place under a mango tree in the soft, green brush a stone's throw from the edge of the sea, Gustave saw the beach laid out before him, a series of wavy silver reflections that illuminated the wax and wane of the tide on shore. The leaves sang their *shhhhhhh shh!* of sides knocking sides, their chorus complemented by the chirp of a thousand invisible island frogs.

When Bang, Cougar, and Nat arrived at the beach as instructed, Gustave went to greet them. An impressive sight he was, flanked and backed by wooden cratefuls of pineapple, so many crates that the chums couldn't tell where the plywood slats ended and the soft, green brush began. Dulled by the sight, the scent, the oddity of the scene, they extended their hands to Gustave with the trepidation of those who, knowing not what else to do, rely on empty formality. Gustave, who had his faults, was not entirely uncivilized, so he met their hands with his own and with a nod.

"Wait here," he said, and headed into the water's shallow edge.

Rooted to the ground like trees, the chums looked at one another in silence until Bang broke it. "Where do you suppose they came from?"

"So many!" Nat gasped, incredulous.

Incredulous indeed. Two acres' worth, picked and packed and transported to the beach and not a single picker, packer or transporter in sight. At no point during the operation that night, however, did they ask Gustave for an explanation, not only because they soon grew distracted by the work at hand, but also because they didn't truly wish to hear one. To the chums' knowledge the only companions Gustave had were the Vilder legends that flew around the island. And though they now believed no supernatural determinant responsible for Puymute's disappearing crops, they were not exactly prepared to abandon the common belief that Gustave still had a few supernatural connections. Some rather strong connections, evidently, if they had managed to pick, pack, and transport two acres of pineapple, unnoticed, to the shore, where Bang, Cougar, and Nat were to help Gustave load them onto boats headed for Killig.

"How on earth are we supposed to manage this lot?" worried Cougar, the most practical of the three.

"I say we make a run for it!" Nat whispered, as forcefully as a whisper allows.

Before they could decide, Gustave's nearing silhouette came back into view. "We'll carry them out to those boats. They'll go back and forth until we've finished."

"What? Just the four of us?" a brave Cougar objected, elbowed by a not-so-brave Nat. "He's barking mad!" Cougar muttered. "It would take days!"

"Don't be ridiculous," Gustave replied, amused. "You underestimate your strength." With that he picked up a crate and held it in front of his body. When he verified that each of them, too, had picked up a crate of his own, he walked toward the beach and soon was heard sloshing into the water where the shallow boats awaited.

"Just humor him till his back's turned and then we'll do a runner," Bang ordered.

As it turned out, a runner wasn't necessary. The three men followed Gustave and soon found themselves sloshing into the sea, Cougar first, followed by Nat, followed by Bang. They watched as Gustave passed a crate from his own hands into the dark, musty hands of a stranger, whose shadowed face they couldn't see. They heard the clunk of wood on wood, slatted crate on slatted boat, then Gustave, empty-handed, turned and emptied the hands of Cougar, who emptied those of Nat, who emptied those of Bang, until all four crates had been passed along to the stranger and had clunked inside his boat.

The passage complete, instinctively Bang turned and walked toward the waiting mountain of packed-up pineapples, his lace-less sneakers full of water and his pant-legs heavy and stuck to his shins. Behind Bang, still incredulous in soggy sandaled feet and short pants, followed Nat. Behind Nat, barefoot so as not to ruin his calfskin shoes, and still directing objections ("Days!"), followed Cougar, who was followed finally by Gustave. But somewhere between the water's edge and the pineapple-mountain's, the original order re-established itself, as it is wont to do, and when the four set out on their second run, Gustave was again in the lead.

Again, too, Gustave passed his load to a waiting stranger's hands, though whether the hands of the same stranger, the chums had no idea. Crates clunked, one, two, three, four. The passage once more complete. Like a music box whose melody never varies, the passage played out over and over (slosh, clunk, slosh clunk), while the four men waltzed in time (step, turn, pass). They danced throughout the night and as they did, the crates grew lighter and the mountain smaller. The strangers' hands were sure and silent; their boats swift and strong. The wooden crafts glided back and forth from Oh to Killig as easily as the tide, emptying their cargo as if the crates were clouds that simply floated to their correct position in the sky. Cougar eventually stopped objecting; Nat remained incredulous, but for different reasons now; and Bang, he sang.

He couldn't help it. The rhythm of the melody and the dance were too palpable and continuous to ignore. The leaves, which always sing on Oh, sang even louder suddenly, in harmony with the cicadas and the hummingbirds who didn't know if it was night or day. The combined song of man, sea, flora, and fauna crescendoed to a frantic, fevered buzz; it fell on top of the cheating chums, like a thick blanket that might smother them.

They could hear nothing for the noise that filled their ears, the living sound that seemed to populate the air around them. They moved in unison with the island's tremble, lifting and turning, passing and pausing, four men dismantling a two-acre mountain and sending it adrift on the sea in sugary snippets. Confused, the chums tried to ignore the noise, tried to escape it by closing their eyes, but in the end they danced—step, turn, pass—as if unawares.

The magic moon laughed at their struggle. The leaves were too agitated, their chorus too loud. Loud enough to drown the chums' collective conscience, which reminded them of Raoul. Had one of the three actually heard it, the heavy pockets of the other two would have brought him squarely back to earth.

The fracas finally culminated in a guttural human cry that confirmed a superhuman deed, a celebratory cheer born of the incidental fellowship created by common objective. The moon, without whose light Gustave and his fellows would never have completed their task, was pleased. Her hands had stripped a garden and carried off its fruit, yanked the roots from so deep within the earthly soil that one would hardly discern which seed had ever been planted there, pineapple, plantain, or almond.

In the dark, they walked home, the chums, now four instead of three. Fresh, cool, their limbs and spirits light. The euphoria of the night's stolen minutes still wracked their bodies, while their minds (three of their minds) still struggled to understand how they had been seduced by the moon's silver glow and the pastels of the island's rainbow bills. The guilt of these same three would rise with the sun on the following morning, a morning dressed up like any other (clear, new sky; fishcakes and herbal tea wafting from next-door Shirley's), the cuckold ignorant of the previous night's betrayal. Like dreamers waking from a hazy, pleasant dream and struggling to return to it, the chums would find instead the gnaw and suck of the truth that tore their edges and rent their middles, devoured them as Nat did the shiny transparent yellow hard candies he kept in his cab.

But until then, they walked. Gustave in front and the others behind. It was Cougar's turn at incredulity. "How do you suppose we managed it?" he asked, his feet dry now inside calfskin. Nat replied only with the squish of his soggy sandals. And Bang, he hummed, in key with the leaves that shuddered a broken battle cry and leaned in respectful nod to the pregnant moon.

As the moon waxed fuller and fuller, proud of the night's doings on her favorite beach, Gustave waxed a bit proud himself. His plan to pull out all the stops was in full swing. Soon the islanders would be too scared to even look at him, let alone keep watch on his every move. Home in his bed, Raoul was happy, too, knowing it was only a matter of time before Gustave tripped himself up with all his boondoggling. The more magic the better, Raoul reflected, for the sooner Gustave would fall. (Had Raoul known already of that night's caper, he would have been happier still.)

As the chums walked home to the song of the shuddering leaves and Bang's hum, both Gustave and Raoul boasted a puffed-up aplomb. In fact, a good many things were puffed up that night: the last bloated boats of the smugglers, the stuffed pineapple depots on Killig, the bulging pockets of four cheating chums.

To say nothing of the swollen tide that assaulted Oh's sandy shores; or the moon. The placid, gibbous moon.

12

There is no shortage of words on Oh. Bounteous as the mangoes or the rain, they are available to all the islanders indiscriminately, though not everyone indulges in them in equal measure. The appetites of some are insatiable, like those of the lonely Pedro Bunch; and of others, easily whetted, like those of the widow Corinna, whose words fall aimlessly from her tongue in the marketplace or in front of the Island Post. Some islanders (like Bang, Cougar, and Nat) prefer a healthy, robust diet; while others (like Raoul or Gustave) opt for slighter fare, their cravings best satisfied by private monologue.

Like legal tender the islanders exchange their words, in sympathy, solidarity, in jest. And in promise, as I've already said. This last part bears repeating, for promises are never contracts to be entered into lightly. Not anywhere. And especially not on Oh.

Abigail Davies and my grandmother Emma Patrice once shared a promise that forever changed the direction my life would take. It was long before my grandmother disappeared on that tall, snowy slope in Switzerland, leaving behind her pearl-handled sewing basket and her two-year-old baby girl. With the sharp edge of a cracked shell, she and Abigail sliced open the dainty brown tips of their nine-year-old index fingers and pledged eternal allegiance, if not in so many words. They mixed their blood, smearing the hybrid droplet into the loops and whorls that distinguished the one girl from the other, declared themselves sisters—blood sisters—and promised to forever treat each other the way that sisters do.

Accordingly, their alliance took many shapes over the course of the years. Playmates turned confidantes, turned rivals, and back, and sometimes months went by during which the two girls never spoke. The reasons for their silences were many and varied, malicious and not: disagreements, distractions, Abigail's pregnancies, Emma Patrice's books. Even then they were her way of escaping, and both sisters must have suspected (known, really, though neither ever said it aloud) that the metaphorical escapes were a prelude to, and preparation for, a full-fledged breakout.

Despite the occasional hiatus, the sisterhood survived. When Raoul returned alone with baby Edda from that first real family holiday, Abigail felt anew the sting of the salty sea in which she and Emma Patrice had rinsed their bloody fingertips that day so many years before. Her sister was gone! No one knew for certain if Emma Patrice's disappearance was willful or willed upon her, but Abigail was certain of the former, and so she chose to rejoice in her sister's new-found freedom, rather than to mourn her demise.

Raoul saw matters in a different light. He, too, suspected a willful departure on the part of Emma Patrice, though he never said it aloud either, and he didn't stop (or for a long time he didn't) hoping she would have a change of heart. Silly Raoul, Abigail thought. He was a good man, as fine as any on Oh, if not better. But he would never have done for Emma Patrice. They should have figured that much before the two ever married. (In my grandfather's defense, I don't think anyone would "have done" for Emma Patrice and her escapist tendencies.) Still, Raoul's glum disposition caused Abigail to wonder if perhaps she shouldn't be mourning a bit more than she was, just in case. After all, her blood sister's departure didn't change the fact that their blood had in fact been mixed. There's no undoing a thing like that. Not even by running away.

So with no blood sister left on whom to lavish her devotion, she turned her attention to the next best thing, her blood sister's baby, Edda. Abigail promised the absent Emma Patrice that Edda would always be happy, that Abigail herself would see to it.

Like her earlier alliance with Emma Patrice, Abigail's relationship with Edda, too, took many shapes over the years. Babysitter turned auntie turned tutor and back, to the extent that Raoul would allow. (She reminded him too much of his missing wife, or rather, of the fact that his wife was missing.) Although Abigail's help was wanted less and less as time went on, she kept her thumb on the pulse of Raoul's parenting—discreetly, from a distance. Keeping tabs from afar is easy on Oh, if you have a knack for it, as some of us do. Midwife Abigail managed it quite well indeed, for her connections and savvy had only increased with each pregnancy she saw to. When they told her it would soon be my mother's turn to deliver, her once-pricked finger tingled and she summoned Raoul.

"Now about your...services," Raoul stammered, seated in Abigail's kitchen. "How would it work?"

"Don't you worry about the details," Abigail replied. "I'll fix everything with Edda, and she'll be well looked after. I can promise you that."

Raoul wanted to ask further questions of this midwife into whose hands he was about to place the future of his first and only grandchild, but ignorance and embarrassment conspired to keep him quiet. That, and the fact that Abigail had always intimidated him just a little bit. He was sure she blamed him for Emma Patrice's disappearance. Not for losing her there on the slope, but for driving her to go. Abigail was the last person he wanted around, but she was Oh's best midwife, and my welfare (and Edda's), thankfully, trumped his pride. He finally stood, resigned if not convinced, and thanked Abigail for taking the time to speak with him, though it was she who had invited him round.

"She'll be well looked after," Abigail repeated, cupping her two hands around the one Raoul had extended to her. "I can promise you that." It was agreed that Abigail would go to see my mother the very next day to discuss the "arrangements" and with that, Raoul left her small but comfortable house. When he had reached the road that bordered Abigail's garden, he almost turned back to inquire about the midwife's fee. He wasn't sure, however, if etiquette allowed for such negotiations, so he kept quiet again, confident (almost) that he would get his money's worth, whatever the cost. Then he headed for Edda's, to tell her the news.

Abigail could not have been more pleased by the outcome of Raoul's visit. She had waited a long time to have a hand again in Edda's happiness. Over the years Raoul kept Edda seemingly *perfectly* happy, leaving nothing for Abigail to do. He taught her to cook and to sew, taught her manners and good posture, even taught her to braid her hair. And in Bang, Cougar, and Nat, she had three of the most doting uncles a young girl on Oh could want. Added to that, Abigail had been pregnant with problems of her own much of the time, and her pledge to Emma Patrice, though never forgotten, had intermittently fallen by the wayside. Until now. Now that Edda was pregnant herself, and Abigail was pregnant no longer, the blood-sister promise could be properly fulfilled.

As agreed, the day after her conversation with Raoul, Abigail paid my mother a visit. She explained that Raoul had engaged her services (as if she would have had it any other way), and she assured Edda that there was nothing to be afraid of. Abigail had training and she could manage the most troublesome of pregnancies, the most delicate of deliveries.

Though it would take some months more to confirm the veracity of Abigail's boasts, she was off to a very good start. My mother was well looked after indeed, better than any pregnant woman that Abigail had attended to before. She devoted herself to Edda and her growing baby, spending almost every day in Edda's company while Wilbur delivered the island post. She sang to her and helped her clean the house, told her stories about her mother Emma Patrice (never mentioning her escapist tendencies), and in between she prepared Edda's meals. This was the hardest part of Abigail's job, for as Edda's belly grew, it grew capricious. Some days her appetite was healthy, robust, and she voraciously satisfied her body's cravings for fresh purpled octopus, sandwiches with peanut butter and pineapple jam, spicy sausages, and turtle steaks; other days her diet was slighter and functional, intolerant of purpled or pineappled dishes, and best satisfied by simpler fare, a mango or bowlful of beans.

Once a week, when Wilbur joined Raoul and the others for their nightly nip at the Belly, Abigail stayed with Edda in the evening, too. Sometimes they would sit on long chairs outside, both with their feet up, the island breeze blowing a fine mist of sand between their toes and inside their skirts. If the light of the moon and the stars permitted, Abigail would sew. While she did, Edda would talk, sharing with Abigail her most intimate thoughts and fears. My mother would almost be sorry to see her pregnancy end, for her days and evenings with Abigail were the closest she had ever come to having a real mother, to experiencing the kind of maternal bond that makes one feel calm and protected and sorted out.

"Abigail," Edda began, one evening when the two were lounging beneath the speckled sky, "will my baby look at these same stars one day?"

"Yes," Abigail answered, then decided that falling stars should be allowed for. "Most of them anyhow."

"Will I have a boy or a girl? Why won't you tell me?" Edda spoke to Abigail but kept her face toward the sky, whose twinklings were reflected in Edda's dark eyes.

"I've told you already, I can't always tell."

"Please tell me, Abigail. You must have an idea!"

"No, child, I must not, or else I would have said something," Abigail lied. She did have an idea. Edda's shape and her demeanor, her cravings, her complaints, all told Abigail clearly that the child was a boy. But even the most astute of midwives could be mistaken, and given Edda's unusually fragile state, Abigail preferred not to share her speculations. The truth was that she had begun to sense real trouble. My mother's was promising to be Abigail's most delicate delivery yet.

"If I have a boy," Edda interrupted Abigail's thoughts, "will he bother about the stars, or will he be too busy?"

"Don't be silly. I imagine he would bother about them just as much as anybody else." Abigail hoped so, at least. She wanted nothing more than for Edda to have the kind of boy who bothered about the stars and cared about the moon. Having only ever met the kind interested in their fishing rods, their pencils, their paintbrushes and pipes, Abigail wondered if the stargazing ones really existed, and if so, where on Oh they hid.

For a while after that Edda didn't speak. She lay rubbing her belly and contemplating the sky, its dark folds and the blinking lights they housed. Like constellations, words speckled the blank thoughts in her head, but though Edda struggled to line them up, she was unable to turn their shapes into sentences.

Thus, the private monologues of Abigail Davies and Edda Orlean, to the rustling of Abigail's stitches on my infamous sunbonnet, until the voices of Wilbur and Raoul, who had finally returned from the Belly, could be heard inside the house, signaling the hour for Edda's repose and for Abigail's leave.

Abigail's devotion to my mother's happiness did not whither after I was born. If anything, it grew. Because of the hand that Abigail had had in managing my birth, she felt a territorial responsibility to protect the interests of our little family. The delicate delivery feared by Abigail had gone better than she dared hope, and though there was still a hiccup or two to quiet (there were always hiccups in this sort of affair), mother and child were doing nicely. So nicely that Edda didn't bother about my pale white skin, and neither did Wilbur. The love that inhabited our dwelling was palpable, like a blanket that threatened to smother us all, which, Abigail feared, it just might do, seeing as how it had already blinded my mother and father both.

Abigail had never experienced this blinding sort of love firsthand, but she had heard of its rumored existence. That its magic could be so powerful as to blot out my birthmark and drown out the chatter of scandalmongers in the marketplace, well, this much she could never have imagined. She was grateful for it, grateful that her charges were lucky enough to succumb to such a spell, for not only did it make our lives easier, but hers, too. We had secured happiness all by ourselves; Abigail had only to safeguard it.

Which explains the dismay she felt when she learned of my grandfather's ad in the *Morning Crier.* She had struck such a delicate balance. Why did Raoul insist on tipping the scales? Had he just kept quiet, the rumors about me would eventually have noodled their way into the casserole of gossip and conjecture on which the islanders inveterately fed, the individual spices (Edda's transgression, or Gustave's) lost in the mix. Leave it to Raoul to stir up trouble and spoil the broth.

Abigail, who never read the paper, preferring to pick up the day's news at the market with her purchases of curry and flour, bought a copy for herself to confirm what the marketplace sources reported. Juggling her parcels and her pocketbook, she opened to the classified section and found it, sure enough. Just as they had told her she would. Jostling her head from side to side, she crumpled the paper, tucked it under her arm, and rushed to the *Morning Crier*'s grimy-windowed office, anxious to displace some of the blame she felt rising in her chest. She had naively overlooked Raoul and his perpetual quest for explanations as plain as noses on faces.

"Bruce!" she shouted, bursting through the door. "Where are you? How could you?!"

Bruce, the paper's editor-in-chief, copyeditor, reporter, and special correspondent, peered up at Abigail from behind the keys of his typewriter. "Abigail! Hello! What a nice surprise!"

"Hello? Is that all you have to say for yourself? How could you, Bruce? How could you let Raoul place that ridiculous ad?" Abigail untucked the crumpled paper and threw it at the typewriter.

"Oh, that."

"Yes, that."

"What was I supposed to do? Raoul came in, had his words, had his money, demanded I put in the ad. I thought it was some sort of a joke, but then I saw he was serious, and I didn't know what to do. So I just did what he told me."

Abigail would not have the blame displaced again so easily. "Did you stop to think for just a minute of that poor girl? You and Raoul have made a spectacle of her!"

"I don't know about that. Seems to me that baby of hers is the spectacle. You can't blame Raoul for wanting to know what's going on."

"I see," Abigail answered softly, too furious even to shout. "And you think this is the way to go about it, do you? Something strange happens, you put an ad in the paper, and in a day or two you have all the answers you're looking for. That's what you think? Since when do things work that way around here?"

Bruce cowered silently behind the bulky typewriter, happy he had never upgraded to a sleeker model.

"You should have talked him out of it!" Abigail shouted. Then she turned and walked out, slamming the door so hard that the grimy office windows rattled.

As Abigail walked home, she wondered how to fix the mess that Raoul had made. She came up with no convincing solution, none of her previous jobs having prepared her for something like this. She could balance accounts and cover things up. She could even keep troublesome things quiet, if she got her hands on them before they were printed in the newspaper. But how to handle a classified ad that had the whole island talking? She could force Raoul to retract it, though that wouldn't undo the fact that everyone had seen it. She could assume a disguise and answer the ad herself, tell Raoul a tale that would placate his curiosities. But what could she possibly say? Or she could wait and hope for some other island drama to begin, one that would steal the spotlight that shone on baby Almondine.

When Abigail reached her house, she still had no plan. But she would come up with something. Some way to protect poor Edda and to quiet the story while Almondine was still too young to bother about it, before the story became who she was, speckling her dark life on Oh like the stars speckled the island's still, dark sky.

A tall order, even for someone as capable as Abigail. She knew in her heart that no matter what she did, I would always have to answer for my white skin and my rosy eyes. There was nothing anybody could do, or say, to change that.

Like the wind that spares no crevice, wrenching the white sands of Oh into every nook and cranny on the island, the rain relentlessly makes its way across the island's shiny surface. It fills the dips in Raleigh Bello's corrugated roof and drowns the moonlight that, gasping and splashing, struggles to dominate the spilling, splintering streams. In a feat of magic typical of Oh, it insinuates itself into the heart of the Belly, in the form of Cougar's watered-down cocktails, which are especially weak when the weather is bad. This doesn't deter the clientele, as you might expect; on the contrary, the Belly is always especially full whenever a storm is brewing.

One rainy night when I was about a few weeks old, my father made (or attempted to make) his weekly visit to the Belly in the company of his father-in-law Raoul. My arrival in the household had not squelched this tradition, nor that of Abigail's visit to my mother while the men were out having their drinks. This particular night the rain was fickle, pelting the island and retreating, threatening and thinning, seemingly intentioned to keep Raoul and Wilbur from their appointment with Cougar and the others. Each time they tried to leave the house, thinking the rain had stopped, it started up again, unleashing a shower more insistent than the shower before.

So Raoul and Wilbur settled in the kitchen, to share a word and a pot of tea, while Edda and Abigail entertained me in the sitting room beyond the kitchen door. Raoul could not have been more pleased by the rain's visit. Since the night of my birth, he had wanted a word with Wilbur in private, but up to now finding him alone had proved a rather challenging task. When Wilbur wasn't delivering the mail, he was busy taking care of me so Edda could nap. When he met Raoul for their weekly nip, Raoul was loath to discuss delicate matters, for Edda's three doting uncles were always close by. Until now. Now that the weather had waylaid their outing, and Abigail had laid out their tea, Raoul's wish for a secret dialogue could be properly fulfilled.

Except that he didn't quite know how to begin. He had half expected that Wilbur, finding himself alone with Raoul, would blurt out those same questions that were buzzing like flies in Raoul's brain. Questions about Edda and Gustave and Almondine. Who seduced whom? And when? Where? How had the deep black eyes of Edda, Wilbur, and Raoul, in Almondine turned to a fiery red? But all Wilbur did was sugar his tea.

"Wilbur, damn it! Aren't you even angry?" Raoul demanded.

Wilbur, who had not been among the flies inside Raoul's head, was puzzled, both by Raoul's fiery question and his even more fiery tone. He waited a moment before replying, trying to discern in Raoul's black eyes a narrative thread onto which he might grapple.

"Angry about what? About the ad? Abigail sure is."

"Not about the ad. About the baby! About Edda! About the whole bloody mess! Don't you know that half the island thinks your wife cheated on you? The other half thinks Gustave has her under a spell!"

"What do *you* think?" Wilbur asked, with a calm that agitated Raoul's flies into a frenzy.

"I don't know what to think! Edda says she's only ever been with you, and I want to believe her. I do believe her. But I refuse to blame what's happened on one of Gustave's spells. You know what I think of magic."

From the sitting room Edda's laughter seeped into the kitchen, like rain through a hole in the roof. "You hear that?" Wilbur spoke to Raoul but kept his face toward the door from which the joyful voice had come. "She's happy. She's really happy." Then turning to look into Raoul's eyes again, he added, "I believe her and I love her. What difference does it make what either half of the island thinks?"

Before Raoul could answer, Wilbur stood and went outside, no longer thirsty, not for a storm in a teacup. The island had quenched its thirst as well, and the sky was bright and starry, the night air hot and still. Raoul peered unbelieving at Wilbur's distorted figure beyond the foggy glass of the kitchen window.

Raoul had never experienced this blinding sort of love first-hand, though he had heard of its rumored existence. That its magic could be so powerful as to blot out my white complexion and drown out the gossip of revelers at the Belly, well, this much he could never accept. Wilbur might not have the courage to stumble down the road to the past, to line up the ugly variables that rotted hidden in pockets and drawers, but Raoul did. Someday

Almondine would look in the mirror and ask for an explanation as plain as the white nose on her face, he was sure of it. If Edda and Wilbur wouldn't give her one, Raoul would. He alone could secure Almondine's happiness; he alone could safeguard it.

Raoul was so moved by his own determination that he announced this promise aloud, although no one was there to hear it. Had Abigail been pressed against the door just then, about to enter the kitchen for some pineapple juice or some milk, she would have heard Raoul's words and been vexed. She would have tried to stop him. Already, she had gone above and beyond the call of duty to protect the happiness of Edda and baby, and Raoul's interference had so far only undermined her efforts.

Alas, Abigail must not have been pressed at the door just then, because nothing stopped Raoul. He rushed outside, compelled to publicize his promise—which he did, in front of Wilbur and the moon, who looked at each other and didn't say a word.

13

Raoul, too, had a vague recollection of my mother Edda's pregnancy. Vague, because like a tiny blemish on a peach, it was the soft spot in an otherwise firm and sweet routine that, once I was born, became a fuzzy memory. Back when Edda's belly swelled, Raoul pondered passports, doled out pineapples, and met his chums for a beer at the end of the day. Back then, his weeks unspooled, one day opening and rolling into the next, culminating in Tuesdays, in his favorite blue shirt with the stripes, and in the library with Ms. Lila. Back then, his favorite book was just that, a favorite book. Now, it was a means to keeping a promise, and a roadmap that was driving him to madness.

Since my birth, Raoul's peachy routine had rotted away, and he found himself in a spot as tough and sticky as the fruit's knotty pit. He still pondered passports and doled out pineapples (that was his job and he had no choice but to do it), and often he still met his chums for a beer at the end of the day. But Tuesdays' neat and regular blue-striped expeditions through the library shelves had disintegrated into variable-seeking scavenger hunts that took Raoul all over the island, on virtually any day of the week when there was time, the book with Mr. Stan Kalpi's silhouette on the cover permanently cocked in the crook of his arm. (My grandmother would be proud; how far Raoul had come since the day he quietly removed his missing wife's books from the house!)

The disintegration of Raoul's routine began with a tiff with Ms. Lila on a thick and foggy morning. The dawn was cloaked in clouds, a rare occurrence on Oh, and one that should have warned the librarian that she was in for an unusual day. She breakfasted and dressed, dowsed herself in honey-flavored eau de toilette, and gave a pat on the head to Fragile, her pet poodle, named for its delicate temperament. Then off to the library she went, humming her way through the fog. Ms. Lila was cheery and keen whatever the weather, so long as in the library no ill winds dared ruffle her pages.

She was especially keen on Tuesdays, of which this foggy morning was one, for it gave her great pleasure to watch, and sometimes take part in, the weekly explorations of Raoul Orlean. None of the other patrons handled the librarian's offerings with such attention and reverence as he did. He handled the covers with care, didn't crumple the corners of the sheets inside them, and never skipped to the ending before it was time. When he was finished, he left everything as he found it, clean and tidy, and always told her "Thank you very much." But lately the poor man had been acting a bit funny. During his last visit he had pounded his fist and played with what was in his pockets, and she had been forced to look at him crossly. There was the ad in the *Morning Crier*, too. She never *had* known what to make of that!

She knew just the thing for him, Ms. Lila thought to herself as she walked to work. Amongst the week's new arrivals were a glossy travelogue of Greenland and a book of poems about the beach.

Both of them had very nice covers and were sure to catch his eye. "That ought to make him forget about his troubles for a little while," she said to the clouds that accompanied her.

The same clouds accompanied Raoul, who had started his Tuesday morning ritual earlier than usual, though not without his coffee and milk and oatmeal, putting himself at the library just as Ms. Lila was opening its doors. Like her, Raoul, too, was keen, keen to roll up his sleeves and dig into his troubles, the very same ones Ms. Lila hoped to help him forget. She was mistaken to think that shiny snapshots and sandy rhymes would hold any appeal for him on this particular morning when there was so much work to be done.

"Morning!" Raoul's greeting caused Ms. Lila to jump.

"Heavens! Good morning! I didn't see you there."

"Thought I'd get an early start today," he explained.

"Yes, yes, please do. I've a lovely new book of poetry to show you."

"Very kind of you, but I don't have time for verse today," Raoul declined. "I'll need some books about mathematics. Algebra, maybe some geometry. There are always curves when you least expect them. And something on criminology. I'll need an atlas, too, or some maps. And some detective books, I think...maybe a spy manual? Have you got one of those?"

Ms. Lila, dizzied by Raoul's requests, turned the key and pushed open the double wooden doors, splashing the dull light of the foggy day onto her desk in the middle of the room. As she did so, Raoul made a beeline for his usual corner table. He sat down, opened up Mr. Stan Kalpi's story, and busied himself rereading it while he waited for Ms. Lila to deliver the books he had requested.

It wasn't long before she did, and soon Raoul found himself

elbow-deep in polygons, parallelograms, pastel seas, and finger-printing techniques. Hmm. All very useful and interesting, but how exactly he might use this information to more quickly detect Gustave's slip-ups, *that* remained elusive. So, like Stan Kalpi before him, Raoul lined up his variables again and decided that the very variables were the problem. He didn't have enough of them. He should take his search for clues outside, beyond the covers of his books, and listen for the songs on the wind that had guided Mr. Stan. "Yes, that's the way!" he said and slapped his palms against his thighs.

At the sound of Raoul's voice, Ms. Lila turned and slapped her own palms against her cheeks in surprise. She tried to shout, but could find no words to do her anger justice. To arrive at his "that's the way!" Raoul had sat down on the library floor and encircled himself not only with the contents of his pockets, but also with his shoes and socks (Mr. Stan Kalpi did his math barefooted with a toe in the mud) and with the most relevant pages from his morning's explorations, which he had gently torn from the books to which they previously belonged.

Gently or no, this was too much, and Ms. Lila finally did justice to her anger thus: "Have you gone mad?! Where do you think you are? *Who* do you think you are?" She scooped Raoul up by the collar, held on to him tightly as he scrambled to collect his things, dragged him to the library door and pushed him out into the noonday fog.

"You can come back when you've learned to behave yourself!" she shouted after him. Then she slammed the door, sighed, and set about mending her torn and abandoned sheets, which Raoul had so lovelessly left on the floor.

Under normal circumstances, Raoul would be devastated to find himself on Ms. Lila's blacklist, but circumstances were growing less and less normal by the day (though I'm not positive Raoul realized as much at the time) and he took his punishment in stride. He had already made up his mind to do some field work anyway, to search for more variables and real clues.

Who knows? he thought to himself. He might find something far better out there than what the librarian had to offer.

You know that on Oh the leaves sing. By day the wind mingles their wafting cries with strains of onion stew and dog's bark to lure the islanders home; by night, complicit with the mischievous moon, their melodies embolden wary lovers and hearten weary thieves on secret beaches. We're used to their songs here; they entreat and encourage, judge and joke. Sometimes their songs are just that. Beautiful songs with no real meaning at all.

But desperate hearts will hear meaning where they want to. They'll discern in the emptiest of tunes a symphony of significance. Had you seen Raoul later that day that witnessed his dismissal by Ms. Lila, I'm sorry to say you would have recognized his tone-deaf heart as one of these.

Raoul was desperate, yes. For variables and clues, for the path that his hero Stan Kalpi had found, the path that would lead him to the true identity of his white-faced grandchild and, he was certain, to Gustave. The variables he had lined up so far had proved insufficient and so some sleuthing was in order. From the detective book that Miss Lila had delivered to him earlier on, Raoul discovered that he needed some tools, which he acquired and now donned with uncharacteristic comical flair.

His black shirt and trousers, designed to melt into the night, were conspicuous in the island sun, as were the binocular and oversize camera that hung from his neck, knocking against each other when he walked (barefooted, of course, to facilitate his maths). His strange appearance was complemented by his even stranger behavior, which consisted in a procession of fits and stops, now to survey some distant movement, now to photograph some passer-by, his jerky march interrupted at intervals for big-toe calculations in the dirt. These Raoul often re-examined with a magnifying glass, which, when not in use, protruded from his back pocket like a big, see-through lollipop. All the while his hands, whenever unoccupied by any of the various lenses he toted, could be found cupped around his ears, where they hoped to catch a snippet of song on the wind.

They were in fact in this very position when Abigail, who was leaving the Staircase to Beauty salon, saw him go by and almost tripped.

"Raoul!" she demanded. "What's wrong with your head?"

"Nothing, why do you ask?"

"I ask because you're holding onto your ears as if you expected the wind to blow them off at any second, that's why. And looking a smidge ridiculous at it, too, I might add." (Her eyes had yet to descend upon Raoul's neck gear, clothing, and lack of shoes, or her smidge would have swelled into a bushel.)

"I'm just listening to the wind. It's all part of an official investigation. Don't bother yourself about it."

"What's all that equipment for?" she inquired sharply, lowering her eyes. "Never saw you use that before in all your years at Customs."

"Never had a case like this one before. Had to pull out the heavy artillery."

Abigail couldn't argue the heaviness of the artillery, for Raoul's top-half was unusually hunched and bent. That the rest of what Raoul had told her was legitimate, well, she would readily have argued with that. Her years of training in plights and cover-ups told her he was up to something odd, and that he wasn't quite himself.

Just what poor Edda needs! she thought. A mad father running around the island chasing the wind! Then again...a mad father was better than an illegitimate daughter, wasn't it? No islander could hold Edda responsible if Raoul started stumbling about with a binocular bouncing on his chest. It wasn't *her* fault he had stopped wearing shoes. Dare Abigail hope that another island drama had begun? One that would steal the spotlight that shone on baby Almondine?

As if in response to her private reasoning, just then four of Abigail's lady friends approached, their giggles and guffaws a harmonious tribute to Raoul's investigative techniques. They had found themselves behind him for nearly half a mile, the entire length of which he had startled and amused them with his antics. Thelma Johnson laughed so hard she had to stop, bend over, and prop her hands upon her knees. Mavis Beech cried in hysterics and used her headscarf to wipe her eyes. Henrietta Williams almost dropped the dozen sugar apples she had wrapped up in the apron around her waist. And Donna Ardeau, the subtlest of the ensemble, bit the inside of her cheek to keep her glee from escaping in more than a dignified titter.

Abigail, who guessed the source of their amusement, looked from the arriving ladies to the departing Raoul with mixed feelings of relief, pity, and foreboding. She almost wanted to hurry after him, though why she was inclined to do so she couldn't exactly say.

Before she could untangle her knotted emotions, she found

herself swept up in the jollity of the noisy band.

"Did you see that, Abby?!" Thelma choked and coughed, still laughing so hard she could barely stand.

"That camera's bigger than he is!" Mavis cried and hiccupped, dabbing her leaky eyes.

"And that magnifying glass! He was looking at his toes! With his backside straight up in the air!" Henrietta's sugar apples resisted no longer and tumbled from her shaking midsection.

"No, no, it wasn't his toes he was looking at! He lined up a bunch of bugs on the ground. And some rocks!" Donna clarified with a civilized chuckle as she helped Henrietta collect her apples.

By this time, Abigail was laughing, too, her worries of a moment before forgotten, her vague misgiving allayed in the wake of the chorus of Thelma, Mavis, Henrietta, and Donna, which was off again before Abigail could decide whether or not to join it.

You're probably wondering how it is that not one of the four women who observed Raoul's behavior bothered to ask if the poor man was alright. This normally respectable, quiet, conservative man who was suddenly acting so strangely. I can't help but wonder that myself. I suppose that when Raoul placed his ad about my mother, he lowered himself in the islanders' regard. Or perhaps their comity discouraged the compassion each would have shown had she happened upon him singly. Maybe, like Abigail, each had her reasons for wanting yet another island drama.

Whatever the explanation, it makes little difference, for had any one of them tried to reason with Raoul, to put herself in the middle of the path he sought, her efforts would have been wasted. At the root of Raoul's mounting madness lay not only his more and more dog-eared copy of Stan Kalpi's story, but his Almondine and the questions she might one day ask. Raoul would never let his little almond flower on uncertain roots. And nothing that Thelma, Mavis, Henrietta, Donna, or even Abigail, could say would have changed that.

If Raoul, for the worthy cause of sparing me a Stan Kalpi journey of my own one day, was resigned to having become an island spectacle, and Abigail, for the equally worthy cause of sparing me undue attention, was relieved to have found a new island drama—not that either of them succeeded in sparing me anything—my mother was reluctant to have her father branded the island fool. My mother was a quiet person, the kind of person life just happens to, not the kind who happens to life. She liked her anonymity (to the extent that anyone could be anonymous in a place like Oh) and she adored her father. Though the blinding sort of love she harbored for me could blot out my complexion and the island gossip, the love she felt for Raoul was different. It only heightened the distress she felt with every snicker snickered at her dear father's expense. She was upset that the islanders should poke fun at him, and poke their fingers into the pie of her family's anonymous existence. So this usually quiet girl was forced to confront her father not long after that unusually foggy day.

It happened one evening as Edda lounged on one of the chairs outside the house, the chairs that saw her tête-à-têtes with Abigail, and Wilbur's lonely stargazing. Abigail hadn't visited on this particular night, and Wilbur had swapped the stars for my shining eyes. Inside the house he gave me my bath, studying the twinkling lights that illuminated my face as if they were suddenly two North

Stars in the Earth's one sky.

Raoul was still in the thick of his investigating on that day, thick, the operative word, for half a week of spying, snapping snapshots, and magnifying the ground had in no way thinned the veil that continued to hide the truth that he was seeking. He hadn't found a single clue.

As darkness neared, my mother heard him approach, his paraphernalia clanking around his neck with every step. When he reached the porch where she lay, neither said a word. He simply bent to kiss her forehead, then sat next to her, and in response she smiled. Under the climbing moon they held hands until finally Edda broke the silent night. "Are you calling it a day, daddy?"

"I haven't decided yet," he answered. "I just came by to see my granddaughter. She isn't asleep yet, is she?"

"Wilbur's giving her a bath."

Raoul rose to go into the house, but Edda stopped him. "Wait," she said. "Daddy, are you alright?"

Raoul sat down again, balancing his binoculars on his knee. His reflection stared back at him from the black of the lenses and he studied it, hoping it might give him the answer to his daughter's question. It's not that Raoul wasn't alright. He was. "Of course I am, dear. Of course."

He just didn't feel one iota like himself. "It's just that, well, Edda, dear, maybe I'm not quite myself these days."

"No?" she asked.

In fact, Raoul felt very much like someone else, though he didn't dare associate himself aloud with the formidable Mr. Stan Kalpi, especially not now, when his road of holes and humps was leading him in circles. He had been around the whole island twice.

"Are you sick?" she insisted.

"Sick? Certainly not! Just a bit more work than usual, but nothing you should bother yourself about. I'm sure it will all be settled soon."

Edda insisted a bit more. "How soon, daddy? I don't like the way people are talking about you. They think you're acting strangely. Are you sure you're alright?"

"Edda! Now who are you going to listen to, them or me? I told you. I'm fine. Once this case is solved and all the guilty parties have explained their wrongdoings, then we'll all sleep easier. All of us." Raoul hugged her, and though Edda had no trouble sleeping whatsoever, at least not as long as her father behaved himself, she decided not to insist any further. Maybe tomorrow Abigail would have something to say about what was going on. Edda would give Raoul the benefit of the doubt for a little while longer.

"You better hurry inside if you want to see Almondine before Wilbur gets her to sleep." Edda patted Raoul's hand, before he made his way into the house.

Wilbur was just coming out of my room. I was already fast asleep and Raoul could do little more than peek into my crib a few seconds, for fear of waking me up. He joined Wilbur in the kitchen, then, which still bore the puddled signs of my recent bath. Soon he found a beer in his hand, for Wilbur was attentive and polite, if not talkative, though Raoul never stopped hoping that on one of his visits, or during one of their weekly nights out, Wilbur would suddenly come to his senses and blurt out the same questions and the same anger that, respectively, filled Raoul's head and heart.

Although this wasn't to be the night for such effusions, not even Wilbur could overlook Raoul's strange and rugged appearance.

"Raoul, are you alright?"

Again. "Of course, I'm alright. Of course I am." Raoul found the sound of his own voice irksome in its lack of conviction.

"It's a warm night. Why don't you leave all that equipment here and go for a walk on the beach. Do you some good," Wilbur suggested.

Whenever Wilbur mentioned the beach, he meant what he called "Edda's beach," that small private piece of the shore where as a boy he first spied on her. The beach the tourists didn't know. The one where he and Edda had honeymooned. It was his favorite, and the only beach he frequented, though it wasn't the easiest on the island to reach.

"Maybe I'll do that," Raoul answered. He liked the idea. Not because of the warm night or the good that a walk on the beach might do him, but because he suddenly realized that despite having circled the island twice, he had never once gone out of his way to check out *that* little bit of Oh. "I'll keep my things with me, so I can take them home after."

Raoul quickly downed what remained of his beer, shook Wilbur's hand, thanked him, and pecked Edda on the forehead once again as he rushed past her and headed out. He jogged in the light of the moon, which had climbed even higher in the sky and followed him, watching and winking. When he reached the coast and bent his head to survey the sandy shore, she splashed her light over the beach before him. Not even with the moon's help, however, was Raoul in any shape to look for variables. It was late and he was tired. His Stan Kalpi journey was taking its toll.

Raoul cleared a space under the mango in the soft, green brush a stone's throw from the edge of the sea and stretched out. In the shine of the morning he would have a look around, but not tonight. Tonight he was sleepy, his energy suddenly gone, his hopes as deflated as the song of the now sleepy leaves. In fact, a good many things were deflated that night on Oh: Raoul's hopes, Abigail's worries, and my mother's anonymity.

Only the moon was full. It perched, high and blue, over Edda's beach, a promise of the secrets that lay buried in the sand.

14

Raoul's obsession with Mr. Stan Kalpi wasn't lost on his three best mates (or on two of them, rather), though the significance of it was. Try though they might, they couldn't figure out what Mr. Stan had to do with anything.

"Stan *who*?" Cougar asked Bang, whose eyebrows were barely visible behind the glossy book jacket with Stan Kalpi's black-on-white silhouette.

"Stan Kalpi," Bang replied.

"Who *is* he?" Cougar asked.

"That's what I'm trying to find out, if you'll pipe down a minute." Bang read while Cougar drummed his hands on the Belly's bar. "Says here he's a maths teacher with no mother and no father who hears messages on the wind."

"Give me that!" Cougar snapped, yanking the book from Bang's hands. "You must have it wrong."

"Read it for yourself then," Bang shrugged.

"What's a mad maths teacher have to do with Raoul? He's been walking around with this book for days."

"Beats me," Bang answered. "The librarian said it's his favorite. Maybe he's just reading to keep his mind off his troubles." It was

Bang's turn to peer at Cougar's eyebrows over the profile of Mr. Stan. "'Course, she did also tell me he ripped up some books last time he was there."

"Ripped up some books?" Cougar repeated, incredulous, resting the book on the bar. "That doesn't sound like Raoul. You must have it wrong."

"What doesn't sound like Raoul?" Nat asked as he slipped into the Belly and looked from Bang, in front of the bar, to Cougar, behind it. "Who's got what wrong?"

"Shh!" Cougar silenced them, or tried to, and put his nose back into the business of Mr. Stan.

"What's going on?" Nat asked. He was confused, and rightfully so. It wasn't often that one found Cougar wrapped up in a book jacket.

"That's the book Raoul won't put down," Bang explained. "About a man who hears messages on the wind."

Nat was still not sure he understood, Cougar in a book and messages on the wind, but as luck would have it, it was an especially windy night on Oh, and so it seemed to him not inappropriate to respond with "He'd get plenty of messages tonight!"

"Don't listen to Bang," Cougar interrupted. "It's not messages he hears, it's songs. He hears songs on the wind."

"Ah, well, that clears it up then, doesn't it?" a cheeky Bang replied.

"You're the musician," Cougar countered. "It ought to clear something up for *you*."

While Bang searched in his head for some musical answer to the Stan Kalpi riddle, or, failing that, a clever retort, Nat nattered on about the wind. Or tried to. Cougar kept shushing him, depriving them all of Nat's account of his take-away dinner the night before on the beach, where the wind was so strong it had snatched away the salt he sprinkled on his fish cakes before the grains could ever grace the golden dough. And in its plastic cup, Nat's equally golden beer had had its head blown off before he could sit himself down in the sand to drink it.

"Not now, Nat," Cougar said. "Raoul will be back any minute."

As if to vindicate the poor shushed Nat, the wind rushed in and blew Raoul's reading glasses across the bar. Bang bolted to catch them before they slid over the edge and crashed to the floor.

"Where is Raoul, anyway?" Nat asked. He couldn't help but feel as if he were only getting half the picture. Maybe the strong wind had muddled his head.

"Toilet," Bang said, as he modeled his chum's rescued specs.

Nat wanted a drink but didn't dare interrupt Cougar's reading one more time. He decided to wait until Raoul reappeared, when presumably the book would be returned to its owner's hands, freeing up Cougar's to pour a shot of yellow rum—rum, Nat hoped, that would undo the wind's damage.

On Oh the wind is shifty. All the islanders know this. It's curious and capricious, advancing and retreating at whim. It spars with the moon and the leaves and trespasses through the islanders' homes and heads. But it was not to be blamed for Nat's befuddlement on this night that found Cougar re-tracing Stan Kalpi's path to the past. No, if Nat was confused, it was because lately he had let the island gossip, as sweeping as the wind though it was, blow into one ear and out of the other, forbidding it to stop in between. He hadn't heard a word about Raoul and Mr. Stan.

I'd like to attribute his indifference to tact or integrity or some emotional maturity that he might have attained, but it was in fact Nat's dishonesty that occupied all his mental faculties, leaving little room for the luxury of idle tales. Yes, he had agreed with his friends that befriending their best friend's enemy was wise, but their wisdom had so far served only to fatten their bank accounts. (Indeed, Nat had never had a bank account before and now he did.) Their wisdom had done nothing for Raoul. Nothing to ingratiate themselves with Gustave. Not really. They were his stooges, not his friends. Nothing to bring anybody any closer to implicating him in Edda's pregnancy. The so-called sleuthing on the part of Bang, Cougar, and Nat was nothing more than a profitable betrayal.

Still, profits were hard to come by on Oh, those rainbow bills never quite numerous enough. And so to avoid the ping-pong of shame-on-me's and yes-but's that bounced inside his head like so many of Raoul's flies, Nat drove his taxi. Since the caper on the beach some few nights before he had driven by night and by day, talking a blue streak with every visitor who graced his cab. Anything to keep his mind off the match going on inside his head. The tactic had worked, sparing him the island gossip, too.

So Nat had no idea that Raoul was creeping around the island with his clunking camera and his Kalpi book, no idea that his friend was the butt of the islanders' jokes. Bang would enlighten him only after the show, when Nat offered Bang a lift home. In the meantime he settled himself at the bar and awaited his rum, confident that his conscience was safe at the Belly, for he knew neither of the other stooges would bring up the matter there, with Raoul so close by. What he didn't know was that each was trying to ignore a ping-pong match of his own, Cougar with his nose in a book and Bang with his eyes glued to a pale blue piece of paper.

"What is it with everyone today? Has the library shut its doors? What are *you* reading now?" Nat asked Bang.

Bang held the page between his thumb and index finger and waved it in front of Nat like a shiny bell. "They reinstated it."

"Reinstated what?"

"The annual marimba competition. This is the entry form. *My* entry form, to be exact."

"You're a shoo-in, but what happened? The contest has been dead for years."

(Remember I told you about the annual marimba competition that Bang's grandfather won ten years running? Well, this is the one. When the pineapple trade on Oh bottomed out, so too did the accounts that the government's Agency for the Promulgation of the Indigenous Arts used to sponsor the annual event.)

"I'll tell you what happened." Bang read from the paper in his hand: "'It is with great delight that the Agency for the Promulgation of the Indigenous Arts announces the reinstatement of Oh's annual marimba competition'...blah blah blah...'historic island tradition'... blah blah blah...here it is...'held under the auspices of Mr. Cougar Zanne, owner of the Sincero Hotel, where the competition is to take place in the Buddha's Belly Bar and Lounge.'"

"Cougar! You?!" Nat knocked on the spine of Raoul's book, still propped in Cougar's hands.

"What?"

"The annual marimba competition. Why didn't you say anything?" Nat asked.

"Wanted it to be a surprise."

Something didn't add up. "Since when are you a promulgator of the indigenous arts?"

"I'm not. I'm a promulgator of profits. I put up the prize money and the space, and in exchange I get a packed house, hot thirsty bodies. I'm working up a signature cocktail to serve in honor of the occasion. I mix up a few batches beforehand and I'll refill their glasses faster than they can say 'marimba.'"

Nat still felt like half the picture was missing, but Raoul returned right then, snatching the book from Cougar's hands, and so Nat's thoughts turned finally to the rum that would soon be burning his throat. He motioned to Cougar to pour him a double shot. Meanwhile Raoul, who had barely muttered a hello, propped the book open on the bar, plucked his specs from Bang's nose, and resumed his reading.

Nat knocked on the book's spine again. "Raoul, you heard about the reinstatement of the annual marimba competition?"

"I heard."

"Bang's a shoo-in. What do you think?"

"Yep." Raoul closed the book with Mr. Stan's story and set it reverentially on the bar, resigned that he would get little reading done that evening. "You enter yet, Bang?"

"Got my entry form right here. I'm taking it into town tomorrow."

"Good luck." Raoul raised his glass, which was met by those of his three best friends. Double rum against water, against beer, against a yellowish concoction in Cougar's hand, murky glasses joined in that most banal of outward signs of solidarity. They had clinked their glasses thousands of times before, but on this particular night the rum and the water and the beer and the yellow goo hovered in the air between them as if suspended in time.

As far as I know, time has never stopped on Oh, but for what they perceived as a fistful of still, dark seconds, the four mates would have sworn that it had. Three of them, guilty-headed, had some idea as to why it might have suddenly halted dead. The fourth could only sense that it had done so, and he made a mental note to note it, for surely it was of importance. It was he, then, who knocked the island clock back into motion. "Cougar, what's that cloudy mess you're drinking?" Raoul asked.

"Mango surprise." Cougar swished a mouthful and then swallowed. "Too sweet. Back to the drawing board."

"The drawing board?" Raoul asked.

"He's working up a signature cocktail for the marimba contest night," Bang explained.

"Ah." Raoul looked at his watch, perhaps to reassure himself that time had kept its meter. It had. "Bang, shouldn't you get a move on?" he said and cocked his head in the direction of the stage.

"Yes sir. I'm off." Bang bounced off the bar stool and was up on stage before Raoul could ask him what he planned to sing about.

Nat knew. "He's singing about money. Must have the marimba prize money on the brain."

"Who could blame him?" Raoul responded.

Indeed.

To witness this exchange between Raoul and his mates, so typical of their nighttime reunions at the Hotel Sincero's bar, you would hardly think that anything was amiss or guess that Raoul was having any difficulty at all in distinguishing Stan Kalpi's path from his own. In truth, things were very much amiss and Raoul very much in difficulty, still scouring the island for variables, but finding more questions than answers in the process (though he *was* making some headway, which you'll hear about soon enough). Even so, like Nat and the others who dodged ping-pong balls at the bar, Raoul found solace that night in the Belly of his friends' company, where he, too, knew that certain matters were certain not to be discussed.

"Ladies and gentlemen, good evening and welcome to the Buddha's Belly. My name is Bang and tonight I'm going to sing about something we all love, something we all need, something most of us on this pretty little island of Oh never seem to have enough of. So hold on to your wallets and let go of your troubles!" And Bang's show began.

When I was just a very young lad,

By now you know all about the silencing, soothing effect of Bang's voice on the noisy, grumbling crowd, the cool coating it splashes, at least temporarily, on the Belly's burning walls. Tonight was no different.

But what of the singer himself? I've never told you what happens to Bang when the music starts, when his voice escapes that vague conjunction of heart, soul, and lung from which the shapeless sounds are born. It's not unlike what happens to you or me when we succumb to sleep at the end of a day, our coursing thoughts relinquished to the custody of the night. Bang's songs take him over like the rhythmic tide invades the sandy shore.

I walked one day with my old granddad.

Like a mindless sleeper who takes mindful part in the dreams that invade his head, so, too, Bang, while his song kept its meter unthinking, contemplated the thoughts that like flies or ping-pong balls played inside his brain. With a mental dexterity akin to the acrobatics performed by his marimba-playing, pineapple-chopping, knife-carving fingers, simultaneously Bang sang and Bang reasoned.

We went to a beach that was still and serene,

Sometimes he calculated the number of people in the Belly, sorted out the locals from the foreigners and decided where the latter were from. He guessed at the topics of his chums' conversations by the bar, imagined Cougar's quips and Raoul's reactions. He observed the dance floor, sized up the expectant men and measured the curves of the ladies underneath their skirts. Sometimes his thoughts wandered farther. Should he re-paint his peeling window frames now or wait until Christmas? How much time until Christmas anyway? Didn't Jacob Wilson's baby sister look mighty grown-up bent over the breadfruit at the market the other day!

The strangest beach I've ever seen.

On this particular windy night, like Nat, Bang struggled to ignore fuzzy and distant recollections of a not-so-distant beach on a not-so-distant night; like Cougar concocting his signature cocktail, Bang toyed with melodies for the marimba competition and with means for spending the profits after the fact; like Raoul, Bang was there at the Belly, physically, but his thoughts wanted to be somewhere else. They were jumbled up, hugger-mugger. Guilt and Raoul and Cougar and the contest and Nat and the night at the beach. Yes, definitely the night at the beach.

Instead of palms on the sandy shore

What bothered Bang about that night on the beach with Gustave was not the same thing that bothered Nat. Bang had entered into the affair light of heart, as he does most things, genuinely convinced of his moral sacrifice, an ugly but necessary deed to help a deserving friend. That Bang should score a bit of cash along the way was just an added bonus, one that meant little to the kind of man who not only knew what the "indigenous arts" might be but even excelled at a few. The rainbow notes he'd ever known were few and far between, but he got by just fine, and without compromising either his melodies or his principles (the latter consisted of two simple aphorisms, "A man's got to walk to his own rhythm," and "Happiness is what life's all about.").

There were money trees with coins galore

What bothered Bang about that night on the beach with Gustave was that something or someone had stolen his rhythm and imposed a new and strange one upon him. His helpless feet had stepped, as if of their own accord, in time to a cadence he had never known before. Bang couldn't figure out how it had happened, how he had *let* it happen, or if in fact it had truly happened at all. Perhaps his imagination had simply played a trick on him.

That dropped like fruits on the soft, white sand

Bang tried to recall the night in all its detail, but couldn't quite. He remembered his first thought when they arrived at the beach to meet Gustave: it was Edda's beach. The beach where she walked as a girl with her hair tied up in a dancing white ribbon; the beach where she walked as a young woman, her hair freed and her arms bare.

And felt so good nestled in my hand.

He remembered the shiny night and the sheen on the moon, whose light rivaled Bang's own brilliant heart. He heard again the *shhhhhhh shh!* of the leaves and the chirp of the invisible island frogs. He saw the wavy silver of the tide and he saw Gustave, surrounded by more pineapples than Bang could count. He sensed again the puzzlement, fear, and awe that was mirrored in the eyes of his mates and he recalled the touch of Gustave's hand on his. He remembered the paralysis that rooted them all to the ground like trees.

"See that tree?" my granddad said.

Bang's mind then fell upon the sea, where bobbed the boat or boats and silent boatsmen who awaited their prickly charges and swept them away, their crafts as if captained by the wind. Into the sea Bang trod all over again, his feet sandaled and soggy, his arms wide to accommodate his load. There his memories faltered. All Bang could recall next was the music. Music, dance, and song. To sloshing and clunking as regular as the tick of a clock, sloshing and clunking that couldn't possibly have come from his own steps and twirls into the sea or from the deposit of crates he himself had borne, to this mysterious rhythm Bang had somehow lost his own.

I saw. In awe I nodded my head.

Next he knew, he was singing in time with the dance. How it all started was fuzzy, as if it had simply always been. The wind shook the leaves and coaxed the cicadas and Bang was surrounded in song. Had he not succumbed, he would have been smothered. So he had opened his mouth and let himself be seduced.

"It's a tree of gold for you and me,

In unison with the island's tremble, lifting and turning, passing and pausing, Bang danced and Bang sang and his burden grew light and his pockets grew heavy and his sacrifices in friendship's name were forgotten. He reasoned that the shifty wind and the meddlesome moon were to be blamed for that night's befuddlement, but his reasonings, he knew, fell short. The crumple of rainbow bills in his pocket and the jingle of island coins was not the kind of music that suited a man of his rhythm, no sir; and yet, he could no more ignore it now than could Mr. Stan Kalpi the songs on the wind. Was this, then, the music to make Bang happy? And wasn't that what life was all about?

A golden tree by a silvery sea."

"It's a tree of gold for you and me,

Cougar and Nat smoked cigars silently (Nat could now afford to buy cigars) as they listened to Bang's song and did some reasoning of their own. If Nat was to remain in the dark about Raoul's strange behavior and about the island gossip until later when he offered Bang a lift, at least the fog was thinning where Cougar was concerned. Promulgator of profits, indeed! Were Cougar's recent patronage of the indigenous arts orchestrated merely for profit, then Cougar could have fronted the money to reinstate the annual marimba competition years ago. Even *he* was feeling guilty, Nat marveled. He was looking for some way to get rid of the cash.

A golden tree by a silvery sea."

Cougar looked and saw the truth mirrored in Nat's eyes. Well, what of it, if he had reinstated the competition? He could hardly donate the money to some orphanage or church school now, could he? That would have been far too conspicuous. Cougar Zanne didn't typically commit such acts of kindness. He only went along with the plan in the first place to protect the others. If any of us ever got caught, my pull would save us all, Cougar had reasoned. But his reasoning, he knew, fell short.

We went to a beach that was still and serene,

Raoul smoked one of Nat's cigars and sang along under his breath. This was one of Bang's old songs and Raoul knew it well. He would have preferred to have his nose in a book, Mr. Stan's book to be exact, but he was enjoying the show and feeling almost lighthearted for the first time in a number of days. He resisted the urge to join Bang on stage and shake a tambourine; for now the urge alone, which he hadn't felt since I was born, was enough to buoy his sinking resolve and shoo his flies.

The strangest beach I've ever seen.

What an idea Wilbur had had the night before to send Raoul for a walk on the beach! Edda's beach. The beach where she ran in her school clothes before returning home to pineapple tartlets and grammar drills; the beach that saw her first steps on the sandy shore, her tiny body shored up by the tired hands of Emma Patrice; the beach where Edda began, in the light of a near-full moon, when the hands of Emma Patrice were still in love and fresh. To the song of the sleepy leaves and doused in moonlight, Raoul had dozed there, and in the shine of the morning he had looked and found it. Finally, a variable. A clue!

A tree of gold for you and me.

Poor Raoul. Mr. Stan's treatise had failed to address the inverse proportion of size to weight in the consideration of variables, and the implications of Raoul's small success on Edda's beach that morning—once discovered—would send his flies into a real tizzy.

But not until tomorrow. He's earned an evening's respite.

A golden tree by a silvery sea.

And so at least for the duration of the show, while Cougar and Nat engaged in silent ping-pong and the shifty wind scattered Raoul's temporarily-homeless flies, Bang reasoned, and Raoul sang.

15

Fred Nettles was a foreman. Oh's best. Time *was* when you'd be considered a right fool to try and build a house without him. He knew the best plumber to lay your pipes, the best gardener to plant your frangipani, and the best mason to fashion you a porch. He knew about sockets and window frames and knobs for your doors, and could pour cement and choose patterned curtains with equal ease. He had proved his varied talents time and again, the length and breadth of all the island. As a result, in addition to a heap of rainbow bills at the Savings Bank in town, Fred had firsthand knowledge of every islander's bathroom tiles and kitchen door.

On the morning that found Raoul variable-hunting on Edda's beach, after his night's rest in the soft, green brush a stone's throw from the edge of the sea, Fred Nettles was at the height of his career. Not a cabinet was hinged without his approval, not a crocus positioned without his say. He knew who had indoor plumbing and who had electric lights, which islanders could afford expensive window-glass, and which ones managed with no window-glass at all. So when Raoul found the clue that he did, it was to Fred that he would turn for help.

Under the full moon, Raoul had passed that night on Edda's beach trekking barefoot from dream to dream in search of answers to the riddles riddling his life. There seemed to be more of them every day, one wrapped around the one before, like the icy flakes he layered into snowballs once so long ago with Emma Patrice. His riddles had grown too big to manage, and the core of the matter had gotten lost in the slush. The core, of course, was me, though my story had become packed in pineapples and variables and binoculars that banged against the buttons on Raoul's favorite shirt.

In his dreams Raoul revisited the riddles. He moved from one to the next as if swimming through the cruel, thick snow that had smothered and stolen his missing wife. He saw my mother holding me, my mouth suckling her breast, my skin new and white against the dark of Edda's, new and white but for the half-hearted mark on one cheek. He saw the blood in my eyes, blood that should have been his own but wasn't. How could it possibly be? Was I testament perhaps to some secret in Raoul's own far genealogical past? Or was I a lie, testament to some far more recent treachery?

Raoul wondered and wandered and by night he came upon the puzzling faces that plagued his mind by day: Wilbur's, blank and unquestioning, full of love and devoid of suspicion, his eyes blind to the appearance of a daughter no one would ever believe belonged to him, his ears deaf to the whispered gossip that swelled into a merciless roar and made Raoul cry out in his sleep; and Gustave's, complacent and resolute, marred by the same scar as mine, while he denied any hand in my creation. It was as if the two men were in cahoots, Wilbur and Gustave, feigning a common ignorance, a common indifference, the sole purpose of which was to drive Raoul raving mad.

As Raoul slept, the wind seduced and twisted the leaves. They shuddered into a cold breath that blew on Raoul's naked forearms and on his feet. He shivered and in his dreams the blinding flakes of snow enveloped him. Visions succeeded one another with rapidity, the rapidity, Raoul thought, of imminent death, the proverbial flashing of life before one's dying eyes. Before he could focus on any single vision it was wiped away, obliterated into whiteness and then replaced by another equally elusive reminder of the troubles he was leaving behind.

If only he really *could* leave them behind! Raoul wasn't dying and even in his nightmarish state he knew as much. Though he lay unable to muster the strength of body and will to shake himself awake and crack the dream's cocoon, he recognized somehow its wrappings around his mind. It wasn't death that lurked imminent on Edda's beach, not the end of Raoul's life, but maybe the end of his sanity, a prospect he feared far more.

Raoul swam and thrashed and through chattering teeth he struggled to call out to the silhouette of Mr. Stan Kalpi, black against the colorless snow, his darkness wrapped in white until only the white was visible. The Mr. Stan Kalpi whose variables had fallen into place, whose mandolin-guitar strummed the music of his once-unknown birth. Raoul looked to Mr. Stan for guidance, grabbed at his heels that he might rescue Raoul from the cold heavy water that froze around him. But Mr. Stan was gone.

In his place, Raoul saw green-gold patches of pineapple and then Gustave's face once more, still unwilling to reveal what magic, if any, it hid. In Raoul's dreams the crops vanished and like them his plans, too, seemed to disappear, useless and vain, his plans to find variables that would implicate Gustave, plans to blackmail him, plans to get the truth from Gustave about little Almondine.

Almondine! Raoul had scraped away the frozen layers and found himself at the core of the matter once more, but how muddled and cold!

Then Gustave was there again, denying Almondine, denying the magic that made her, touting the magic that swept away the fruits of the green-gold acres, more acres every day and Raoul less and less poised to discover the truth, to ever unblur the mingling of magic and mundane.

The moon watched over Raoul's fitful repose, splashing her light on his curled body and following him on his journey that not even sleep could still. She was worried, the moon was. If Raoul's wits slipped away from him and into the still, dark night, then who would be left to unearth the truth? Who would discover the seed she had planted, or unfurl the leaf she had sewn of stolen sides? No other islander would be as anxious as Raoul to make sure certain mysteries were solved. What pleasure in trickery if trickery is never unveiled? To what end the moon's magic, if not to relish the islanders' defeat? To revel in their realization that they've realized nothing at all?

So for now the moon retired, relinquishing Raoul to the charge of the new sun. The leaves stopped their shuddering and withdrew their cold breath. Raoul's body stopped its shivering. As the sun warmed his skin, the snow of his dreams melted and pooled, and then it was gone, evaporated.

Raoul woke and despite the restless night he had passed in the moon's care, he felt calm and pleased, a marathoner who at the finish is worn but proud. He stood and dusted the grass from the front of his trousers and stretched his arms high in the air to call to attention the tightened muscles of his back. He rubbed his eyes, and looked out at the sea, calm and brilliant in the early sun. Raoul saw what promised to be a perfect day.

The morning was quiet and soothing, the beach deserted but for a sniffing stray dog and a clump of three enormous spindly palms, the scene spectacular in its barrenness and geometric in its beauty. The sand was a flat white plane that bordered another of wet turquoise, both ending in triangle points where Raoul's line of vision ended. Triangles of climbing green hillside and light blue sky intervened at the same distant point toward which the dog's lolloping rhomboid body made its way. Nearer to Raoul, the palms bent at angles of 65, maybe 70, degrees, adjusted by the gentle wind, their bushy heads points on a vast, invisible graph. "So simple," Raoul breathed.

Raoul knew something of geometry. He had devoted more than one Tuesday to it some years ago, back when in his mind I was not yet even a fantasy and Stan Kalpi was little more than a well-crafted one. The purity of the shapes had always fascinated Raoul, their naked simplicity and the basic tenets that governed their existence, their variation, their cohabitation. He stared at the rippling plane before him and looked at his feet in the sand. Sunk down into it up to his ankles he was nothing but a line, half a right angle on the plane that was Oh itself, which in turn was but a dot on the circumference of the earth.

"So simple," Raoul breathed again, looking at his feet and observing his position amidst the immensities of the universe: light, air, water, life. Suddenly the mathematics of Mr. Stan Kalpi were clear. Why, it was all a question of perspective! Of knowing when and how to fit the variables into the bigger picture. Raoul had been going about it all wrong, focusing on the minutia. He paced up and down the sandy beach, tapping his index finger against his chin, elaborating aloud a mathematical proof that would have made even Mr. Stan proud. The minutia still mattered, of course (don't let's forget that Raoul was a philosopher of the plain-as noses-on-faces school), but perspective mattered, too. The perspective that turned a plane into a triangle, that reduced the world to simple, mathematical absolutes. Standing on Edda's beach that day, Raoul felt as if he were an absolute himself, in tune with the other absolutes of the island, in perfect harmony with the songs on the wind.

Even as he formulated his thoughts, Raoul wasn't quite certain that he understood them all. The variables would fall in line, this he now realized, for they were governed by rules that were timeless and pure. But they implied a philosophical adjustment on his part, an element of the abstract, of faith, that he decided he would have to allow. Raoul was heartened by this new discovery, the details of which he'd have been hard-pressed to put into words (had you asked him), and ran from the sandy shore to the mango tree in the soft, green brush to gather up his belongings and go home. A new reading of Mr. Stan's story was in order, in light of Raoul's new realization about the mathematical-musical order of things.

Illuminated in the sun, their lenses starbursts and mirrors, Raoul's oversized camera, his binoculars, and his magnifying glass struck him as artifacts from an earlier time, though only the night before he had been unable to part with them at Wilbur's. In a fit of giddiness he grabbed them up and dashed to the sea, prepared to hurl them into the rippling waves in a grand, symbolic gesture. But at the last Raoul changed his mind. Faith was one thing, foolhardiness another. Not only had the costly equipment been requisitioned from the Office of Customs and Excise, which would have demanded reimbursement, but—more importantly—it might be wiser to keep the gossiping islanders thinking him mad. Yes, definitely wiser. Which is why later that same day at the Belly, though he was feeling almost lighthearted and though he yearned to join Bang on tambourine, Raoul had hidden his hopes from his friends. And rightly so. For though things had taken a turn for the better, they were still far from sorted out.

In full regalia then (barefoot with camera and binoculars around his neck), Raoul hiked up his trousers and stepped from the sea's edge, about to turn away from it, and stopped. Something in the sand just below the water's surface caught his eye. An arithmetic error? The solution's next logical step? Raoul moved closer. He bent to meet the sand, nearly dunking his paraphernalia into the tide. Just in time he clasped the lanyards in his left hand, and with his right he fished around in the shallow water. The tide ebbed and flowed, invading and retreating, its foamy edges distorting Raoul's view and drowning his boon. His fingers dug deeper. When they finally closed themselves around the object Raoul hoped he was seeking, he pulled his hand from the water. The rising sun played tricks on his eyes. His fingers appeared to hold a rainbow tinged in blood.

Raoul closed his right eye and looked with his left, then he tried it the other way round. Finally he turned his back on the morning rays and in the shade of his body the vision was clearer. Not a rainbow, exactly, but a prism of sorts. Had Raoul happened upon a crystal washed up from the bottom of the sea, or carried to Oh from some distant land, a gift of splendor and light from a mermaid or a muse? As Raoul examined his hand more closely, he realized he was cut. His blood drizzled over the sharp edge of what was in fact nothing more than a broken chunk of glass whose bevels split the sun into a painter's palette. He saw that now. He saw it very clearly.

"Bloody...!" Raoul cursed. Still holding the glass, he rinsed his hand quickly in the stinging water and held the dripping piece up to the sun. With every tilt it spilled another rainbow into the sea.

"Fantastic," he whispered, dazed that an object of such beauty could cause him so much pain. Raoul stuffed the wet prism into his pocket, delighting in his ache, and squeezed his fingers into his palm to stop the bleeding.

Before long, he was back at our house, hollering testily as he climbed the front steps.

"Hello! Good morning!" Though Raoul had been awake since sun-up, pacing and reasoning on the beach, the household was still rubbing the remnants of sleep from its eyes. "Good morning!" He was a walking ruckus, shouting and stumbling into one of the lounging chairs on the porch, his dangling equipment ringing out like a windchime fashioned of plastic and metal. "Helloo!"

"What's all this fuss?" Abigail shouted back. She appeared behind the screen door just as Raoul pulled on it and went inside.

"Morning," Raoul replied sheepishly, embarrassed to find that his rough tone had fallen on Abigail's ears. But his sore hand was beginning to make him cranky.

"Morning to *you*," Abigail answered. "What brings you by so early, and making so much noise?"

Raoul might have asked Abigail the same question (to which she would have answered that a delivery of still-warm pineapple-upside-down cake for breakfast brought her to see "the children," as she referred to the three of us, Edda, Wilbur, and me), but instead he simply told her that he had come from a walk on the beach, where he managed to cut himself on some glass in the sand. Edda's house was closer than his own, and he needed a bandage and some alcohol.

"Looks like alcohol is the last thing you need, not that it's any business of mine," she told him. (You have to forgive Abigail her harshness: Raoul did look to be in quite a state. He was still wandering shoeless, with all his equipment in tow, and he had spent the night shivering in the grass, much of which still clung to the back of his trousers.)

"Wilbur's washing up and Edda's dressing Almondine," she said. "Let's see if there's some antiseptic in here." Raoul followed Abigail to the kitchen where she sat him down at the table and with some water from a bowl began to cleanse his hand. "How's the official investigation going?" she asked.

"The what?"

"The official investigation? The heavy artillery?" With a nod of her chin she indicated the tools that hung from his neck.

"Oh, that. Fine. Fine. Just fine," Raoul answered, wincing less from pain than in an effort to change the subject of the conversation.

As Abigail worked on his hand, she studied him. She was satisfied that he continued his antics, his new island drama that drew attention away from Edda, but she was suspicious, too, that he might have spent the night up to no good. A mad father was one thing, a debauched one something else altogether.

"Shouldn't you be spruced up a bit more for an official investigation?" she ventured. "You look like you slept under a tree."

"I did, now you mention it."

"Where's that?" She dabbed alcohol on Raoul's cut.

"Sinner's Cove." Sinner's Cove was the map's name for what in the Orlean family we have always (at least as long as *I* can remember) referred to as Edda's beach, because it wasn't thinkable that my sainted mother should spend her every free moment in a place with such a sinful name. Exactly which sins prompted the unfortunate designation that time made official, no one seems to be able to tell me for sure. Maybe the seedy port girls from the seedy port bar (a locale not far from the Cove) were responsible for the name, or maybe it was the indecent name that still lured the girls there on occasion.

Abigail, in her professional capacity, knew all about the seedy port girls. She knew about their tight jeans and complicated strappy sandals, and about the trouble they got themselves into. She didn't like the idea that Raoul might be frequenting them, though she could imagine no other reason for which he might have spent the night under a tree at Sinner's Cove (nor why, on this morning, he wouldn't have called it "Edda's beach").

"Why on earth would you do that, spend the night there?" she asked.

"No reason," Raoul replied. "I went for a look around last night and got tired, I guess." He knew that his behavior must have seemed odd to Abigail, but if the rest of the island was still to think him a bit mad, then she might as well do the same. Raoul couldn't be bothered to apprise her of his quest and his recent discovery, of the hopes and difficulties that remained. Her questions, he was convinced, were prompted only by want of gossip, not by any real interest in his work, his reputation, or his well-being.

But Raoul misjudged Abigail's motives. What prompted her questions was not a craving for tales to tell in the market square. On the contrary, she knew how the seedy port girls liked to talk, and she feared that where Raoul was concerned, they might do a little too much of it.

"You see anybody else on the beach?" Abigail asked, as she dried Raoul's wound and started to bandage his hand. "I'm told it's busy there at night sometimes."

Abigail's veiled reference to the seedy port girls and their nighttime cavorting eluded Raoul, who merely replied with a puzzled "no." Which only convinced Abigail further that he had something to hide, that she had caught him, literally, red-handed. Heaven knows how he got that cut! she thought to herself. But no use pressing on a fruit that wasn't ripe. If Raoul wouldn't talk, others would, others who Abigail knew well.

With a satisfied sigh she stood up and waved her hands at Raoul as if to dismiss him. "It wasn't much of a cut. I don't know why you came in hollering and pitching such a fit before." She cleared away the bowl and the bottle of alcohol, then said her goodbyes to Wilbur, who had just then entered the kitchen. "There's warm cake for you. Tell Edda I'll look for her later." And Abigail was off. She had things to attend to.

"Good morning, Raoul." Wilbur tried not to look surprised by Raoul's ruffled appearance. "This is an early pleasure."

Raoul explained again that he had come from a walk on the beach, where he managed to cut himself on some glass in the sand, that Edda's house was closer than his own, and that he had needed a bandage and some alcohol.

"You look like you've been out all night," Wilbur said. "Are you okay?"

"Yes. Fine. Just fine," Raoul answered. "I went to the beach last night like you suggested. I guess I fell asleep."

Wilbur stifled a smirk. He envisioned Raoul, bivouacked under a palm tree, hugging his binoculars as if they were a stuffed toy. "I wouldn't have suggested it if I knew you'd stay all night."

"Well, I didn't plan to, but I was tired," Raoul said. "It worked out for the best. It was a good idea to go."

Wilbur didn't know what Raoul meant by that and he was afraid to ask. For a second he too entertained the notion of a seedy port girl, then just as quickly he dismissed it. It was far more likely that Raoul referred to some development in his official investigation, of which Wilbur wanted no part. Better to change the subject, he decided. Which is what he did, or so he thought. "How did you hurt your hand?" he asked.

"On this." Raoul pulled the jagged prism from his pocket. He hadn't examined it or pondered it further because of the cut in his hand, which now looked—and felt—almost as if it had never been injured. Abigail really *was* adept at covering things up nice and even, wasn't she?

"What is it?"

"I thought it was a crystal of some kind, but it's just a piece of broken glass."

Wilbur took it and turned it over in his hands. "Pretty fancy glass. Looks like the stuff in those big doors at Puymute's. You know the tall ones they always keep open? Where the curtains are?" Wilbur didn't know about the islanders' light sockets or about their indoor plumbing, but thanks to his daily mail route, he did know about their front doors. Even as the words left his mouth, he was sorry he had mentioned this particular one.

A fly awoke behind Raoul's eyes.

Wilbur changed the subject again, or so again he thought: "Fresh pineapple cake! You picked a good day to come by so early." And he put on the kettle for tea.

But it was too late. Raoul had already made the connection between Puymute's doors and Gustave. With a satisfied sigh he stood up and waved his hands at Wilbur as if to dismiss him. "Enjoy your cake. Tell Edda I'll look for her later." And Raoul was off. He had things to attend to.

The Raoul of a few days earlier would have meticulously studied the newfound variable, examined the broken chunk of glass from every angle. He would have measured it, polished it, photographed it, and ultimately catalogued it useless. But the

Raoul of this perfect day saw the bigger picture. Not just a piece of glass, then, but glass just like that which adorned the door of the manor house on Puymute's plantation, where Gustave worked every day, and where island phantoms were swiping acres of island pineapple, to the detriment of the Customs and Excise coffers.

At the thought of Customs and Excise, Raoul remembered the airport, looked at his watch, and quickened his step. His flies hurried their pace as well. Was the glass really from Puymute's? And how had it gotten broken? Was there an unreported burglary? A kerfuffle on the premises? Wilbur hadn't mentioned a busted door. Had Gustave had it secretly repaired? How had that one piece ended up on Sinner's Cove? Had Gustave inadvertently dropped it there? Why carry a chunk of broken glass? And why on Edda's beach?

Despite the progress of the previous night, Raoul realized that many questions remained, more questions than answers by far. His geometry was muddled, his perspective distorted. Gustave and the glass were dots on a graph. Now Raoul must draw the line to connect them. Which is how Fred Nettles fit into the ever-spreading bigger picture. If anyone knew about the glass from a door on Oh, it was he. In this instance Fred would be of more help to Raoul than even Stan Kalpi himself.

Though Raoul longed to speak with Fred Nettles that very minute, to learn the significance of this latest variable and move the story forward, it was late and there wasn't time. Raoul sighed. He would have to wait and see Fred before work tomorrow (Fred went to bed too early for Raoul to visit him at night).

Right now, the morning's passengers were about to arrive. About to make their way through the zigs and the zags and the grit of Oh's airport floor, to Raoul's frustrated huffing and the dizzying pineapple perfume.

STILL WANTED: information concerning circumstances surrounding recent pregnancy of Edda Orlean. If you were party to/witness to/privy to details/events/evidence explaining origin of daughter of Edda Orlean you are STRONGLY urged come forward. Please. Call evenings 45468.

Not many little girls—black, white, or otherwise—can say they made their local paper *twice* before they were two months old. This dubious honor is yet another I discovered on my own road of holes and humps into the past.

I'm far more like Raoul than he could ever dream, far more Orlean than Vilder, despite my pale-white skin and his convictions to the contrary. Somehow that night on Edda's beach, when the Almondine seed was planted, the moon gave me a few Stan Kalpi tendencies of my own. *I* heard songs on the wind, too; I must have, or my unfinished mosaic would have suited me just fine. I had a mother and father and grandfather who had nurtured me better than any could have. And a grandmother who wasn't a grandmother, but a magical, faraway snow-fairy who may or may not have existed. *She* is the one I'm really like, what with my escapist tendencies.

Yet in spite of the latter, I went back to Oh, and still go back again from time to time. First, I went to find my missing variables, or as I like to think of them, my missing tiles, a colorful indulgence I hope the mathematical Mr. Stan wouldn't mind. Once all the pieces were stuck in place, I realized that mothers and fathers and grandmothers were as changing as the moon, and now I suppose I go back to show where my love and my loyalties lie.

As to my genes, the marrow and blood that make up my own, I'm pretty sure there is no trace left to be found on Oh. Raoul had a hand in that, it seems, and even now I struggle to forgive him his involvement. But he was well-intentioned; that's what you have to remember. And as luck would have it, Oh is Oh, so the traces that can't be found, they aren't really gone. They're written on the moon, if you know how to read them, and sometimes the leaves talk of little else; others, the wind has whispered in my ear. So I stuck them on my mosaic and every day I put them in my paintings, where they take whatever shade and depth I fancy.

When I'm not struggling to forgive Raoul his well-intentioned folly, I worry about him. Not the everyday Raoul, just fine now in the arms of one honey-dewed librarian who lets him out at night to drink at the Belly. No, I worry about the plain-as-noses-on-faces Raoul, who still has the odd nightmare of unsolved riddles wrapped in snow. As unlike him as I am in complexion—as unlike all of them, my mother, my father, the neighbors—I belong to the island as perhaps no one does. Certainly more than my dear grandfather ever could. If for *that*, Oh hasn't told him the secrets it's told to *me*, is it *my* place to ignore the island's whims?

You'll see for yourself. My Stan Kalpi mosaic is almost finished, the last secrets almost out. From that tree in the soft, green brush a stone's throw from the edge of the sea, the last mango is almost ready to fall.

16

The Government Mail Boat stopped at Oh once a week. It came from nearby Killig and was piloted by a man named Jack. The islanders all called him by name, though they suspected he deserved some loftier title, but whether "captain" or something more postal, nobody knew. Jack's craft, though official, was unassuming, which confounded the matter even more.

Whether in any given week Jack arrived on a Monday, a Wednesday, or at all, depended on what he ate for breakfast. If his wife gave him pancakes with butter, he took her back to bed, their stomachs heavy with sleep. If she made him toast with jam, he took her back to bed the same, their inclinations sweeter and stickier. If, though, she fed him farina, he climbed atop his bicycle and pedaled straight to the Post. There the sacks of mail awaited, for delivery to Oh and Walou and Esterina, Killig's tiny island neighbors. With the help of the Postmaster, Jack dragged the sacks to the dock nearby, and in his burdened government vessel set off on his rounds.

Oh was always Jack's first stop. When he arrived, two men from the Island Post pulled the sacks meant for Oh from the Government Mail Boat, while Jack bought coffee from a bar that was a window in the side of a house. He dribbled two coins into the palm of the man seated inside and two capfuls of Killig rum into his coffee (Jack never set sail without his flask). Then while he proceeded to his remaining peregrinations, the contents of the sacks began their own. Letters were divided by village, and packages were sent to the office of Customs and Excise, which in turn dispatched notices to the lucky addressees.

With your Customs notice in hand, you could claim your package, open it for inspection, pay what duty was due and carry home your prize. So you see how a bowl of farina was needed to produce your new shortwave radio or pair of shoes.

It was according to some similar faulty logic that Raoul decided to place *again* the advert about my mother's pregnancy. The ad would remind the islanders of Raoul's feigned feeble mental state (by virtue of which he could behave as oddly as his investigation required), and, more importantly, he was sure it would produce a pineapple smuggler: his phony madness, he hoped, would stir pity in at least one of his cheating chums, who would be moved to confess his betrayal, to open his guilty heart to the inspection of Customs and Excise Officer Raoul, like a package with shiny new loafers inside.

When, exactly—and how—did Raoul find out that his chums were cheaters? To explain what prompted his logic and his ad (his farina, if you will), we have to get back to the airport and pick up the story from the gritty floor. The morning's passengers were due at any minute, remember? And Raoul was running late.

He managed to get to work on time and cleaned-up, if barely, and spent the day consumed by the piece of glass in his pocket. It was a tangible tie to Gustave, of this he was sure to have confirmation from Fred Nettles the following day, and he couldn't get it out of his head. Now perhaps even Stan Kalpi himself, forced to wait a full 24 hours to determine a variable's value, would have lost sight of the bigger picture, or at least of the solution's next logical step. Heaven knows that by the time Raoul went round to see Fred Nettles the next morning on his way to work, his flies had worked themselves up into a terrific frenzy. And when Fred identified the glass! (He held it up to the light and rubbed its facets, but nothing is what it appears to be on the surface, I can assure you.)

"Sure, I know this," Fred said. "Not too many people around here who can afford it. I just had to order some in for...what's his name...it's on the tip of my tongue, you know." Fred held the broken piece to his forehead as if the information he sought might be transferred from the chunk of glass directly into his brain. "Begins with a G..."

Raoul felt like Mr. Stan Kalpi, spilled at the gates of his village on the morning after a long night's rain. He shifted his weight from one foot to the other and back, not daring to put any words into Fred's mouth, and stifled a smug grin.

"The Gentle contract! There you go! That's who I ordered this for."

"The Gentle contract?" Raoul said the words without hearing them, so deafening was the silence in his head (in utter bewilderment his flies had come to a sudden and dead halt).

"Yes. Gentle. Nat Gentle. Said he saw it over at Puymute's and had to have it. He's been doing some work on that cottage of his, you know. It's starting to shape up real nice."

If Fred Nettles said anything else after that, Raoul didn't notice. He was busy lining up his variables, fitting them into the bigger picture that was getting uglier and uglier. What was Nat doing at Puymute's? And why hadn't he mentioned his recent renovations when they talked at the Belly? Raoul had gone to Fred hoping to learn about some trouble at the plantation, hoping to incriminate Gustave, and instead he had implicated one of his very best friends.

Uglier, indeed.

But then life rarely reads as smoothly as your favorite book. That much, Raoul should have guessed. Though he longed to speak to Nat right then, to confront him with this latest variable and to exact from his friend what duty was due, it was late and there wasn't time. The airport's gritty floor again awaited and Raoul hurried off, wondering if he had bothered to tell Fred "thank you" for his time.

Raoul has to make his way to work, but *you* might be interested to know how Nat's piece of glass came to be lodged in the sand on Sinner's Cove in the first place. It was the fault of the shifty wind, the same shifty wind that Nat had on the brain last time he was at the Belly. It had kept him twisting and turning and wriggling on the beach the night before to shield his dinner of fishcakes and beer from its gusting sandy glaze, and in the process the rainbow chunk had fallen from his pocket.

Nat had just come from his cottage, where he had capped off a day of taxi-driving with a debate on the merits of frosted glass, Fred Nettles having in surplus something in a stylish and subtle green. But Nat wouldn't crack, and in the end Fred Nettles agreed that beveled glass better suited the front door's decoration. That Nat had a sample of Puymute's glass to show him was sheer and innocent serendipity, of the kind fitted so perfectly into the bigger picture you can't help but wonder how serendipitous it really is.

There had been no burglary at Puymute's, and no kerfuffle, only the careless swing of a machete by a hearty and inebriated gardener named Bud.

As luck would have it, when Bud smashed the glass door at the manor house, Nat was there, exacting his due from Gustave, who had paid him heftily for his night's work on the beach a few days earlier, and paid him now for his promise of more nights' work to come. Curious Nat. He had picked up a few of the pieces and, admiring their prismatic effects, decided to install the same glass in his own front door. He took one of the chunks with him, to show Fred Nettles what to order, and so with a rainbow in one pocket and rainbow bills in the other, Nat went home. When he and Fred had finished discussing Nat's new glass, Nat went out to get some dinner.

He ate his takeaway on the beach—with the wind—tilting his body to withstand its breezy affront, ignorant of the clue that the wind's tricky fingers had fished from his jeans. The islanders tolerated the wind's assault, as they did that of the tide and the noisy leaves (what choice did they have?), and though the gusts blew the salt from his food and the foam from his beer, Nat resigned himself, and settled in to enjoy the wind's company. It blew sand in his ears to drown out his conscience and cooled the heat of his remorse.

Like a storm forgotten in the face of a rainbow, Nat's guilt was drying up a bit more with every colored bill from Gustave that he stashed away. It dried up until all that remained was the slightest puddle, which Nat avoided by driving his cab.

Simple, that.

Things were not so simple for Raoul, who couldn't simply drive away his troubles. For one thing, like many of the islanders, Raoul didn't own a car. For another, neither did Mr. Stan Kalpi, whose journey to the past might have taken a different turn entirely had he set out in a noisy vehicle. He mightn't have heard the songs on the wind, and he certainly wouldn't have made the leaps and bounds that finally got him home. No, Raoul would have been loath to find escape behind the wheel.

Instead, he found escape at the airport. Not by plane, but by pineapple. While he worked at his typewriter, flanked and backed by wooden cratefuls of the spiny fruit, his hands completed triplicate forms and doled out sticky gifts in a manner so automatic it allowed for flights of fancy to Puymute's, to Sinner's Cove, to Nat's cottage, to the Belly, and back.

If Nat had been at the manor house to collect his piece of glass, Raoul reflected, he must have gone there to see Gustave. (Puymute himself spent all *his* time in the patch. Everyone on Oh knew that.) But why would Nat ever go to see Gustave? Creepy, that's what Nat called him. So why on earth pay him a call?

Raoul passed a pineapple to a man from Canada, who dropped it on the floor. Of course! Nat must have been dropping off a passenger when he saw Gustave's broken glass. He must have dawdled to chat with the girl from the foyer, the one who answered the phone and sat in her sandaled feet, and serendipity had put a rainbow in his pocket. A rainbow that he lost to Sinner's Cove. (Nat often went there to eat his dinner alone. Everyone on Oh knew that, too.) Perhaps the bigger picture wasn't so ugly after all, Raoul surmised as he sized up a Japanese businessman's passport. Aaah-huh-huh. And yet.

A muffled buzz hummed in Raoul's brain, a niggling suspicion. In his mind the bigger picture was a jigsaw puzzle that he did, un-did, re-did. There were pieces missing, but what they depicted Raoul couldn't know. Why didn't his theory of Nat's passenger and the sandal-footed girl, of serendipity and Sinner's Cove convince him? He was overlooking a variable, a point on the graph, but which one? Raoul checked his watch. He wanted to smoke, but the stream of incoming passengers continued to trickle. So he continued to check and to stamp, while his buzz continued to hum.

He thought about Nat's front door, about how spiffy the cottage would look with its new beveled glass. 'He's been doing some work on that cottage of his, you know,' Fred Nettles' words came back to him. 'It's starting to shape up real nice.' Why had Raoul learned this from Fred and not from Nat himself? Topics of conversation at the Belly weren't terribly numerous. Surely in between cricket and signature cocktails Nat might have mentioned his refurbishments. Maybe it was meant to be a surprise? Maybe he was planning to invite them all for a little lime once the place was tidied up. Yes, that must be the reason! There could be no other to account for Nat's secrecy.

But Raoul lacked conviction in this theory, too, and the suspicion in his brain niggled more and more. He saw exactly what was going on. He saw it very clearly. Nat had come into some money. Money for redecorating, money he kept a secret, money that must have something to do with Gustave. Raoul's mate was in cahoots with the local smuggler.

Wasn't he? Like the zigs and zags of the visitors arriving on Oh, Raoul's thoughts shilly-shallied. So Nat had some extra cash. Did that naturally denote a connection to Gustave? Of course not! So Nat had passed out expensive cigars at the Belly. Did that mean he was up to no good? Not necessarily! Still the buzz in some far niche of Raoul's head would not be silenced. He was missing something, it said. His geometry was skewed. Raoul checked his watch again, his urge for a cigarette growing, but the watch's old hands were reluctant to scale the Roman numerals the years had faded. Time seemed to stand still. Raoul sized up the slow-moving line before him, just a few stragglers more, and shook his head in resignation. Perhaps the shake jarred loose a cog or agitated whatever fly buzzed inside his skull, but suddenly Raoul understood. Suddenly he was back at the Belly and it was the night before, and his glass hovered in midair, suspended in time along with those of his very best friends. At the time he hadn't been able to put his finger on it, but now, now Raoul identified the wrench in the clock's works, the sand in the gears of his friends' solidarity. The reason time had seemed to stand still.

Guilt.

Gentle, cautious Nat was in cahoots with the local smuggler, and the others must know something about it, too. What a fool Raoul had been!

His buzz was strong and decisive now. Not that of a fruit fly or a housefly or even a blowfly, but that of a taunted and hairy bee. Raoul had to sting or get stung, it told him. So like Jack on a farina-filled stomach pedaling straight to the Post, Raoul hurried the stragglers and stamped their forms and rushed off to place an ad for a smuggler.

Now as Raoul makes his way to the grimy-windowed offices of the *Morning Crier*, ostensibly to further his investigation into where

I came from, let me tell you what *I* discovered about my birth, a happy (for some) and moon-blessed event, in counterpoint to Raoul's sad discovery that his loved ones have fallen short.

It was a shiny night when I came into the world. The gibbous moon waxed high in the still, dark sky and beckoned my mother, who went to stroll in its light at Sinner's Cove, her own Edda's beach. It was there, while walking with her naked arms bent at her sides and her gauzy, transparent skirt entangled in her ankles and thighs, that she felt the first assault inside her swollen belly. Like the salty strike of the waves upon the shore, a watery tongue prodded her rent middle until she yielded and folded, compliant and pliable host to the tide that splashed and stormed her body's threshold. She cried out and fell, into the very sand where on her wedding night, to the accompaniment of the singing leaves, Wilbur had first discovered what lay past her hem.

As luck would have it, when Edda collapsed to the ground with a cry, Abigail was there, exacting her due from the moon, whose affairs the midwife often minded, now covering things up nice and even, now balancing both sides of some account. Clever Abby. The island's nighttime magic, in her had found its match.

Though Abigail hadn't expected to find Edda at Sinner's Cove that night, having altogether other business to attend to there, find her she did, and just how fortunate a finding it was, probably only I can appreciate. Abigail had known since early on in Edda's pregnancy that this delivery would be more delicate than most. She feared for Edda's health and for the happiness of her blood-sister's little girl. But not even Abigail had dreamed of the lengths she would need to go to to save Edda's life.

Had Abigail not intervened, Edda would most certainly have lost her baby. I would have succumbed to the sand as my grandmother succumbed to the snow. My mother would never have survived the sadness of another loss; she knew nothing of the nature of lost people and things, of how they sometimes struggled to misplace themselves, or struggled once they were found. She knew nothing of Mr. Stan Kalpi, of how a man (or woman) can find the way home if he (or she) really wants. My grandmother taught me that to be lost is not always a bad state, and I figured out for myself that to be found is sometimes unsettling. There really are some prisms better left buried in the sand.

Where was I? This part of the story always gets me out of focus. It splits the light of my attention into so many rainbows on the beach. Suffice it to say that I did not perish in the sand that night. I could not count myself among the lost. Abigail harvested what the moon had sown and, happy, the moon took its leave. In the morning my cry marked the end of Edda's travail, her joyful tears christening the dawn of my journey. Together we rested, then with Abigail's help we found our way home.

I know. You're thinking I left out the best part. The guts and the gore, the blood and the marrow. I'll come back to them, I promise. But my story belongs to Raoul a little longer, and if he thinks newspaper ads stir confessions and one crime solves another, then who am I to question?

"Bruce! Bruce, where are you?" Raoul burst through the door, his enthusiasm propelling him right into the desk of the *Morning Crier*'s editor-in-chief, copyeditor, reporter and special correspondent.

"Raoul! Hello! What a nice surprise!" (Bruce always officially classified unannounced visits this way.)

"You remember that ad I placed a couple weeks ago?" (Both men knew that he did.)

"I remember," Bruce replied.

"I need to run it again. With a few changes. Here you go." Raoul stretched his arm past Bruce's bulky typewriter, and handed him a piece of paper.

"Uh, what's that? Run it again?" Bruce recalled the visit Abigail had paid him a few days earlier. He wasn't scared of a lady, not exactly, but it was always best to stay on the good side of a woman of Abigail's repute. Although he had defended his journalistic integrity against her accusations once, he shuddered to think what she might do to his integrity should he see fit to run the ad a second time. "It's only been two weeks," he stalled. "You can't expect to get a call so quick, Raoul. These things take time. Maybe a month. Or more!"

Not normally prone to violent outbursts, or indeed to outbursts of any kind, Raoul listened startled as his voice reprimanded Bruce with a vehemence in complete disproportion to the crime. While Raoul ranted, Bruce recalled again the visit from Abigail, weighing the wrath of the one versus that of the other and deciding ultimately that his health would be better served by obeying Raoul's request. When Raoul finally stopped his shouting, Bruce accepted the piece of paper, along with payment of a rainbow bill, and thanked Raoul for his custom. Raoul thanked Bruce in turn, and left the *Morning Crier* for the still dark of evening.

To clear his head of the flies and bees that populated it, Raoul took a walk, feeling a proper fool for his explosion in front of poor Bruce. It was fine and dandy, nay, helpful, for the islanders to think him mad, but it was another thing entirely for them to think him a thug.

Raoul was unduly hard on himself. The weeks since my arrival had been tough. He had juggled the demands of a public smuggling case and those of private turmoil. And he was troubled to find them more intrinsically linked than he thought, the common denominators none other than Bang, Cougar, and Nat. On top of that, Raoul had gotten himself black-listed at the one haven Oh ever offered him, the Pritchard T. Lullo Public Library.

What right-minded, dark-eyed, bespectacled Customs and Excise Officer of the plain-as-noses-on-faces philosophical school, when faced with a red-eyed, cheek-stained, white-skinned grandchild; a red-eyed, cheek-stained, white-skinned smuggler; pineapple-poaching pals who betray him; a blind and desperate daughter; an indifferent and starry-eyed son-in-law; a midwife who won't go away; a barefooted mathematician-musician mentor; and a ban from the public library, *wouldn't* be moved to threaten the editor-in-chief, copyeditor, reporter and special correspondent of the local paper who had qualms about placing an ad? A blow-up was long overdue.

Raoul's walk didn't take him along Edda's beach, or indeed along any beach, where the geometry was too stark and the secrets that lay buried in the sand too shocking. Instead Raoul walked through town, his legs carrying him, as if by instinct, past the public library just as Ms. Lila was locking up. She pulled the heavy doors shut with a thunk and turned to the road in a hurry, late for her appointment with the hairdresser. When she saw Raoul she gave a start. "Oh! Good evening," she said.

"Good evening," replied Raoul, who had been tempted to turn away and avoid her gaze. It wasn't that Raoul didn't want to see Ms. Lila. He very much did. But recalling his fit of madness—real madness—on the Tuesday before, and her subsequent fit of pique, he felt a proper fool for the second time that day, and simply couldn't bear for her to see him. He had been wrong to think there was something better out there than the librarian's usual offerings.

You can imagine how great his relief when she addressed him: "Raoul, I'm in a bit of a rush, I'm afraid. If you'd like to keep me company a piece, I'm just walking to the next gap ahead."

They were a perfect match that night, Raoul and Ms. Lila, as Ms. Lila was feeling a bit of a fool herself. No one had ever shown more respect for her material than Raoul, and if something had moved him to tear up her sheets, she might have tried to find out what it was instead of just kicking him out. The shade of the cookery shelf was dark and drab without him, and she waxed nostalgic for Tuesdays past.

Raoul tried to speak, but the apology in his head wasn't quite sure how to displace itself. Thankfully, Ms. Lila was a clever chickadee, who sensed his embarrassment and remorse even as she struggled to communicate her own. Perhaps if his words and hers were insufficient, those of loftier minds might do. From her bag she removed the book of poetry that he had refused when she offered it on Tuesday, the book with the poems about the beach and with the very nice cover. Raoul accepted it with a grateful nod, one that Ms. Lila returned.

At the gap they parted. Ms. Lila climbed the Staircase to Beauty and Raoul continued his walk, his thoughts momentarily distracted from his earlier outburst and from poor Bruce. Raoul's right hand clutched Ms. Lila's gift, his fingertips gently rubbing the cloth of the book's spine, his head gently mulling the book's endless and various implications, some heavy and sleepy, some sticky and sweet. It was a promise, the book was. Mysterious, exciting, unexpected; a Customs notice, and he, the lucky addressee whose prize awaited.

17

Gustave Vilder possessed a strong work ethic that was not, as you might suspect, at cross-purposes with his moral slackness. If his deeds and objectives were questionable, the zeal with which he went about achieving them was not. Did it matter if he orchestrated Agustín Boe's snakebite or pumped a few pickers full of beer before Puymute hired him? He got the job he wanted, and had done it well for a very long time. But Gustave was tired of managing another man's money, tired of keeping the plantation "up and running" and answering to its ostrich of an owner. Ten years of that was quite enough. Instead, Gustave wanted to make some money of his own, and to do so he would draw on every resource at hand.

A firm believer that one man's mealybug is another man's meal ticket, he first hatched his plan to get rich when he heard of the blight on Killig. Oh had plenty of pineapples to funnel to its island neighbor, and who better to finagle the funneling than Gustave himself, what with the many and varied forces at his command? He could arrange in a few weeks what it would take months to arrange via diplomatic channels, and for a bigger bite of the profits. He had tried to explain as much to Raoul, but Officer Orlean wouldn't be bought off and he wouldn't be bartered with. He had no head for business or economics, that one. No appreciation for the fact that Gustave was single-handedly expediting the resolution of a potential produce crisis of potentially global proportions.

Of course, Raoul would prove no obstacle to Gustave's determination. If Gustave couldn't boldly sail past Customs with his paperwork seemingly in order and his pineapples all aboard, then he would spirit away the fruit by dark of night. What other choice did he have? It was hardly his fault if he was forced to dabble in magic. So dabble he did, and a few days later, right on schedule, two of Puymute's acres were infamously picked clean.

Before Gustave could see to the clearing of two acres more, his pineapple plan had required a bit of fine-tuning. For one thing, Raoul had been snooping around, poking his nose the way up and down Dante's Mountain. For another, half the island (or more) was certain that Gustave had fathered Edda's baby. Though Gustave wasn't nearly as certain of this himself (and was, frankly, miffed by the distraction just then when he had business to conduct), he feared (and rightly so) that Raoul would pursue his Customs investigation with unusual rigor, to exact revenge for the presumably-ravaged Edda.

To escape the clutches of Customs and Excise, Gustave might have suspended his Killig business straightaway, after just the one transaction—at least for a little while. But the variables (and those marbles!) he pulled from his desk on that day Raoul paid him a visit, they had advised him otherwise. Like Stan Kalpi with his toe in the mud, Gustave saw the solution's next logical step. Not to back down, but to flummox the islanders with magic so dazzling they would be frightened even to meet his gaze. He would spirit away Puymute's whole plantation if necessary, manor house and all, and would do it with the help of Bang, Cougar, and Nat.

Thus in the light of the complicit moon, Gustave got the next two acres carried off, a second coup that left the policemen and the excisemen shaking their heads in wonder. You know all this already, I realize, but it's just the start. Gustave's story and Raoul's are still intertwined. Gustave is trying to flummox and dazzle and Raoul is stalking and waiting, hoping his adversary will stumble. Not that you should expect this to happen, for Gustave was feeling very sure-footed after two successful heists and with three marbles for collateral in his pocket. So sure-footed, in fact, that plans for his biggest sting yet were under way.

It would take him almost two weeks more to pull his resources and coordinate his forces with those of the moon, which would be just full enough by then to provide the light his nighttime operation would require. Gustave would double the take this go-round, haul out four acres at once, which meant securing twice the pickers, packers, and transporters to get the goods from plantation to beach. There Bang, Cougar, and Nat would again lend a hand carrying the crates to the boats, their presence only insurance should Raoul get wind of the scheme. For brute strength and stealthy speed, Gustave would engage other, more expert, hands. Instead of sending the fruit to Killig in the swift but small wooden crafts that glided as easily as the tide, Gustave would get three properly-sized boats, big enough for all of his cargo. The smaller crafts would shuttle the crates to the bigger ones, whose bulky bodies would be camouflaged by their distance from the shore.

Gustave made notes and diagrams, drew maps and added up figures, designed every detail with the accuracy of an engineer. Had he and Raoul ever shared a common aim, or labored toward a common end, the combination of their accidental science and their incidental philosophies might have shamed even the likes of

Mr. Stan Kalpi. I like to think that, had things ended differently, they might have joined forces one day, for my sake if for nothing else. That they were ever at odds with each other still strikes me as the most terrific of ironies. Raoul had no reason to blame Gustave for who I was. There had been no ravaging and no magic spell. Only the careless sleight of hand of a hearty midwife, inebriated by the moon.

Abigail stumbled through the soft, green brush a stone's throw from the edge of the sea, her arm pulled taut by that of the seedy port girl who held onto her, leading the way. "Hurry, Abby! We're almost there. She's under the mango."

Although the islanders who spoke of the seedy port girls made no distinction between them, Abigail, no doubt owing to her own pregnant past, treated them with respect and decency, extending the further courtesy of knowing each of the girls by name. The one who tugged her arm was named Lilly. The one that lay writhing under the mango tree, Claudine.

Abby (that's what the seedy port girls called her) knelt at Claudine's side and touched her brow. It was wet with sweat, but little cause for concern. The night was hot, and Claudine in the throes of labor.

"How long have you been here?" Abby asked. She addressed her question to Lilly but studied Claudine's face, measuring the girl's pulse while awaiting an answer.

"Her water just broke. We were here walking. When I realized, I just laid her down and ran to get you. Is she alright?" Lilly was crying. She had never seen a woman giving birth, and she was scared.

"She's fine," Abby lied. "You did good." Claudine still had perhaps hours to go, but Abby's intuition already told her something wasn't right. It would be a delicate birth, but nothing she couldn't manage.

"It hurts, Abby." Claudine's voice was a whimper. Abby soothed the girl with warm words and tucked soft leaves under her head and under her knees. She told Claudine to relax and to breathe slowly, to fix her gaze on a single star, or better yet on the moon. The swollen moon that waxed high in the still, dark sky and beckoned.

Lilly stretched herself out beside her friend, holding Claudine's hand and whispering into her ear. Telling her she would be fine, believing she must surely be about to die. Abby said it was too early for Claudine to push, and so Lilly tried to focus Claudine's thoughts on other things.

"Look at the stars," Lilly said. "Do you know about the constellations?"

Abby nodded at Lilly's efforts. Good, Abby's nod said. But before Claudine could tell them that when she was a girl she could pick out every constellation in the sky, before she could say that she'd learned them from a book her best friend gave her for her birthday, a terrible cry split the air, drowning out the song of the leaves that had gained volume and force in the few minutes since Abby had arrived at Claudine's side. Abby recognized the cry, though she couldn't fathom its meaning or explain its presence there just then: it was Edda's.

"Stay here with her," she commanded Lilly, who gazed in horror as Abby's silhouette rose and retreated into the night.

In the sand not too far away Abigail found Edda collapsed and gripping her belly. Her water had broken, too. Abigail mumbled a curse to the moon and set about comforting her charge.

"Abigail...." Edda tried to speak, but couldn't. Abigail cooed reassurances into Edda's ear and stroked her hair, stretched out the girl's body and laid her hands on Edda's swollen middle.

Both the beach and the brush had fallen into darkness by this time, though the evening's curtain was thinned by the moon. It had risen up fully now, exerting its pull and release on the waves that crashed loudly and rolled to shore. Abigail raised Edda's skirt. Edda gasped for air and Abigail saw the blood that poured from Edda's body, seeped through the cotton of her panties. Abigail's thoughts flew far off, to Emma Patrice, to her blood-sister who had gotten away and left Abigail home to take care of things.

Their struggle began.

Edda's hair mingled with the damp sand, Claudine's with the dry twigs of the brush. One called out. One pushed. Blood spilled onto the sand and onto the brush beneath the mango. Abby, as if a spirit possessed, divided herself, attending to four lives at once.

The mischievous moon smiled down on them all and sent the sea into a violent, enchanted rush, guiding the female contractions that mimicked the waves. Spurred by the sea's urgency and assisted by the wind, the leaves sang even louder suddenly, in harmony with the cicadas and the hummingbirds who didn't know if it was night or day. While Lilly watched Claudine and cried, the song crescendoed to a frantic, fevered buzz; it fell on top of the women, like a thick blanket that might smother them.

They could hear nothing for the noise that filled their ears, the living sound that seemed to populate the air around them. They tried to ignore it, to escape it by closing their eyes. Claudine concentrated on the body inside her. Edda rocked her body in time with the island's tremble.

Claudine was the first to find escape from the noise that drowned her baby's cry, her eyes opening again only long enough to steal a glimpse of her little girl. Abby laid the baby at Claudine's side and tried to rouse her, but in vain. When Lilly realized her friend was dead, she fainted and left Abby alone in the wild darkness, cursing the devilish moon, who had hidden behind a cloud.

The magic moon laughed at the women's struggle. The leaves were too agitated, the wind so strong it ripped them from the very trees that bore them. Then the fracas suddenly culminated in a guttural human cry that would confirm a superhuman deed.

Edda!

Abigail left Claudine's child in the arms of its dead mother and ran the length of the beach to where she had left Edda a moment before. She threw herself into the sand, feeling in the dark for Edda's body. Edda was unconscious, but breathing. The baby between her legs was not. Edda's little boy was dead.

Abigail jerked the child to her chest, trying to coax it to life, but its limbs refused to stir and its voice refused to sing. She had already let two lives get away, but she wouldn't let a third be destroyed. Edda wanted a baby. Edda needed a baby. And a baby she would have, the baby left at the mango tree. Abigail moved with new resolve and cleaned Edda's body and that of her dead son as best she could. She ran to the brush with the dead child in her arms and prayed to the darkness that Lilly hadn't awakened from her swoon.

The darkness complied, and when Abigail reached the mango tree, Lilly was still unconscious. Abigail laid Edda's baby under the already cool flesh of Claudine's arm and picked up Claudine's wriggling orphan (the babies of seedy port girls almost never had fathers, that much Abby knew).

Back and forth, Abigail moved again between the brush and the beach, her eyes adjusting to the night just enough to get her through her task. She revived Edda and placed the newborn in her arms, then she let them both doze again in the sand. She revived Lilly and told her that both Claudine and her baby were dead. She handed her the corpse that had come from Edda's belly and sent her off to make arrangements. She cleaned and composed Claudine's body, lowered Claudine's skirt over her like a blanket, closed the sprawled legs, adjusted the feet in their complicated strappy sandals. She stroked Claudine's forehead and told her goodbye, then returned to where Edda lay sleeping on the beach, with me, Almondine, in her arms.

The mighty moon was pleased. On Wilbur's wedding night, her finger had poked a hole in the soil of an earthly womb and dropped a seed into it; tonight she had reaped an almond from a mango. Contented, the moon finally took her leave. It was morning, and time for Abigail to take us home.

Once she had eased my mother and me into bed, Abigail's plan required a bit of fine-tuning. For one thing, one very important thing, the morning light had revealed that I was not one of those seedy port babies without a father. My parentage was clear. When Abigail realized the truth, it was too late. Edda had already bonded with the child she believed to be her own as she lay sleeping on the beach, my tiny self warm on her chest. Abigail had been forced to let her bring me home. That Edda seemed not to notice anything amiss only made matters worse; Abigail would never, ever, pry me from my mother's arms now.

While my mother and I slept that first day of my lucky—if black-and-white—life, Wilbur and Abigail conspired. Abigail told him everything: where I came from, how Edda's baby and

Claudine had both died on the beach, what Abigail had done. Even someone of her caliber needed help once in a while, and Wilbur proved a ready ally. He had seen Edda and me together for only a few moments before we fell asleep, but in those moments he had seen his wife happier than he had ever known her. He couldn't bear to take me away from her. And I *needed* a mother, didn't I? If Edda could live with my white skin, my reddish eyes, and the half-hearted mole on my cheek, then who was Wilbur to question?

"If Edda's happy, then so am I," he said.

Together, Wilbur and Abigail reconstructed the circumstances of my birth to be reported to the rest of the islanders. To allay any suspicion of Edda's presence on the beach that night, they would say that she had given birth at home, and that she had had a very easy and normal delivery. To cinch the charade Abigail would burn behind the house the sheets that Edda's labor had supposedly soiled. When Edda awoke the next morning, they planned to tell her she had dreamed her walk to the beach and her delivery there, but in the end there was no need. Edda had no recollection whatsoever of the night and the evening before.

Her unwitting cooperation and Wilbur's espousal of Abigail's scheme began to erase the doubts Abigail had experienced in the daylight that first shined on my almondine skin. Any doubts that remained could be explained away by generic island magic, which was abundant on Oh. Abigail's plan was working. Only she and Wilbur knew the truth, and both loved Edda enough to take it with them to the grave.

You're thinking that Gustave must have known the truth as well, known that he fathered a child with poor dead Claudine. But he didn't. When Gustave discussed mealybugs with Raoul over Puymute's finest wine and swore he knew nothing about me, he was telling the truth. He knew almost nothing of Claudine either; she was merely one of the girls from the seedy port bar among whom he made no distinction, their prices being equal. Even less did he know of her pregnancy, for the seedy port girls hid such matters ably.

So you know now where I came from, but that's not all there is. What matters is that *Raoul* find out the truth, that he reconcile it with his Stan Kalpi notions of identity and the bigger picture we all fit into, like the misshapen bits that latch onto each other to form the whole of a jigsaw puzzle. To do so, he must still corner Gustave, or so he believes, because on Oh, like farina leads to packages and adverts to smugglers, just maybe the threat of arrest betrays paternity.

If you feel sorry for Gustave, who when cornered won't know to confess his inadvertent crime, don't. Not yet. Though I'd be the first to forgive him his indiscretion that night under the mango, he *is* still a thief who bribes a man's best friends, and worse, if you believe the tales the islanders tell. Before he can evoke pity, Gustave has a long legacy for which he will have to atone.

In the bedroom of his small, simple villa with indoor plumbing and wispy fabrics, Gustave sat at his desk near the window. By moonlight he scratched pencil notes on lined paper, elaborating his smuggling plan. To make certain that he had omitted no detail, he constructed a rudimentary model with boats of folded newspaper, olive-bodied men with toothpick legs, and peanuts for pineapples. The paper boats and peanuts were for measuring whether Gustave's big boats would be big enough to accommodate the crop that must cover four acres. The olive-bodied men, because Gustave was hungry.

As he mulled over his plan, he stood and paced the length of his room, piercing fat purple olives with a toothpick and pulling them out of the jar he carried in his hand, brine dripping onto his fingers and onto his shirt. He stopped at the desk to scoop a fistful of peanuts from one of the boats' hulls and noticed, square on the side of the newsprint craft, Raoul's second ad about Edda. Gustave read it and shook his head. He had already seen it of course, but in the heat of figuring the footage and tonnage of what he was about to steal, he had almost forgotten the other dilemma that occupied his mind. Since the day he spotted my blond locks in the market square, locks so like his own, he had thought a lot about me. Part of him was as sorry as Raoul that the ads had elicited no answers.

When I said before that Gustave was miffed by the distraction of Edda and her baby, that wasn't exactly right. He was more than miffed. He was flummoxed and dazzled by his very own magic. More and more he believed me to be his own. My eyes were the eyes that met his every morning when he looked at himself in the mirror. Mine, the blotch on his face that he rubbed like a talisman, and mine, the skin of his brow that was unlike that of the other islanders. He had only seen me once, for a few moments that day at the market, but in those moments he felt a magic greater than any he had ever known. How he had made me, he had no idea. But he knew that somehow he had. And if I was his, he wanted me back.

But Gustave was mixing his flies. He had started the evening preparing one crime and now he found himself contemplating another. The mathematical Mr. Stan Kalpi would never have approved of this. One polynomial at a time is all that you should ever ponder. Your process must be logical and your calculations orderly, if you're to harbor any hope of defining your undefined variables. Would Mr. Stan Kalpi have re-claimed his family had he galumphed sentimentally from plantation to shore and rushed cock-a-hoop into the scrapping tide?

Why, most certainly not.

18

Raoul, too, possessed a work ethic nothing to sniff at. The devotion with which he applied, and applied himself to, the principles of Kalpi maths was but one example of it. Indeed, since that morning when the sun revealed the triangle that was Sinner's Cove and the treasure that lay hidden in its sands, the enthusiasm with which he treated, and treated himself to, the pursuit of Gustave—and his cohorts—was but another.

Mind you, Raoul had no desire to see his friends behind bars. Rather his efforts were spurred by hopes that in cracking the case he would disprove his own suspicions, for surely his friends weren't really stabbing him in the back. Surely there was a logical explanation for their apparent and utter disloyalty. In his philosophy Raoul stood firm: there wasn't a mystery anywhere on the island that couldn't be explained, no truth that, like the raw cashew, couldn't be freed of its shell, roasted, and rendered agreeable.

Three weeks had passed since Raoul's fingers plucked the sandy prism from Sinner's Cove, three weeks since he had spoken with Fred and placed the second ad to induce the regret and confession of his three best friends (not one of whom had been induced to either, but I'll get to that in a minute). Three weeks, now, too, since Gustave had hatched his pineapple plan, pleated his newsprint boats, and bloated them full of peanuts. Both men had spent the interim days in furious activity, Raoul investigating and Gustave orchestrating, while the rest of the islanders thought and spoke of little but marimbas. The revival of the annual marimba competition, and Cougar's generosity in hosting the affair at the Sincero, had in fact so captivated the attention of Oh that, as if in jealousy and neglect, the island rebelled, pelting the inhabitants with a persistent and unseasonable rain.

An inconvenience, yes, but not enough to dampen the merry spirits awake and awaiting a dead nice party. The islanders made friendly bets on whose marimba-playing would win, drank bottlefuls of beer and rum in the days' run-up to the show, and generally ignored the island's tantrum. If one of the islanders grew impatient and complained about the showers, another was quick to note how very lush they were making the hills. When Cougar griped about the outdoor tables the rain would make obsolete, Bang pointed out the merits of a Belly tight with ladies in festive skirts. It didn't happen often, but now and again the islanders made their own fate, relegated Oh to the rank of scenery. There was magic in the air, and marimba songs on the wind, for which a bit of thunder in the dark was no match.

Like the triangles that grace Sinner's Cove, the scenery of the story as it nears its end is delineated by three vertices, the Belly, Puymute's Plantation, and Edda's beach, defined and familiar variables in the polynomial of Raoul. So as not to mix my own flies, I'll report on them singly, at least for as long as their stories will be kept apart.

To the Belly, then, where, contrary to Raoul's hopes, newspaper ads do not evoke pity and penitence. Or not *enough* of the former to inspire the latter. Raoul's mates were certainly sorry, sorry that their friend was still making a fool of himself and sorry that Edda's circumstances were what they were. Their involvement with Gustave was another matter entirely. It had started innocently enough, and if Raoul's mates' plan to get information from Gustave had failed (though none had ever posed even one question to him about my mother), the mates saw no reason to give up their extra cash. Even Cougar, who didn't really need it, had fallen irretrievably under the spell of all those rainbows, with which he planned to purchase embellishments for the Sincero that justified higher nightly rates.

Whether, as in the case of Bang and Nat, doing business with Gustave was blamed on fear (and maybe a little greed), or, as in Cougar's case, on a silly and convenient delusion (Cougar had to go along, remember, so his island influence could protect them should they ever get caught), the important thing was that no one was smuggling for the sake of smuggling, conspiring with Raoul's declared enemy just for the thrill. That would have been too striking an affront to their friendship.

The night before the marimba competition found Bang, Cougar, and Nat gathered at the Belly's bar, where, after closing, Cougar was perfecting his signature cocktail.

"Try this one. Think I've finally got it now."

Bang took the glass Cougar extended. He held its cloudy golden contents up to the light and twirled the glass for effect. Then he raised the drink in quick salute to Nat and downed the icy mix.

"Bloody hell!" Bang slammed his fist onto the bar. "A bit strong, don't you think? What do you call it?"

"Pineapple Slam," Cougar replied.

"You feed the audience drinks this strong, they'll be under the tables before it's even my turn to play!"

Cougar passed a taste to Nat. "What do you think? Bang's used to water."

Nat tried the drink and scrunched up his face as he swallowed. "Bang's right, man. Too strong."

"Okay, less rum, more fruit, and we downgrade it to Pineapple Sting." Cougar set about mixing one last prototype.

"You guys hear from Gustave?" Nat's voice hung in the hollow of the Belly. The bar was closed and empty, but even so, to speak of Gustave so openly and so close to home left all three as if sprinkled with a soft and eerie dust.

Bang coughed the discomfort from his throat. He looked at Cougar and then at Nat and said, "No, not a word. Wonder what's going on. There was supposed to be another load going out this week."

Cougar shook his cocktail and shrugged. "Probably the rain. Bet he decided to wait until it dries up a bit."

Nat shrugged a silent reply and paged through the *Morning Crier* looking for something. When he finished, he sighed.

"What?" Bang asked.

"Nothing. Just making sure Raoul didn't go placing any more ads. He's out of his head, you know."

"He's fine," Cougar insisted. "Just a little desperate, that's all. This baby business has him so mad he can't see straight. He just won't admit it. So he's playing dumb, placing his ads, hoping some fool will feel sorry for him and spill the beans. He should know better than to think anyone on this island would rat out Gustave. If Raoul would just keep quiet about it, it would all go away. All you need on Oh is a little time."

"I guess," Nat said. "I just feel bad seeing him act a fool. And the three of us making a fool out of him too, as if he weren't doing a fine enough job of it on his own."

"How do you figure we're making a fool of him?" Bang's inquiry was genuine.

"How?! Are you as mad as Raoul is? By smuggling pineapples with Gustave, that's how!"

Cougar intervened. "No one's making a fool of Raoul but Raoul. Babies are one thing, pineapples are another. This has nothing to do with him. It's not his acreage we're carting away, is it?" Cougar put three mugs on the bar. "Here. Make sure this is okay, so I can mix up a few batches before the competition tomorrow night."

Bang picked up one of the mugs. "Cheers."

"Cheers," answered a reluctant Nat and a relaxed Cougar. Then the three men sat in silence, sipping their still-bitter Pineapple Sting.

At Puymute's Plantation things were not going smoothly at all. The rain had turned what should have been a two-week job into a three-week job, seriously testing even Gustave Vilder's proven organizational skills. He had put off some of his orchestrating, in hopes the rain might stop before he should strike his next pineapple blow, but as the marimba competition and Gustave's rescheduled coup grew nearer, the rain merely thickened. As it appeared it might never stop, the strike could be postponed no further.

Gustave had garnered the boats to flit away his booty to Killig, boats that had now spent two days waiting and bobbing just beyond Oh's coast. Their crews were bored and restless and threatening to abandon ship, so to speak. Gustave had to hand over some cargo soon or he'd owe more to the crews in payment than what the heist was due to earn in profits. He would have to move his fruit the very next night.

Although Gustave had already laid the groundwork for much of what would be needed that next night, firming up arrangements on a day's notice was no mean task. The plantation was soggy and Gustave felt himself slip at every turn, both muddily and metaphorically. A muffled buzz hummed in Gustave's brain, a niggling suspicion he couldn't put his finger on. All systems were go, all his personnel poised, but rather more like sticks in mud than militiamen primed to the attack. There was magic in the air, and impatience on the wind, for which, Gustave feared, his plans in the dark were little match. Which is why the night before the marimba competition found him tentative, preoccupied, and prickly as a soursop.

Raoul was prickly too. Three weeks gone by and his ad had yet to bear the fruit he'd hoped, that of his friends' confession. He had mixed up his own pineapple sting, and Bang, Cougar, and Nat were three ingredients too many. Gustave's bobbing boats had not gone unnoticed by the Customs Office, and the bigger picture, elucidated by the loquacious and simple-minded Pedro, suggested to Raoul that victory was nigh. But his thrill at the prospect of cornering Gustave, of bartering Gustave's freedom for information about *me*, was soured by the thought of his friends. How could he protect them from the law if they wouldn't come clean?

To minimize the risk that his friends might be arrested, and convinced, still, that some explanation for their conspiracy would ultimately surface, Raoul conducted his operation subtly and secretively, calling on a bare minimum of back-up and informing the called-on officers of as little detail as possible. Thanks to Pedro (who had no idea of the amount of information he'd been tricked into revealing), Raoul confirmed his hunch that the suspicious crafts loitering beyond Oh's coastline belonged to Gustave, at least for the duration of the crime. Raoul learned, too, that the boats were awaiting cargo to carry off to Killig. Raoul didn't know the timing of the transaction, but even Gustave could only keep his boats afloat and idle for so many days. The strike couldn't be postponed much further now.

So like ripples in one of the many puddles that dotted the sodden island, the crescent shore at Edda's beach was encircled by the crescent of Gustave's waiting boats, which were encircled in turn by the crescent of Customs and Excise, a semi-circle of small, manned crafts far enough way that they shouldn't be seen, close enough that, on Raoul's signal, they should easily block the path of escape. Raoul had only to wait. Soon, Gustave would be his. Soon, his, the answer to the riddle of Almondine. All that Raoul needed was a little time.

As if by magic, shortly after the mention of his name in the quiet, empty Belly on that night of the Pineapple Stings, Gustave appeared there in person. Although Bang, Cougar, and Nat were now more used to, if not more comfortable with, his nearness, they tended to tread lightly when Gustave was close by. Which is why they greeted him in complete silence and with blank faces, their mixed feelings of fear, expectation, and discomfort too complicated to express in words, or in any single conjunction of the muscles and wrinkles of jaws, lips, and eyes.

"I know this is short notice, but we're moving tomorrow."

"Tomorrow?! No way!" Bang slid off his bar stool in one fluid motion and thudded onto the floor. Not even fear of Gustave could keep him from his marimba. "Tomorrow's the competition. I'm a shoo-in to win, and even if I wasn't, I can't miss it! What would people think?"

"He's right, Gustave. I'm the one hosting the contest tomorrow. I can't leave the bar," Cougar added.

Nat watched them all and said nothing.

Gustave wanted to protest, to throw his weight and scare all three of them into compliance, but he realized they were absolutely right. It would be suspicious indeed if Cougar left his bar on the biggest night of the year and if Bang, of all people, were not to compete for the marimba prize. Better to keep things business-as-usual.

Gustave could scare Nat into coming along, but would Nat alone be enough collateral if Raoul and his colleagues should catch them? He wasn't rich like Cougar or flashy like Bang. Then again, there was no reason to think Raoul might know anything of the next night's plans, so the muffled buzz humming in Gustave's brain told him better-than-nothing Nat would do. Gustave put a hand on Nat's shoulder, high up, at the base of the neck, and pressed the flesh with his thumb. "What do you say, Nat? Just you and me then?"

The next night finally came, its arrival marked not only by strains of melodious marimba, but by thunderclash and rainsong as well. The jealous island still raged, its noisy fit a culmination of the previous weeks' pouting and pouring, of Gustave's offensive maneuvers on Puymute's Plantation, and Raoul's defensive ones at Sinner's Cove. The gibbous moon waned high in the cloudy sky, though hidden as it was by the storm's watery curtain, you'd never have known so. Likewise, the voice of the leaves, if they sang on that night, was trapped and smothered in the curtain's heavy folds. On the waters beyond the island, boats bounced, empty ones hungry for pineapples and Excise ones starved for revenge.

Inside the Belly, the air was dry and fresh, the storm's inadvertent breeze purifying the space as it made its way through one entrance and exited from the next. The mood, too, was light and winsome, untroubled by the outburst of the wet, dark sky. Every table was full and at the edges of the locale the islanders leaned in little groups along the walls, chatting and smoking and downing batches of Cougar's signature cocktail. On stage a marimba glistened under blue and yellow lights, awaiting the touches of the first marimbist's hammers. Ten finalists were slotted to perform, starting at ten o'clock (which on Oh means 11:30, if you're lucky).

At the Plantation, the atmosphere hung somewhere between anxious and enervated. The patches were drenched, as were the men collected to clear them and carry them off. Despite the urgency of the task at hand, the weather dampened the spirits gathered at Puymute's, and a sluggishness reigned. It helped matters little that Gustave was hardly himself, slipping in and out of the stalks as if in a trance, mumbling barely audible orders and directions that were, consequently, barely obeyed. If a crew is as good as its captain, you'd have wagered this one gone down with the ship before night's end.

As thoughts of his Almondine multiplied in Raoul's head, where the flies were looking forward soon to a good long rest, in Gustave's head, too, I figured prominently. No longer just the silly baby of a silly pregnant girl he barely knew, I had become for Gustave the only family he had left. He thought of me day and night now, to the detriment of his smuggling plot, which was shaping up sloppily at best. Why I should disturb his thoughts so much just now, he couldn't say, but disturb them I did. Perhaps it was the lonely moon stirring trouble from behind the rain's curtain, or perhaps Edda was to blame, for parading her brand new baby all over the island. Gustave had seen us both a number of times by now, and each made him more convinced that I was his.

Then there was the ad. Gustave couldn't stop thinking of that, either. He hoped as badly as Raoul that someone would come forward and explain what was going on. Maybe he would go to Raoul himself when the night was over, confess to a crime he knew nothing about, and take his little girl home, stop all this mixing of mangoes and almonds.

While Gustave waxed sentimental under the rain and the hidden moon, trudging through the tall plants and muddling through his operation, Raoul hid behind the mango tree at Edda's beach, hoping this would be the night when from the soft, green brush a stone's throw from the edge of the sea the truth would finally emerge. Both men were glad for the marimba competition, for it would keep the attention of the island diverted and its music would drown the noise of their misdeeds. Bang and Cougar were glad for the marimba competition, too, neither much fancying a night's work in the pouring rain, no matter the number of rainbows to be pocketed at daybreak.

Poor Nat. He wasn't glad at all about the way things were shaping up. Not only would he miss Bang's marimba performance (and his likely victory) and the most festive night of the year, but he would spend the night in the rain, working with frightening men (were they?) who seemed to float and glide above the ground, bearing heavy burdens without the slightest strain. It hardly seemed fair. How much help could he really be, he alone? What would happen, he wondered, if he simply didn't show? Did one skinny Nat Gentle make that much of a difference?

At nine o'clock, under cloak of the wet, dark sky, Gustave set into motion the workings of his plan. By ten, it was clear that the plan was flawed, in its implementation if not its design. The rhythm that typically characterized Gustave's heists, the waltz of turns and passes, was out of time with that of the rain; the slosh-clunks of the crates as they were carried through the water, out of tune with the nightsongs of the frogs and the wind.

The trouble lay in the transporting of the heavy cargo. The picking and packing went easily enough; a bit more slowly than usual, perhaps, but that was the fault of the weather. Getting the fruit from the plantation to the shore, however, was taking far too long. The crates piled up, creating a bottleneck at Puymute's, while on the beach the boatmen stood idle and angry, waiting for wares to shuttle to the bigger boats that hid beyond the coast. Nat, whose courage and rebellion thrived only in private rumination, waited, too, his part in the dance that of carrying the crates from shore to ship. That Nat shouldn't bump into Raoul, who waited eager behind the mango tree nearby (puzzled, by all the inactivity of the actors pacing the sand), was thanks only to the wet, dark sky, which rendered the stage so gray and blurred.

Piecemeal the pineapples appeared on the beach, sometimes

accompanied by Gustave, sometimes not, and Nat did his part to lift and pass them on to the next set of hands. But on that gray and blurred night he struggled, the crates heavy, unlike the other times when Bang sang, and the moon shone down, and the music of the leaves and the cicadas drowned Nat's grunts and erased his efforts. What was going on?

"What's the hold up?" Bang shouted across the Belly to Cougar.

It was nearly eleven now and the stage still glistened silently under its blue and yellow lights, showing no sign that the contest was soon to start. Normally an hour's delay would mean nothing to Bang, but tonight he was keen, for victory was nigh.

Cougar was less keen. The longer into the night he stretched the concert, the further he stretched his profits and his popularity. But he knew he wouldn't keep Bang off stage much longer, and so he nodded at him to get the ball, or the marimba mallets, rolling.

"Good evening, ladies and gentlemen, and welcome to the Buddha's Belly." Bang stood at the microphone under the multicolored lights. "How about a round of applause for our benefactor tonight? Cougar Zanne, ladies and gentlemen." He stretched his arm toward the bar, from behind which Cougar, smiles and silk, waved to the crowd.

Bang continued. "My name's Bang and I'll be playing for you a bit later. Right now, let's welcome our first contestant."

While Kalvin Jones regaled the Belly with marimba love songs, on Edda's beach Nat's frustration grew. He was doing more standing around than helping and his back and shoulders ached. With his mounting frustration his courage and rebellion grew bolder, and in his head he composed a telling-to for Gustave, for whenever the latter should next appear.

Aha! There he was. "Gustave!" Nat shouted.

"What is it?" Gustave walked toward Nat, wiping his brow. He looked as if his back and shoulders ached as much as Nat's.

"It's a mess, that's what it is. What's going on?"

"Just a few hiccups," answered Gustave, seemingly still in a trance. "A few hiccups is all."

When he turned to walk away, Nat grabbed his elbow and pulled him back. "What's wrong with you?" Nat asked. "At this rate we'll be here all night! Someone's sure to spot us. You'll get us all arrested!"

"If it's Customs you're worried about, don't be. I'd like nothing more than to run into Raoul tonight." With that he dusted his hands on his jeans and set off for the plantation again.

As luck or magic would have it, and despite the rainy curtain that muffled the night's sounds, Raoul's ears captured Nat's "Gustave!" and most of their ensuing conversation. So Nat was a willing participant, not frightened of Gustave after all! (He wouldn't have spoken to him so brazenly otherwise, Raoul reasoned.) And Gustave was as interested in confronting Raoul as Raoul was in confronting him! Raoul's mind struggled to decide on which of these two pieces of information to focus.

While Raoul struggled and Nat stood around, and Gustave hoped for a chance to claim his Almondine, at the Belly Bang and Cougar began to worry. The contestants shuffled across the stage, each showcasing his dexterity and his charms, the crowd drank, and the time passed. Soon Bang's turn would come, and still there was no sign of Nat.

Troubling, this. Gustave's capers never took so long.

More troubling still, though neither Bang or Cougar could bring himself to mention it to the other, was Raoul's conspicuous absence. What could possibly keep him away from the Belly on a festive night like this? On a night when one of his very best friends was a shoo-in to take first prize?

Nothing would have made Raoul happier, it's true, than to drink a beer and watch his friend on the stage. To sit unfettered from the search for variables and crooks. To be warm and dry in the Belly instead of muddy and wet under the mango tree at Sinner's Cove. But funny things happen on Oh sometimes. Funny, out-of-the-ordinary things that dictate behaviors astray of the islanders' desires and their routines.

Which is why on that blurred and dreary night Raoul's heart was too heavy for marimba music, too full for signature cocktails. Why from under a crying mango, a soggy Officer Orlean radioed to the crescent that lay in wait, giving orders to block the path of the boats that piecemeal had stuffed their bellies and their bows. Why Gustave meandered, his hands in his pockets, pining for his little almond instead of minding his pineapples and their soon-to-be-foiled journey to Killig. Why gentle Nat was sure he'd spend the rest of his life in jail. Why, after so many days in hiding, the moon finally fought its way from behind the curtain of rain, ready now to see how the story would end.

19

"Encore! Encore!"

Nat slipped into the Belly just as Bang, the last contestant to participate in the revival of the annual marimba competition, finished his set. To the applause and cheering of the crowd Bang responded with a dramatic pose, marimba mallets raised high above his head, his form a silhouette against the backlit stage, where the colored lights had spent themselves as Bang banged out his last note. It was hours past midnight, but the audience showed no sign of wear, their jovial spirits owing in no small part to the no small quantity of Pineapple Sting that poured within the Belly all night long, persistent and thick as the rain that fell on the island outside the Belly's walls.

Nat squeezed his way through the crowd, through the whistling, yelling, jumping bodies that smelled of sweat and soap and boozy revelry, until the human swell finally deposited his light frame at one of the short ends of the bar. There, it took him a few minutes to catch the eye of Cougar, who had interrupted his bartending and was gesticulating instructions to Bang on stage, telling him to switch on the loud, recorded music that would occupy the crowd while the judges voted.

"Where've you been?" Cougar demanded when he finally saw Nat. "We were getting worried, you know." Even before Nat could answer, Cougar realized that his worry had not been misplaced. "What's wrong?" he continued. "You look like you saw a ghost."

"Feels like one followed me all the way back from the beach," Nat said. "Give me a rum, man. Double."

Cougar complied. "What happened? Everything go off alright with Gustave?" Cougar was beginning to get scared.

"No. No, it didn't. Anyone asks, I was here all night. You never saw me leave the premises." Nat downed his double rum in a single swallow. "Give me another one."

Cougar complied again. "Where's Gustave? Did he go home?"

"He's under the mango at Sinner's Cove. That's where Raoul put him."

"*Put* him? Raoul? What the hell are you talking about, Nat?" Yes, Cougar was most definitely scared now.

While Nat gulped his second double, Bang bounced over to him and patted him on the back. "Now, there's a friend for you. I knew you wouldn't miss my set. Wish I could say the same for Raoul." Bang turned to Cougar. "Coug, glass of water."

"Raoul was at the beach" is all Cougar said in reply, his tone conveying the height to which his fear had climbed.

"Edda's beach? Did he see you?" Bang cautiously asked Nat.

Nat nodded his head. "He told me to come here. He said if anyone asks, you and Cougar should say I was here all night, I never left."

"Did he see Gustave?" Bang asked.

"He saw everything. He knew what was going on. He was there waiting. It was a mess. Gustave was...was...I don't know what was wrong with him. I told him to snap out of it, but he didn't care.

Said he wanted to see Raoul. And out of nowhere there's Raoul, too, and he tells me to sneak back here and stay put. Then these characters come out of the tide and start fighting. And Gustave, Gustave's down."

"What do you mean, 'down'?" Cougar asked.

"On the ground. Dead. Maybe."

"Dead?! How? You're not making any sense." Bang was scared now, too. "Who came out of the tide?"

"Men, I guess. It was raining and then it just stopped and there they were, like they came right out of the rain, or out of the sea. They had knives!" Nat struggled to spit out frenzied details in a whisper loud enough that his friends—but only his friends—would hear, while Bang and Cougar exchanged glances that said "what should we do?"

"Where's Raoul now?" Cougar wanted to know. "Is he alright?"

"I don't know. He had blood all over him. But he was talking and walking. He said we shouldn't go to the beach. He said for all of us to stay right here. He made me promise."

Bang and Cougar exchanged glances again, glances that said "we should go to him anyway," then they looked away from each other, knowing they wouldn't budge. Their curiosity and concern for Raoul were no match for their worry and their fear for themselves. They would do as Raoul had said and stay put at the Belly. For once, these fair-weather friends would keep a promise.

They sat at the bar in silence as the marimba-contest judges deliberated, feigning interest in the music that blared from the speakers on stage, watching the crowd on the dance floor, the atmosphere painfully unsuited to quiet contemplation. Now and again Bang, or Cougar, would pose some question to Nat, who would reveal one detail more, his words like brushstrokes on a painter's canvas, hiding the bare, coarse truth underneath. Each new random fact that Bang and Cougar collected and tried to reconcile made the two men shrug, their perplexity directly proportional to their enlightenment.

Singly they arrived at a common thought. They decided that Nat was a little shook up is all. That his head would clear in a while. That no one (especially not Gustave) could possibly be dead. They decided, too, that, after the judges announced the winner and the winner played one more time, they would take Nat for a walk. In the coolness of the night air, they would ask for his story again, for the bigger picture, starting from the beginning. Then they would decide what they should do.

A common mistake on Oh, this thinking that people know more than they do. Nat knew as much about the facts of that night as Gustave knew about *me*. Nat had seen steel knives and blood; Gustave, sharp white skin and blood-red eyes; and both had made their deductions. Neither knew a thing about the bigger picture. Neither knew the truth. Thus, there's no point to your hearing the sketchy version Nat will tell Bang and Cougar later when they walk. The bigger picture, the puzzle pieced together, looks like this.

For the first part of the night the rain continued to pour down, scouring Puymute's acres and the geometric palms of Edda's beach. It washed off the singing leaves and the stalls at the market, the library's heavy doors. It rinsed the dust from Fred Nettles' truck and the sand from Lullaby Peet's new shovel, and cleaned up the Sincero's sign. It even scrubbed the gutters of the seedy port bar. So persistent was the rain, it agitated the island itself, which found little consolation in the play of warm marimba and directed its restless energies elsewhere.

You know already about Gustave's distracted state, about his heartfelt and sentimental inklings and his murmured, half-hearted commands. You know that Nat was short-tempered and tired, and that Raoul was now sure of at least one friend's deliberate betrayal. You know of the crescents that like misshapen horseshoes wrapped themselves one around the next, boats around boats around the sandy shore. You know, too, that Raoul had finally had his fill of the so-called magic that had been going on since I was born. At last he had all his variables in line and was about to even the score; real police back-up was on the way.

From his hiding place under the mango, Raoul moved—agitated—to set his sting in motion. He had called to his boats by radio and instructed them to block the exit of Gustave's boats from the cove. As if Raoul had radioed to the moon itself, the moon began to break free of its watery curtain, thinning the rain and showering the beach with light. The light fell on the bothered features of Nat, who stood, hands on hips, waiting for Gustave, waiting for pineapples to carry, waiting for someone to tell him what to do.

Raoul complied. "Nat!" he called, dashing from his hiding place onto the shore.

"Raoul! What are you doing here?" Nat was too startled to try and offer excuses for his own presence, there on Sinner's Cove just then.

"I'm working," Raoul said. "Get out of here. Run, do you hear me? Go to the Belly and stay there. If anyone asks, tell Bang and Cougar to say you were there all night and never left."

Nat wanted to ask Raoul what was going on, but the urgency in his friend's voice told him the time wasn't ripe for questions. So

Nat nodded in obedient and frightened agreement and turned to leave. Raoul added in a strong, throaty whisper as Nat walked away, "And stay away from the beach. All three of you!"

Nat got as far as the soft, green brush a stone's throw from the edge of the sea, when his frightened obedience abated, like that of a child whose shame diminishes with each step that parts him from his angry mum. Instead of running to the Belly like he was told, Nat took up Raoul's post under the mango tree, from where he spied, hidden, the moonlit stage; and Raoul took up Nat's post in the sand, where he stood, hands on hips, waiting for Gustave, waiting for pineapples to catch, waiting for something to do.

It seemed that Oh itself waited with him, holding its breath, its rains ever-slowing, its leafsong ever more audible. But none of them would wait for long. Not Raoul, not the palms, not the cicadas or the pregnant mango. Gustave was but a few steps away, his slow cargo by now having mostly made its way from the plantation to the boats that promised passage to Killig. The squeeze of the Customs' crescent around Gustave's pineapple-burdened fleet would break soon upon the sandy shore. So soon, in fact, that Gustave would happen upon the hullabaloo in fullest swing.

With the rain suddenly and finally stopped, the tide revealed itself just as Nat had described it to Bang and Cougar. It spit onto Edda's beach a number of angry bare-chested contrabandists, their heads wrapped in braids and bandanas and their necks ringed in gold chains of varying weight and worth, the overall impression one of latter-day pirates. They were the sort of men ruled by blades, not books, by money rather than moonlight. If ever they bothered about the stars, it was not in awe or enjoyment, but in service to their nefarious navigation between Oh and Oh's island neighbors.

The leader of these modern-day brigands who stood in a pack behind their captain called to Raoul from the tide. "You know anything about the boats in the cove? My men are locked in."

"You, your men, and your crafts have been detained pending an investigation by the Office of Customs and Excise of Oh."

"Investigation? I don't submit to 'investigations' in general, and certainly not by you. I've got produce on those boats. I don't intend to let it rot out there."

"You have the Customs documents to account for that produce, I presume?" Raoul taunted. "Or did you harvest it on the high seas?"

"Of course I do. I'm not some common thief. See for yourself." The leader, whose given name was Dennis but was known by his cohorts as Dutch, turned to one of the men ranked behind him, his arm extended and his hand opened as if in wait of the documents to show Raoul. Raoul (naïve Raoul!), meanwhile, ventured into the tide where Dutch and his band of men stood.

When Dutch turned back around, the credentials he presented were not of paper, as Raoul had expected, but of steel. In the palm of his pirate hand, he held a knife that gleamed silver under the moon's white gaze. "This is my right of passage," he said, holding the blade at chest-level between himself and Raoul. The men ranked behind him displayed equally incisive dossiers.

What happened next is hard to describe, even from the vantage point of a bigger-picture view, so striking are the distortions effected by the various angles of observation. Raoul didn't see a knife in Dutch's raw and weathered hand. He saw, rather, a deadly, saw-toothed mirror, and in its reflection, the unsuitable and unacceptable end of a too-long quest for answers he owed his granddaughter; and so he lunged, careless and determined at once. Nat, from his hiding place behind the mango, saw the swirl of gold and silver that had issued from the tide, Raoul at its center; and so he cowered, disbelieving and aghast. For Dutch there was little more to the story than the foolishness of a wild, middle-aged man; and so he reacted as his gut commanded. Gustave, who just then arrived at Sinner's Cove, having put the plantation and its sluggish activity to bed, Gustave saw a skirmish between his bread and butter and his flesh and blood; and so he, too, lunged into the tide, careless and determined, and commanded by his gut.

I suppose you can decide for yourself which perspective you find most appealing, which the most fair. Me, I always defer to the moon, who, still nearly full, illuminated the happenings on the beach that night from a distance more permitting of objectivity.

She saw Raoul rush toward Dutch and Dutch reply in kind, saw Dutch's knife stab at Raoul's heart and fail, repelled as if by Raoul's sheer force of will. Encircled by the other bandits who watched but did not intervene, the fighting pair grasped onto and hugged each other, spun in a demented and vicious dance. When Gustave arrived and spotted the commotion, he hurled himself into its midst, his gut instructing him to protect Raoul, not the evening's profits, the former representing his surest course to his misplaced daughter. Which is why, when Dutch struck a second blow at the flesh around Raoul's brave heart, Gustave heaved his own thick torso into the path of the knife, whose blow, this time, didn't fail.

As Dutch's blade pierced Gustave's body, saturating his shirt with the blood that oozed from the fresh, raw wound, for a fistful of still, dark seconds, time on Oh seemed to stop again, as it had when Raoul and his friends shared a drink at the Belly some weeks before. The gang of Dutch's men slowly broke up, revealing as it did the crumpled body of Gustave over which bent the figure of Raoul. Moved—agitated—to action at the sight of this gruesome picture, Gustave's pickers and packers, who had arrived then at the cove for a cool swim after a long evening's work, retaliated. They set upon Dutch's men with fists and kicks and stinging words, indignant and in staunch defense of their employer.

As Gustave's men swept through Dutch's bandits, Raoul did what he could to save the operation. All around him blows and blades sliced the air, shouts and grunts washed away in the splash of the knee-deep water that hosted the maelstrom of fighting men. His hands and knees in the tide, Raoul used his body to protect that of Gustave, who still breathed, if laboriously, and still held the answers to Raoul's questions—not least of which, now, why had Gustave risked his life to save Raoul's?

While Raoul sheltered Gustave, simultaneously bobbing and leaning to keep his own body whole as well, he fumbled to keep hold of his radio long enough to call for help, the back-up required now on shore. But neither Gustave's men nor Dutch's were eager for the help Raoul might summon, and so they knocked the radio repeatedly from his hands.

Meanwhile back at the mango tree, Nat did some bobbing and leaning of his own as he strained to get a glimpse of the bigger picture through the squall of arms and legs and blades that unleashed itself on the beach. He contemplated nearing the fight, but before he could muster the courage to do so, the fight came to an end. Like birds scattering at the shot of a pistol, the men that had encircled Gustave and Raoul took abrupt flight and were gone. Raoul had at last managed to keep a firm grip on his radio and help was on the way. Before the beach should teem with policemen and excisemen (and possibly men in locked cuffs), both Gustave's posse and Dutch's fled the scene.

With the beach quieted, and the shore emptied, in the clarity of the moon's glow Raoul took stock. Gustave was unconscious and breathing still, if barely, but Raoul feared for his survival. If Raoul's own perishing was an unsuitable and unacceptable end to a too-long quest for answers he owed his Almondine, equally unacceptable was it that Gustave should perish when Raoul was so close to getting a confession from him. Though Raoul wished to remain on the shore and await the reinforcements he had called for, though he longed to oversee the clash of crescents in the cove, he knew he must leave the scene and seek out a doctor, or all his efforts would be for naught. Delicately he pulled Gustave's fading body from the shallow water and onto the dry sand. He turned and looked around, examining the beach for something on which to prop Gustave's head, but he saw nothing that would do. No rock, no shell, no debris. Under the mango Raoul had left his copy of the story of Mr. Stan Kalpi (yes, he still carried it with him), and so he ran to get it and make of it a makeshift pillow.

At the mango tree, Raoul found Mr. Stan in the company of Nat, who was so startled by the sudden departure of the men from the beach, and so frightened by the bloody clothes of the two men left behind, that he stood rooted to the soft, green brush, his arms hugged around the tree's trunk.

"Nat! What are you doing here? I told you to go to the Belly!" Raoul shouted at him.

Nat didn't answer. He looked at Raoul's shirt, red with Gustave's blood, and sunk to the ground, whimpering.

"Nat!" Raoul insisted. "Get a hold of yourself and go – to – the Belly!" He jerked Nat to his feet, but still Nat said nothing. "What's wrong with you?" Raoul spat. "Come on! Snap out of it! The police are coming. Get out of here!"

Nat slid to the ground again, his whimper turned to tears, his hands over his face. "Raoul, are you alright? I'm sorry. I'm so sorry. I didn't mean to. I shouldn't have, I know."

"Nat, listen to me." Raoul pulled him from the ground again. "I have to get help. I have to get a doctor, and the police are coming. Do you understand me? You have to get out of here or they'll find you and arrest you." Raoul gripped Nat's shirt tightly, keeping him on his feet.

"They should arrest all of us!" Nat screamed. "We deserve it. We tricked you!" Nat was hysterical, alternately crying and screaming, falling to the ground and letting himself be pulled to his feet by Raoul.

Raoul looked to the beach, worried. If he didn't bring a doctor soon, Gustave would die. And if Gustave died, the truth Raoul sought would die with him. But Nat was blubbering under the mango tree, and if Raoul left him there alone, he would surely be found and charged. If only time had stood still in *that* minute, that fistful of still, dark seconds when Raoul balanced the weight of his friend's life against that of his enemy's, when he chose between Nat's freedom and his own.

Time did not stand still (I told you it almost never does on Oh) and whether in those few seconds Raoul "chose" or simply "did," moved—agitated—by years of island friendship, I doubt if even he himself could say.

Whichever the case, it was Nat who benefited from Raoul's immediate attention during those critical few minutes. Raoul tried to calm Nat's screams, to stifle his repentant sobs, to pardon his admitted sins. But nothing he did could shrivel Nat's hysteria, nothing he said could provoke even a slight diminuendo of his frenzy. Raoul nearly became hysterical himself, nearly cried as he watched

Gustave whither on the beach. Helpless, he looked to the moonlit clouds, hoping that like tea leaves they would tell him what he should do.

The clouds complied. So did the wind, who blew the clouds furiously across the moon, eclipsing the moon's face. Raoul reached behind himself, gathering all his forces, then swung his arm and eclipsed Nat's face in a fierce and furious slap. Not a choice, but a pure doing. The clap of flesh on flesh scattered the clouds again, frightened them back to their proper place in the sky, and exposed the moon anew. She illuminated Nat's face, and Raoul saw that Nat was himself again. If he remembered his wild behavior of a minute before, he made no show of it in front of Raoul.

"Go to the Belly," Raoul told him again. "Stay there with Bang and Cougar. Stay away from the beach. Promise me."

"Okay, okay," Nat said, moving slowly as if awaking from sleep.

Raoul left him and ran back to where Gustave lay in the sand, so that he could prop Gustave's head on the book of Stan Kalpi before running to call a doctor. Raoul didn't know how much time had passed, but he felt certain it was less than what it seemed. There would still be time enough to save Gustave.

As Raoul reached Gustave and knelt at his side, a breeze chilled Raoul's body, damp from the tide and from the sweat of the evening's trials. Hopeful, denying, Raoul lifted Gustave's head and slid the tattered volume underneath it. Alas, Mr. Stan's mathematics were of no use. Gustave was already dead.

Uncertain of the disruption that would take place when the police arrived and pushed Gustave's boats ashore, Raoul thought only of safeguarding Gustave's remains. (As to his legacy, Raoul would reflect on that when the sting was done.) He left his book behind and dragged Gustave to the soft, green brush a stone's throw from the edge of the sea. Raoul left Gustave's body under the mango tree, which now sheltered my dead father as it had sheltered my dead mother some months before.

Nat, who was still making his sleepy way out of the brush, watched Raoul compose the body and walk back toward the tide. Was Gustave wounded, or was he really dead? Was it Nat's fault, what had happened? Though he didn't recall his hysteria or the minutes he had cost Raoul under the mango, Nat knew that somehow he had done it, had hurt Gustave, or killed him. By conspiring, by double-crossing, by pitting Gustave against Raoul. Somehow Nat was to blame. They all were.

Nat turned and ran. He ran from the brush all the way to the Belly without stopping, putting Gustave's death as far behind him as he could. But there's no getting away from a thing like that. Not even if you run.

"Raoul! Raoul!"

Bang, Cougar, and Nat called out to their friend as they reached Edda's beach at dawn. They had walked the whole night (what was left of it, after Bang won the contest and played his marimba once more), listening to Nat's sketchy story, fitting themselves into it, and deciding in the end to go look for Raoul.

They found him seated in the sand amidst the rubbish of the night before, watching the sun climb over the water. His sting had been a huge success from a Customs point of view, less so in terms of Kalpi maths and island logic, for Gustave was never cornered and the truth about me never revealed. But a dozen smugglers or more had been arrested, and Raoul was looking at a fat promotion.

"What are you doing here?" Raoul looked up at the three of them.

"We were worried about you," Bang said, stooping to better meet Raoul's gaze.

"Did you win the contest?" Raoul asked, his eyes directed now at the sea.

"Yeah," Bang replied. He wanted to tell more, to say how sour had been the sweet victory he had anticipated. But he added nothing.

"What happened here?" Cougar asked, looking at the sloppy shore.

"All in a day's work," Raoul sighed. "The smugglers have been stopped. Gustave's dead. No more magic from *him*." Still he kept his eyes on the sea. "I lost my book. You know, the one with the black and white cover?"

Bang, Cougar, and Nat looked at each other, not knowing what to say, not knowing if they should say anything at all.

"Looks like the rain's let up for good," Raoul went on. "The sky's clear."

"Have you been here all night?" Nat asked. Raoul didn't answer, but stared into the waves. Bang might have suspected Raoul's head full of private flies, had it not been for the eerie quiet that fell on the beach that morning, like a thick blanket threatening to smother them all, a quiet that couldn't have camouflaged even the tiniest of gnats.

"Come on, now! What's this moping? Congratulations are in order!" Bang jumped up out of the sand and put his hand across his heart. "Ladies and gentlemen, I give you Raoul Orlean, Esteemed Officer of the Highest Order of Customs and Excise of the Kingdom of Oh!" Then Bang began to sing the island's national anthem.

Cougar and Nat surrounded Raoul, one on each side of him, and they pulled him awkwardly, unevenly, to his feet, Cougar's side benefiting from greater muscular bulk. Raoul almost toppled over but caught himself, though not before losing the contents of his shirt pocket.

"What's that?" Nat asked.

Raoul bent and retrieved from the sand the lucky harmonica he carried with him every day, ever since Bang had given it to him what seemed like ages before. He wasn't so superstitious as to believe in its properties, don't think *that*. He just never wanted to hurt Bang's feelings, was all. It was dented now, marked by Dutch's knife, which had stabbed and failed. Raoul rubbed his thumb over the instrument's new notch. "Sorry about that. Guess I won't be needing this anymore, now that Gustave's gone." He held it out to Bang, who was still singing the island anthem.

"Let me see it," Nat said, grabbing it from Raoul's hand.

"You can't play," Cougar objected.

Nat's rebuttal was an elaborate arpeggio that sent Bang into a cartwheel of delight. (He couldn't state his enthusiasm, his mouth still occupied in song.)

On Raoul's face a reluctant smile started to break. (Bang had that effect on him.)

"Well, well, Nat!" Cougar exclaimed. "Keeping secrets from us, are you?" The sun had risen, lightening the humors of the island and the islanders alike, so much so that Cougar didn't notice his own risky quip.

Likewise, Nat, who answered with a spontaneous "Never!"

On they marched, Raoul and his three best mates, Cougar shoring up Raoul's tired frame, Nat playing the harmonica, and Bang singing Oh's national anthem. They crossed the sand and stepped onto the soft, green brush where under the mango tree Gustave's body lay still, halting their procession instinctively but not their concert, for Bang had reached the verse about heroes who defended the island from threats in the night. When the verse was over, he stopped, and Nat did, too.

"It's alright," Raoul said. "We can go. I've sent someone to make arrangements."

So the men took up their procession and their processional again, putting the mango tree behind them. Raoul marched. Cougar shored up. Nat played. And Bang sang.

20

The rest of that next day, the day after the revival of the annual marimba competition, Oh was shiny and wet. The island's puddles had yet to dry. The wounds of the night before, those real and metaphorical, had yet to heal. But the sky was clear, as Raoul had so clearly put it, and there was every reason to believe that like the island's puddles, so too the blood and the scandal, after their initial gush, would dry and flake, and be blown away by the wind.

When the islanders spoke of what happened that night on Sinner's Cove, and to varying degrees they always would, what they remembered most was the rain. The way it had come down for weeks, merciless, and then had simply and suddenly stopped, as if having drowned whatever beast, what sin, in need of drowning. The rainy scenery always began the tale, theme on which to base the variations. The rest of the story would undergo innumerable changes, be corrupted by its tellers and bent by their leanings.

Some would say that Gustave had been long misunderstood, that he had saved poor Raoul's life; others would say that Gustave had gotten served his just desserts—"comeuppance long overdue, that!"; still others (imagine!) would say that Raoul was a murderer, that he had stabbed Gustave in a mad and deadly rage to avenge my mother's rape. The more salacious the reasoning and the sharper its tang, the better and broader it spread (islanders do like their spice, after all). But like passions and novelties and the moon itself, fiery tastes wane, and gentler, blander versions of the story were served up soon enough.

I won't bother you with too much else of what the future held for Oh after that, just enough that my story, and my grandfather's before it, might finish properly. Besides, unknowing, you may care to imagine things turned out differently than they did. Rosier and more brilliant, or more wretched, the whole island swallowed up by a giant wave perhaps, pushed into the depths of the sea where not even the moon's pervasive gleam could reach it. No harm in that, that the story should be hewn by its readers. Myself, I can't take such liberties, for neither Raoul nor Gustave would forgive me a finish as cheap and facile as a hungry wave. Like Abigail and Lullaby and Alejandro Creek, they've both known the resilience that only Oh inspires, that pliable spirit bequeathed by each generation to the next.

So I, too, must bow to the fitful island winds and shape the contours of my sandy tale to the doings of the tide and moon, however accidental and undue.

Hear.

The Belly seemed less festive on that next day. Its floor was littered with the scraps of the marimba contest and its stage was disordered and silent. Its emptiness called to mind a wedding hall after a wedding, the confetti tossed so gleefully now mocking bits and pieces of real life to be swept away. Broom in hand, Bang shuffled along the floor arranging the dirt into neat, gritty piles, that they might be collected and disposed of more easily. Now and then he stopped to have a rest, propping his broom against a wall and puffing into his now certifiably magic and life-saving harmonica. If you arrived at Oh on that particular day, you wouldn't have found him at the airport chopping his wares and dazzling you with his shiny, gold tooth. He was too sleepy for that, not having shut his eyes the whole night, and something in his gut said the Belly was where he belonged.

Cougar's gut told him the same, and so instead of dozing or doing his daily accounting in the Sincero's cluttered office, he too spent the first half of the day cleaning in the lounge with Bang. Each found the company of the other soothing, though neither said as much, or indeed said much of anything at all. Not even Nat spoke, when he arrived soon after, not to comment on the night before, not even to relate some oddity of the passenger he had picked up that morning (and each of his passengers was odd). He simply took up a towel and scrubbed the tables. The three of them scoured and polished, dusted and wiped, a silent catharsis they hoped would wash away their sins.

Whether or not they achieved the redemption they sought, it's hard for me to say, and frankly I'm not sure they deserved to. But by noon the Buddha's Belly Bar and Lounge was spotless, shinier than it had been in a very long time. As if by magic the three chums were less tired than before they had started, and they sat at the bar to share a drink. Anything but Pineapple Sting, they all agreed. Cougar poured and together they sipped, blissful in their easily-donned ignorance, for none had yet—nor ever would try—to grasp what Raoul had sacrificed in the name of their friendship.

Ignorant, too, was Raoul, if truth be told, for he had no idea where the truth really lay. On that same morning he stood at the airport pondering the fact that Gustave was gone, and with him, any chance for answers about my beginnings. He couldn't have imagined that Gustave was as ignorant as he.

While the passengers slid through the grit on the airport floor, a distracted Raoul studied their faces and the pictures in their passports, tried to size them up, wondered to what lengths his misjudgments must stretch, to what extent his miscalculations, seeing how very far he had strayed in his jumbled appraisals of his enemy and his friends. The latter had cost him the truth (or so he thought), while the former had paid with his life. The irony of the loss, so final, so complete, might have made a lesser man bitter. But an islander knows to move with the tide, and Raoul admitted that some polynomials were simply too complex to solve. He was tired of trying to reconcile reality with Stan Kalpi maths.

I suspect it didn't hurt matters that Gustave—that my father—had saved my grandfather's life. In so doing, Gustave had at least validated my parentage in Raoul's eyes, mysterious though it remained in its mechanics. Raoul would never tell me any of this; he wouldn't speak of it at all, as a matter of fact. He had come to no real conclusions, and had cost me a father in the process. For a while after that, he couldn't even look me in my Vilder eyes, so great was his shame. Eventually, he would resume his visits to the library (it would soon be Tuesday again), and though the book of Stan Kalpi with its silhouetted cover had been washed out into the sea, Ms. Lila would have plenty else to show him. Raoul would give up on his variables in her company, and would relax—for a little while—his strictly plain-as-noses-on-faces philosophy.

Like Raoul at the library, Bang, Cougar, and Nat would resume their routines, too. Bang would smile at the tourists, entertain them with his pineapple tricks and sell them his hand-carved pen-knives by day, his words and his melodies by night. Cougar would furnish his hotel guests with charm and with overpriced maps, while the Belly's visitors and the island girls would get rum and romance, respectively, overpriced as well. And Nat, Nat would drive his shiny taxis all around the island, one day picking up a girl, or a lady, who would indeed be satisfied with market-day t-shirts, a diet of fish, and his cottage with its new front door. Then at the end of the day, all four mates would meet for a drink at the Belly, none so petty as to forsake a friend over a dented harmonica or a bit of smuggling. Could Oh's sandy shore ever forsake the vicious tide?

Second chances on Oh are as prevalent as promises and mangoes, and Raoul—and his cohorts—had been so shaken up that none would keep a secret from the others ever again. Rainbow bills and back-stabbings would come between them no more, nor would adverts in the *Morning Crier*. The island daily, of course, will outlive us all, for the islanders care to know exactly what's going on and require the inaccuracies of the paper to confirm their private convictions on matters from Parliament to pineapple. (If you were wondering, by the by, Oh's Parliament never did respond to Killig's request to purchase Oh's pineapples. The case was suspended pending the Customs and Excise investigation into the island's missing crops. By the time Parliament remembered to resume its deliberations, Killig's blight was gone and the point moot.)

Cyrus Puymute assumed for himself the General Manager position vacated by Gustave and kept up-and-running the plantation, which Pedro haunted, sharing the odd beer and odder word with Puymute's pickers. Abigail, after Gustave's death, restricted her midwifing to the demands of the so-called seedy port girls, dividing her time between them and me (and I got the lion's share of it, I'm happy to say).

With Gustave gone, the island's appetite for magic, if by no means starved, was at first subjected to a stricter diet than usual, for in dying Gustave had wiped the Vilder lineage officially from the island's plate. Unofficially, I carried on the Vilder line myself for nearly twenty years, with all the whispers and attention and finger-pointing that that entailed. The islanders all assumed I was Gustave's daughter (and so did I), though none of us knew how this had come to be. I did ask sometimes, my mother, my father, Abigail. They all claimed to know nothing and were quick to respond with worried questions of their own: "But aren't you happy as you are? Don't you want to be here with *us*?" Though I wasn't always happy being who I was, I *did* want to be there with my mother and my father, and so to spare them any further discomfort, I finally stopped asking why I was different. Raoul and I never discussed my pale white skin or where I came from. For as long as I can remember, I knew—though I'm not sure how—that this was a subject I could never bring up in his presence.

Happy as I was otherwise with my grandfather, or with Abigail or my three favorite uncles (Bang, Cougar, and Nat), outside the loving and colorful home that Edda and Wilbur had made for me, my world was black-and-white, and lonely. Or, rather, my world was black, and *I* was white and lonely. All I ever wanted was to blend in.

So like Emma Patrice before me, and at about the very same age, I traded island sands for mountain snows in Switzerland, that mysterious land that had once swallowed up my grandmother, land of my childhood fantasies and landscapes as white as my skin.

I bought a house with some money that Abigail gave me and made a modest living as a painter, as I told you before.

But like Mr. Stan Kalpi who awoke one morning dissatisfied with mere mathematics and pork, I began to wonder who I was really. I wasn't an islander like the others, yet at times I felt like more of one than they could ever be. I must be a Vilder, but what was a Vilder anyway? I was like the polynomials that Mr. Stan Kalpi taught his students at school, a string of unidentified variables that together equaled Almondine Orlean.

My father would be a variable, and my mother, too, but those were dead ends, for Gustave was dead and Edda, for all her motherly love, had never looked into my eyes and seen that they were red, not black like hers. Then there was Raoul, and Abigail. They were variables, too. They had dodged my questions before, but maybe it was time to insist. I thought maybe I should lock up my small house, take a leave from my colors and canvases, and go back to Oh to attend to my past. An almond couldn't flower hidden deep in the snow.

As luck or magic would have it, the moon and the wind had never lost sight of the fruit they left at the mango tree. They had never stopped watching over me, never stopped playing their tricks. So when I could no longer resist the gibbous moon's shine or the songs and the scents on the meddling breeze, when I finally recognized that I was a mosaic full of holes, wind and moon conspired and dropped a variable at my door. One evening dressed up like any other evening (cold, gray sky; goat cheese and chimney-smoke wafting from next-door Maxim's), as I packed up my belongings to go back home, my grandmother knocked and asked to buy a painting.

I knew her at once, for despite her age Emma Patrice bore a striking likeness to my mother Edda, or vice versa, I suppose.

Emma Patrice was well preserved, her smooth skin spared all those years of island sun, and she was eager to tell her story to her granddaughter. Emma Patrice hadn't perished that day on the slopes, she said, hers was escape not demise, not a choice but a pure doing, selfish and selfless both, motivated by the simple island philosophy that "happiness is what life's all about." Had Emma Patrice remained on Oh, she said, her island fever would have burned permanent scars into Raoul and baby Edda. For her own sake and theirs, she had to get away. She might have taken her baby with her, Emma Patrice admitted, but then what would have come of poor Raoul all alone?

You probably don't understand this kind of reasoning, especially not after seeing how devastating and permanent an effect a missing mother had on poor Edda. But Edda's loneliness is what saved my life, and because of that and my own escapist tendencies, I subscribed to my grandmother's belief that one might justify betrayal for the sake of a loved one's best interests (so had my loved ones done to me my whole life, as I was about to discover). All the same, Emma Patrice was saddened to know of the pain her absence had inflicted on Edda; she had rather hoped my mother would be emboldened by her state, broadened, forced to allow for circumstances that cracked the island's usual molds.

Emma Patrice's theory, a farina philosophy of sorts, panned out, she saw, but with a generation's delay. I was the bold Orlean, the broadened one. Me with my Vilder mole and white complexion. So bold must I have seemed to Emma Patrice, in fact, that she felt an immediate kinship with me, though of course we were not at all related.

Like me, perhaps Emma Patrice was more islander than she admitted, for my presence triggered in her an irresistible urge to indulge in island gossip, something I typically avoided, provoking as much of it as I did. Imagine my surprise when Emma Patrice knew more about Oh than I, thanks to the give in that fabric of history and lore with which the islanders inveterately cloaked themselves. Apparently, it stretched over oceans and across continents, unfrayed by blizzard or drought. She even knew she had a red-eyed granddaughter.

Emma Patrice had a friend on Oh, a friend with a secret. Henrietta Williams was her name. (You might remember she dropped her sugar apples once, laughing at Raoul.) Secrets on Oh—*kept* secrets—are even harder to come by than those elusive rainbow bills, and their purchasing power far greater. In youth Emma Patrice had had the good fortune to happen upon a secret of Henrietta's, spotted it like a shiny penny in the sand, she did, and with it years later she bought both information and guaranteed discretion. Henrietta was the only one on Oh to whom Emma Patrice had confided her whereabouts, the only one to be trusted not to reveal them, for Henrietta's youthful indiscretions had earned interest over the years and that Emma Patrice might splash her secret across the island was a gamble Henrietta couldn't afford. (I have yet to coax Henrietta's crime from my grandmother, but I will one day, rest assured. When the wind is right and our hot chocolate, hot enough.)

Well, thanks to this mutually profitable arrangement, from a distance Emma Patrice had followed the developments of her abandoned island home, the magic and the mundane, the gossip and the rumor. She knew that Edda was well looked after, knew that Abigail had honored their blood-sister pledge, knew that Edda had given birth to a baby named Almondine. She knew who fell in love, who fell into money, who fell drunk across the threshold of the seedy port bar. Henrietta's missives spared no islander and no detail.

Emma Patrice's only regret, were she forced to admit to one, was that Abigail had never known the truth for sure, never known that Emma Patrice had escaped the island strictures and thrived in the shiny snow, though Emma Patrice was sure Abigail must have guessed it. To tell her outright back then would have been too cruel, to expect her to lie to Edda about her missing mother, too unfair. "Then once Edda was grown," my grandmother explained, "too much time had gone by." She was right. Abigail would indeed have considered such a tardy truth an offense.

Emma Patrice and I talked through the night. She told me about everything from Agustín Boe's death by snakebite to Ms. Lulu Peacock's activities by night. When the sun finally rose, I had enough defined variables to fill my suitcase and then some, but the mosaic was still incomplete. I still didn't know *who* I was really, and the wind wanted me home, to find out.

My grandfather Raoul Orlean, on the other hand, had had the good fortune of a well-ordered childhood, his past and his future stretching before and behind him like sharp rainbows spilling from clouds. That's probably why the story of Stan Kalpi, and the rough and rugged journey on which he embarked, captivated Raoul so, for the sheer contrast they bore, the disorder, when measured against his own predictable and orderly life. In Raoul the tale evoked fear and wonderment. How close Stan Kalpi had come to not knowing who he was! How brave that he should have journeyed so far to find out!

Raoul, uncertain that I would be as lucky and as courageous as Mr. Stan, and (though he would have been loath to admit it) unwilling to accept unquestioning such pale, red-eyed disorder in his dark-skinned, black-eyed, plain-as-noses-on-faces kind of life, had attempted a similar journey on my behalf. Lineage was a matter of history and pride on Oh; no mingling of roots among family trees could go officially undocumented. As head of the family, Raoul had had to try and see to that. He had worried that one day I would see myself in the mirror and know that I didn't belong (which is precisely what I did), and that I would ask him where I came from (which I never dared).

When I went back home again, it wasn't Raoul to whom I finally turned. I arrived at Oh and pulled the bits and pieces of the story from my bag, and I laid them out before Abigail. She must have wondered how I knew as much as I did, but she never asked me about the variables I brought from Switzerland. She only added to my mosaic those misshapen tiles she had fashioned herself. Although she loved Edda enough to take her secret to the grave, Abigail's love for me, her rescued almond, was even greater. And so she passed her secret on.

If I have two fathers in Gustave and Wilbur, my mothers are three: Claudine, Edda, and Abigail, the one to whom I owe my livelihood. She taught me to paint, having had her bit of training in brushes and colors, and she secured my inheritance after Gustave's death. That night of the sting he had hidden away his money, removed it all from the bank and instructed Pedro to use it to secure his release from jail, should Gustave have been captured by Raoul. Talker that he is, lonely Pedro, he told Abigail where the money was hidden and she swiftly stole it. Years later she gave it to me, saying only that she had saved it on my behalf. Her painting may be rudimentary, but she knows how to balance accounts.

I have never in turn passed on my secret to Raoul. He remains partial to absolutes, though he seeks them with less rigor these days, and if he thinks that the truth died absolutely with Gustave, then that's just as well. At least it's dead and Raoul can relax. No one can know more than he, and he knows all that can be known. Not even Stan Kalpi would pursue a dead end. Raoul has recognized, too, that behind Gustave's slouch-shouldered legacy there stood a tall man, with broad-shouldered inclinations. For years now I've been plain Almondine to Raoul, no more the creature with the red eyes and the skin that isn't his own. To tell him the tardy truth now would be an offense.

Our common quest is over, mine and Raoul's. What missing pieces Emma Patrice and Abigail couldn't supply, I managed to scrounge on my own. It's amazing what you can find—and find out—if you know where to dig in the sand and how to listen to the leaves. After defining the variables of the polynomial that is me, I went back to Switzerland to put together my mosaic and to care for my grandmother, who isn't my grandmother at all. But our escapist tendencies keep us strangely bound. When Emma Patrice is gone, I'm not too sure where I'll go. Back to Oh perhaps, or maybe to a city where the lights outshine the invisible stars. Wherever I end up, the wind and the moon will find me, and will have a hand in what I do.

And every now and again, they will insist that I come back home.

When you leave from Oh, your memories begin to wane, memories of a place—my place—too ephemeral to survive in the concrete world of indifferent winds and pacified moons. In time you will forget your visit entirely. Your verandah with the dancing curtains and smell of gardenia, the chill of the night's kiss on your sun-baked shoulders, the chirping frogs, and the mangoes in more varieties than you knew existed. It will seem very far away and you will wonder, were you ever really there at all?

When *I* leave from Oh, the wind is still. The tourists notice the attention I get from the airport staff and wonder who I am. They assume it's my scar that makes the islanders stare, think them insensitive or rude. That's not it. I am proof of the magic of Oh and my departure always leaves the islanders torn. Between fear and relief, between the desire that I stay and preserve the island's gentle balance, and the desire to be rid of me and what most of them think I represent. Do I belong to the seductive moon? they wonder. Am I capable of casting spells?

The truth may well be entirely different from what you're thinking, or different from what the islanders believe. Maybe it lies somewhere in between. Truths get lost as they age. They wrinkle and whither, grow distorted by the filter of the years and the prisms I carry in my pockets. I can never be sure of them.

I can never be sure of anything. Not the oils on my palette that blend and bleed. Or even my Almondine mosaic, with its chipped and sandy tiles that sometimes come unglued. Like the wind, friends can turn in the space of a breath. Almonds can sprout from mango trees and thrive. Too many pineapples might break your heart, especially when it rains.

And one windy evening, when the moon is right, a long-lost grandmother-who's-not-really-a-grandmother could knock on your door, and ask to buy a painting.

Acknowledgments

It is impossible to acknowledge all the blessings—the people, the places, the occurrences—that conspired to make this book a book, for they are as many as the pineapples on Oh. They are writing teachers and writer friends, friends who live on islands, and friends who *were* islands when I needed a sunny shore; they are beaches and rum shacks, coffee bars and yoga classes; stellar alignments (I can only presume) and proverbial bullets dodged. They are little towns on tops of hills, and one very real and bounteous mango tree.

For their help and their handholding (book-related and otherwise), they are most definitely Priya Balasubramanian, Patricia Gillett, Marie Lamoureux, Dee LeRoy, Kristin Stasiowski, and Kari Winter; for their heart and their artistry, Andrew Bly (cover design) and Patti Schermerhorn (cover art); and for everything, always, my mother, MaryAnn Siciarz.

I am grateful for all of it; I hope I put the pieces where they were meant to go.

About the Author

Stephanie Siciarz was born in the US and is a graduate of Georgetown University and The Johns Hopkins University. She is a writer and translator and has worked for high-ranking officials in international, government, and academic institutions in the US and Europe. She currently resides in Ohio, where she is on the faculty at Kent State University. *Left at the Mango Tree*, her first novel, was shortlisted for the Dundee International Book Prize.

CPSIA information can be obtained at www.ICGtesting.com
Printed in the USA
LVOW05s1925221113

362500LV00001B/32/P